CONQUEST: KAI'S STORY

Kaden Shay

Supposed Crimes LLC • Matthews, North Carolina

Published in the United States.

ISBN: 978-1-944591-29-8

www.supposedcrimes.com

This book is typeset in Goudy Old Style, licensed by Ascender Corporation.

CHAPTER ONE

FOLLOWED

KAI'S JOURNAL - *Spring Cycle, 2606 – 220 years after the event:*
Weather seems to be tracking normally, usual spring storms rolling in. I've been spending time out scouting the city for supplies. Most of the buildings were stripped bare decades ago but every now and then we find something useful. I've been going alone despite Luke's protests and insistence I take guards with me. Heading out again tomorrow but it looks like we might get some rain.

A flash of bright white lightning backlit the ruins of what had once been a great city. Three seconds later a clap of thunder shook the dusty remains. I turned my face up toward the night sky and the clouds overhead blotting out the moon and then took a deep breath. A hint of moisture in the air made the whisper of a sigh escape my lips, the sound one of relief. Rain meant the four men who had been tracking me all day would have to find shelter and I could finally head home. Home sounded more wonderful by the second the longer I was out in this wasteland.

I'd been due back hours ago but I knew better than to lead them right to our home base. No chance I'd make it so easy on them, they probably didn't even realize I knew they were following me. Silly humans. I allowed a smirk to tweak up the left corner of my lips and then ducked around a crumbling wall and sat down on a hunk of broken concrete. No point in continuing to wander in the wrong direction now.

I leaned back, intent on relaxing and waiting for them to take cover. Only then would I make my way back to where I belonged. I had a report to deliver and surely someone would be missing me by now. A second flash of lightning, this one brighter than the first, struck close enough to make the hair on my arms stand on end. The clap of thunder accompanying it sounded at almost the same moment.

The rain I'd been expecting would begin any time now and the small contingent which had been following me all day finally seemed to register the fact. The sounds of bodies scrambling over piles of debris and rocks being kicked free to tumble down them told me the men were done with being subtle. I couldn't hold back the chuckle which broke free. Their mad scramble for cover was the entertainment I had needed to break the tension of the day I'd had. I almost shifted to a new spot to try and watch them in their attempt at hiding but decided against it.

I had always been amazed at how easily some creatures could be sent into a panic. A little radioactive rain and humans suddenly scattered to hide like small animals running from wolves. The echo of scrambling footfalls ceased but I decided to wait until the rain was falling to move, for the sake of safety. Ten minutes later a steady sheet of rain bathed the drab ruins in a shimmering layer of water. The area around me seemed to glow as small breaks in the clouds allowed slivers of moonlight to cascade onto the gathering moisture.

After using the runoff from the rain to wash the dirt from the day off my face, it was time to get moving. I pushed myself to my feet and stepped out into the cascade, letting it soak through my clothes. I took a minute to enjoy the chill the storm had carried in with it. Refreshed and more than a little drenched after my time out I took stock of my surroundings and then figured out which way was north. With my sense of direction sorted out I turned toward the east and began my trek home.

I used the time to really look at the ruins of the city I had known so well. Dallas had been a thriving metropolis once upon a time. Now the empty shells of office buildings and hotels stood as a ghostly reminder of what we had let happen. I ran my hand over the trunk of a tree which had sprouted up in the middle of what had once been a street, and one I knew well. I had lived in a home at the end of the block for several years before everything went to shit. I turned my gaze up into the branches, the leaves giving no indication of being affected by what had happened here.

No matter how bad we took advantage of our poor planet, when we failed to keep our foothold, nature resumed its steady march forward. I shook my head as I plucked a wet leaf from a low hanging branch then continued on my way. Each wall I passed had seen the return of the flora the area had once been covered in before we paved it all over. In a way I was glad for the collapse of our 'revolutionary new electrical infrastructure' which had wiped out most of the human population. Cutting down our numbers meant things could be as they were meant to be again.

"Kai! Holy shit where have you been? We've been worried sick!"

I managed to get one foot through the gate before the booming voice of Luke, my second in command and Captain of my guard, shook through the area. I rolled my eyes at him but smiled a little anyway, it was always nice when he worried about me.

"Relax man, just had a tail and ended up running in circles for a few hours. Rain sent them running."

"Thank goodness for the storm, then! Though now you're soaked. Come on, we'll get you dried off. Any news?"

I waved off the concern I saw flickering in his eyes over what I may have found in favor of getting into some dry clothes. Updates could wait.

"That will hold until I'm not standing around with chattering teeth. Dry now, news after." Luke laughed but nodded and I let him lead the way through the compound to my quarters so we could chat on the way.

"So you did find something then?"

"Luke, really, it can wait. I'm freezing."

He held up his hands as if conceding defeat and kept walking.

"Okay then, what about this tail you had? Can we talk about them?"

I nodded to the inquiry and stripped off my drenched sweater as we continued past several of my soldiers.

"Yeah we can talk about them. Four of them, definitely trained. They were on me no matter what I tried. Thank goodness for this storm otherwise I'd still be out there trying to get away from them."

"You can usually outrun them."

"I know I can, these were... Different. Faster, more agile." I caught the panic on Luke's face when he stopped and turned to face me. I knew him well enough to know he was thinking the same thing I was. "I know, trust me, I thought the same thing you're probably thinking. Maybe they weren't fully human."

"They've been able to keep up with you better in the last several years. And not just you either, Trista and Lila reported the same thing." My brows furrowed with the news and I stopped dead in my tracks, Luke doing the same several steps later when he realized I wasn't moving.

"What about Thea?"

"Thea? Ha! First she'd actually have to leave her compound for something as menial as scouting. No, Death doesn't do her own dirty work, she has lackeys for that shit."

I glared at nothing in particular since he was right on. Thea, also known as Death by the other side, never had liked getting her hands dirty. Anything she could pawn off on someone below her she didn't do herself. She differed from the rest of us in the habit. I took a deep breath and released a slow, shuddering sigh on the exhale.

"Hey, try not to overthink it," he said.

"No, this needs to be overthought. Something isn't right here. Send a runner with a message to Trista. We need a meeting, this crap is getting weirder the longer we leave it unchecked and it might be time to figure out what the hell is going on."

"Are you sure that's a good idea? I mean, Trista will definitely go for it and Lila can be persuaded, but there's probably no chance with Thea."

I knew he was being honest with me and simply pointing out the hurdles awaiting the endeavor, but I hated being second-guessed. It was time to be his superior rather than his friend.

"Luke." My voice was stern and sharp as I stepped up beside him and grabbed the handle on the door of my quarters. "Just do it, that's an order." I turned a heated glare on the larger man and watched as every bit of the extra eight inches he had on me melted away.

"Yes, ma'am. It'll be on the way as soon as the storm lets up."

"Good. Now go on. I'm changing and getting warm. I'll be down to brief you and the team in a couple hours. Nothing I found will make any difference in this storm."

He nodded, turned on his heel and trekked back the way we had come.

I shook my head as a grin slipped onto my features then turned and let myself into the small concrete room I called home. I knew he was only doing his job, looking out for me and trying to keep me from making a mistake which might land me dead or worse, captured.

Ten minutes later, I had changed and settled myself in front of a fire I'd managed to get going in the small fireplace in the corner. Finally warming up as I went over what I had learned while out scouting, I wondered what the other scouts had come across, if anything. I leaned back against the wall and watched the red and orange flickers cast dancing shadows on the drab gray walls of the small twelve-by-thirteen room. I followed the shadows as they moved around the space, my gaze landing on the only book I still owned, one of the few books still known to exist, my Bible. It was one of the only examples of the written word which remained other than our occasional handwritten communications.

CHAPTER TWO

BRIEFING

I MUST have dozed off. A pounding on my door ripped me from a dream and I sat bolt upright from the floor. I took a steadying breath, rubbed my eyes to clear them and then levered myself up to my feet and went to the door. I never locked it but my people rarely burst in without knocking first. I opened it to find Luke and his oldest son, Bradley, standing on the other side. They both looked at me expectantly as I yawned, ran my hand through my storm and sleep tousled hair then shrugged with a sleepy, "What?"

"Sorry to wake you but you said you'd be down to brief us in two hours."

"Yeah." I yawned again, failing to see the purpose of their visit to my room.

"It's been four." Oops, guess I'd been pretty tired.

"Sorry, come on."

I pulled my boots back on, happy to find them dry if a bit cold thanks to the fire having died while I'd been asleep. The three of us headed down to our meeting place which consisted of a large makeshift lean-to propped against the side of the building. It was big enough to keep the ten of us present out of any inclement weather which might spring up. I let another yawn slip free as I made my way to the old tree stump I used as a chair and settled onto it.

"Luke tells us you managed to get yourself a tail while you were out earlier."

I nodded as my gaze drifted over the group, making sure everyone was present. I scanned back until I found the person who had spoken, one of my guards.

"Yeah, Marcus, I did. Four men, all dressed like Purist soldiers, but something was off."

"Off?" He raised an eyebrow at me as Luke took his usual place on my left.

"That's what I said, off. They were faster. They kept up with me, they were winded but I couldn't lose them. I had seriously started to wonder if they were really humans when the storm kicked up and they ran for cover."

A murmur went up through the small crowd. They all knew what Luke and I did, Purists were human. While they were completely immune to the latent radiation which had affected the rest of us they still stayed well clear of the rain when it fell. Few people really knew how a massive dose from a direct hit of radiation or being soaked in the stuff would affect them. Other than the minor immunity, they weren't anything special.

The fact I had encountered this group, all of whom had kept up with me was something to investigate on its own. Add to it the several I'd run across who seemed to possess the same abilities in the last handful of years and we had an issue. We were stronger, faster and able to heal ourselves in ways they couldn't but if they had begun to mutate we could have some big problems.

"I think you should see this; it came in while you were out."

A hush fell over the room as Steph stepped up and handed me a slip of paper. As my head runner she would get any messages coming into the compound and bring them to me herself. I took the paper from her and unfolded it, quirking a questioning brow at her as she stepped back without a word. I looked down and read the note, a quick communication about an encounter between Trista and a small group of these not-so-human Purist soldiers.

"Did you read this?" I directed the question toward Luke, knowing Steph had already read it before bringing it to me.

"No. Why?" I handed it to him and he read it over quickly. I watched his forehead crease and his brow furrow as his eyes darted over the words on the paper. "How is this even possible?" He handed the note back to me as I shook my head, worrying our worst fears were becoming reality. Seeing the looks the rest of the group had on their faces, I knew I needed to share what we had read.

"It seems Trista encountered a group of these scouts recently as well. While we knew she had come across a few of them here and there it's picked up recently. It seems she ended up in a scuffle with this group. She claims she kicked one of them in the nose, broke it then dealt with his buddies only to find his nose had already healed."

A muffled gasp went up around the small group.

"I only see one explanation, Kai."

I turned to face Steph again and as much as I hated thinking what I was sure we'd all had run through our minds; it was the only thing which made sense.

"So do I. They had to be Regens. Only we heal that way."

Nervous shifting and throat clearing swept the space and I met the eyes of every one of my people present. "Look, if they're using our own against us, I wanna know how and why. They hate us, they've done everything they can to exterminate us. It doesn't make sense that they would have Regens in their ranks, but the speed and healing don't make sense any other way. Bradley?" I turned to the young man, only twenty-five but already the leader of my scouts.

"Yes, ma'am?"

"I want you to take your three best and head out toward the old airport where I was earlier. The storm hasn't completely let up and those four that were tailing me should still be there. I want them here, immediately. It's about time we get some answers."

"I'll get them and we'll head out right now." I gave him a nod which he returned before he turned and left the space to follow my orders.

"Kai…"

"Don't, Luke. I know he's your son and he might get hurt, but he wanted this position. I can't baby him and keep him out of harm's way because you don't like it."

"Dammit! Why do you have to be all business all the time? He's my kid for fucks sake!"

"I understand that…" I didn't even get to finish my sentence before he cut me off.

"Do you? Honestly, do you really understand? Because I don't think you're capable of understanding. You don't have kids, never had a family. You don't know what it's like to--"

"Enough!" I stepped up to the larger man, my finger meeting

him center mass and backing him across the space. "I've had it with your attitude when it comes to Bradley's assignments. The fact that I grew up without a family has nothing to do with my decisions when it comes to what needs to be done. He's the leader of my scouts and that means he's the best I've got. He has a job to do. I have a compound to run here and I can't start playing favorites because of family involvement."

"You're practically his aunt, Kai!"

"No, Luke, I'm his commanding officer, just like I'm yours. Now you need to shut up and stop questioning my orders or you and I are going to start having issues. Am I clear?"

He muttered something under his breath and it added fuel to the fire of anger already burning in me.

"Am. I. Clear. Soldier?" My jaw was set, my voice cold, hard. I was done taking his crap and I was pretty sure he knew it.

"Crystal, *General*." His inflection rubbed my already raw nerves but in the interest of preserving some kind of civility I shoved it aside before continuing.

"Good. Now get the hell out of my sight before I say or do something we'll both regret." He opened his mouth like he had the urge to say something else but then shut it, turned and exited the space. I took a breath to clear my head and then turned to face the rest of the group. "Anyone else want to question me today?" Seven heads shook their response in the negative and I nodded in reply before I waved them off.

After the space was clear I settled back on the stump, my forehead against the heel of my right hand, my head pounding.

"Kai?" I raised my head enough to see Willow, Bradley's wife, standing a few feet away and heaved out a sigh.

"Christ. Willow, look if you came here to go at me about your husband's assignment I'm really not in the mood."

"No, not at all. Actually he loves it when you give him these kinds of responsibilities, it excites him."

I couldn't help the chuckle which broke free, Bradley had always been eager to please and ready to prove himself. It had made him an exceptional soldier, his agility and stealth had made him a good scout and moved him through my ranks quickly.

"I only wanted to tell you to not let Luke get to you. He loves Bradley but he knows that he has a job to do. At the end of the day, you know he's on your side."

"Of course I do, he wouldn't be my second if he wasn't. Try

not to worry. I do what I can to keep Bradley out of harm's way as much as possible. Not because of who his father is but because I need him. He's damn good at what he does and no one I have here can replace him."

She flashed me a small smile then nodded and walked away, leaving me alone again. I pulled one foot up onto the stump and wrapped my arms around my knee, my chin on my right arm. Trista's note floated around in my head, bothering me more and more the longer I thought about it. I couldn't imagine any circumstances under which the Purists would use our kind to fight for them. After decades of capturing us and killing us off why would we suddenly become a viable weapon?

The better question would be, who in their right mind from our side would agree to such a weird alliance. As much as the Purists couldn't stand us we felt even more negative toward most of them. We'd been singled out, herded like cattle and slaughtered for decades because we were different and we scared them. I couldn't imagine any of my people even considering joining their side after the things they had put us through. I had to believe one of the other generals might have done something to run a few people off.

Somehow I knew if it had to do with one of the four of us, Thea was the winning choice. The more I thought about the whole thing the less sense it made. A distinct pain had kicked up in my right temple warning me of an impending migraine. I released a ragged breath and pushed off the stump, standing there for a bit as I tried to decide what I needed to do next. I started back toward my room but then stopped short as an idea hit me. I did an about-face and headed in the opposite direction, catching Bradley as he and his group were about to leave.

"Bradley!"

"Ma'am?"

"These are your top three?" He nodded his affirmative and I looked the scouts over, trusting his judgement on them. "Okay, I need names for your next four before you leave. I have another assignment for them." He thought about it and then spouted off four names. I gave his small squad leave to go start their mission and made my way toward the scouts housing complex. I pushed through the door and my presence stopped all activity in the room within fifteen seconds.

"General. What can we do for you?" The young woman who spoke to me first couldn't have been more than twenty-one but she already held the appearance of someone who had seen too much to ever look at life the same again.

"I need Greer, Kymbal, Justin, and Xander up here." My voice echoed through the space and the confused pause only lasted a few beats before three bodies made a mad dash for the front of the room.

"I'm Greer." The woman who had greeted me when I entered answered as she was joined by three young men all around her age.

"Alright. I have an assignment for you four. Follow me." I whirled and exited the building, not questioning for a second whether or not they would follow. Making my way back toward the meeting place I'd been in a short time earlier, I kept quiet until we had reached the space. Once under the cover of the lean-to, I turned to face them. "Your squad leader gave your names as his next best four. He and the group he hand-picked are heading west. I need you four to head to the south."

The confused looks they were giving me told me they didn't understand why I was sending them in that direction.

"We've searched everywhere else recently so it's time to hit the one place we haven't looked yet. It would put them right the hell under our noses but when we tend to venture out a day or two looking for them it would be smarter to stick closer. I hate the idea they might have found a way to outsmart us, even for a little while but I'm not too proud to give it a shot. So, south it is."

Four understanding nods met my idea so I continued with their orders.

"I want you to go see if you can find anything. Even if you can't find a base, maybe you can catch some of their soldiers out and about. Even a scouting party would be fine with me. Capture, detain and bring them here. Do not engage them physically unless they give you no choice. Understand?"

"Yes ma'am. You want someone to talk to that hasn't had the crap kicked out of them yet." I smiled at Greer, she was quick and she seemed to understand my motives perfectly. If she was Bradley's number four pick I could only imagine how good the three he had taken with him were.

"Good, now gather what you need and head out."

"Duration ma'am?" The question stopped me since I hadn't decided how long I was sending them out into the wilds. Our scouts were well trained and could live off the land for a fair amount of time.

"As long as it takes. If you find yourself unable to obtain supplies, return and restock then get back out there. I want you on alert until we find a second group to question." The more bodies I had in holding cells the better the chance I'd get some answers. Greer and the three men nodded before making their way toward our supply building.

"Oh, and Greer?" She turned back and raised an eyebrow at me. "You're in charge. You make the calls on this one." A quick nod was the only response I got before they were gone. I hoped I hadn't made an error in sending them out without a true squad leader but I needed answers which meant I needed the people who had them.

CHAPTER THREE

PROPHECY

I NEEDED a break from the disaster forming in my world and there were a couple ways I'd found which worked. Before giving into the draw for a very long nap I took a detour to the stables and slipped through the door. The squeak of the hinges gave me away but even if they hadn't the head which popped over the wall near the door would have still appeared. I smiled when the pure white muzzle raised and a whinny sounded in my direction. With a quick wipe of my boots on the mat inside the door I crossed to the stall and reached a hand toward the massive horse.

"Hey, handsome boy."

My soft words elicited a small snuffling noise from the solid white animal before he stretched his neck out and pressed his velvety nose against my palm. The contact made him nicker at me and I slid my hand up under his chin, giving him a good scratch. I used my free hand to reach down and pull the well-aged slide lock on the stall door. We'd been lucky to find a usable stable on the grounds, the other generals had to toss theirs together out of parts and pieces. I pushed the door open and turned, walking toward the workout pen at the other end of the building.

The horse followed me like a small puppy, not the giant animal he was. Once we were in the pen I kicked the door closed to keep it from getting in the way and walked toward the opposite wall. I dragged my beat-up saddle off the rail as the horse stopped beside me. After tossing it over his back and securing it I glanced around, unsure of where his bridle had ended up. I discovered it tossed in a heap on the other side of the door we'd come through and got it on him as well.

He let out an excited neigh as I pulled myself up into the saddle. I had to laugh. He always got so excited when we went anywhere and I assumed he was glad to be out in the fresh air. I hated not being able to take him out but I couldn't risk another venture into the storm still blowing outside. He would have to wait until it passed but in the meantime I would run him in the training pen. He needed the exercise anyway so I settled into the well-worn leather and nudged him with my heels.

After making a dozen passes in various patterns across the pen a voice professing, "I always forget what an amazing looking animal he is," caused me to pull him up short and look for its source. I found Steph leaning against the top rail near the door and walked him over to her.

"He is a looker, isn't he?"

"That he is." Expressive biohazard green eyes fixed onto my friend as he stretched out his neck and nibbled on her sleeve.

"Prophecy, cut it out. That isn't food, you walking stomach."

He looked back at me as if trying to decide what to do with what I had said to him and then turned, grabbed Steph's sleeve between his teeth and gave it a hard tug, unbalancing her. When she lost the fight with gravity, tumbled over the rail and landed ass first in the dirt he whinnied and tossed his head like it was the funniest thing he'd ever seen. I winced at the thud the contact produced but still barely held back the laugh trying to break free.

"That horse is an ass."

"Oh come on, that's not nice. He was just having some fun." I gave her a very fake pout and she rolled her eyes at me as she stood and dusted herself off.

"Yeah, loads of fun." She turned her narrowed eyes on Prophecy, hands on her hips as she huffed at him. "Jerk."

I hadn't been around any horses before the event so I couldn't tell if the normal versions ever showed the kind of emotional awareness our horses did. I couldn't imagine a regular horse being like Prophecy. At Steph's jab he dropped his head and let out a soft nicker as he shuffled his way up to her and bumped her shoulder with his nose.

"No, go away. I'm mad at you."

Seemingly unwilling to take her dismissal, he plopped his chin over her shoulder and nudged at her cheek, nuzzling her. I watched her face as she attempted to maintain the glare and set of her jaw as he gave her the horse equivalent of a purr. Her resolve broke a piece at a time but within two minutes she had a smile on her face and was scratching his nose. He gave her a happy huff and then pranced around like he'd won the argument, which I would hold he had. A soft gasp coming from the door to the pen made us both turn toward the opening. One of the teenage girls who had relocated to my base with her family from a renegade camp in what had once been Oklahoma stood staring at my horse.

"Hi. You can come on in." She took a tentative step forward without saying a word, then another but stopped after the third, keeping her distance. "You're Faith, right?"

"Uh, yeah."

"You can come closer; he won't hurt you." I dismounted as I spoke, flipping the reins over his head and leading him a few steps closer to the girl.

"What's his name?"

She looked up at him in awe and I couldn't blame her for it since the radiation had done some crazy things to the animals as well as us. Prophecy was part of a line of Arabians who had all taken the same traits as those of us Humans who had mutated. His pure, snow white coat was only broken by the streaks of brilliant green in his mane and tail. His bright, expressive green eyes the same color as those streaks and were almost glowing.

"His name is Prophecy."

"That's a weird name."

I laughed and shook my head, supposing it could be a strange thing to name a horse, but it had a story behind it.

"Might be, yeah. But it suits him. I'm Kai."

"Oh," I watched the realization of who she was speaking to alter her expression before she stammered out, "I... I'm so sorry, General. I didn't mean to intrude, I should go." My brow furrowed as I watched the girl for a moment before I reached out and stopped her from hightailing it from the pen.

"It's fine Faith. You can stay, I don't mind. And please, call me Kai, only the soldiers call me General."

Ever since I'd achieved the rank it had made me itchy, I hated the sound of it but couldn't shake it. I'd be General forever so I had to let it slide sometimes, but not every time.

"O... Okay. He uh, he's big."

I chuckled and turned to look up at Prophecy. He was rather large and I'd been told normal Arabians were an average of fifteen hands high. My horse stood a massive, gleaming, snow-white eighteen hands. His shoulder reached almost four inches over my head.

"That he is. But he's a big ol' baby. Wanna pet him?"

Her eyes went wide and I bit back a laugh, not wanting to make the poor girl self-conscious. She gave a small nod then stepped forward and reached a hand out. Showing himself to be the wonderful animal he'd been since the day I'd received him, Prophecy leaned down and touched his nose to her palm.

"Wow, his nose is really soft."

I nodded as I patted his neck, making sure he knew what a good boy he was being.

"How old is he?"

"That's a really good question. I haven't got a clue." She giggled as Steph and I both laughed. It was the truth since I'd been given the horse as a gift from my mentor when I'd made the rank of General in the resistance. No one had any idea how old he'd been then so I couldn't even begin to make a guess on his current age. As the sound died away a voice called Faith's name from somewhere inside the barn and she offered me a sheepish look.

"That'd be my mom. I sorta wandered off. I should go."

"Yeah, probably best. Come back and see him whenever you want though." She beamed at me and nodded as she turned and charged back through the door toward her mother's voice. I shook my head, let out a sigh and turned toward Steph. "Come help me get him settled for the night?"

"You just don't wanna do it yourself."

"Crap, you caught me. So I'm being lazy, so what? You gonna help?"

"Sure, come on."

She laughed as she grabbed his reins from my hand and started out of the pen and back toward his stall. I trailed behind them a few feet, knowing he'd get up to something before we made it all the way. Sure enough when they hit the halfway point he butted her shoulder with his nose, sending her sprawling into a pile of straw outside one of the empty stalls. In usual Prophecy fashion he tossed his head and whinnied like he was oh-so funny. My laugh caught her attention as she turned over in the straw and she glared at me.

"Some friend you are! And you!" She turned her gaze on Prophecy who I would have sworn was smiling at her. "See if I sneak you anymore treats."

I knew he'd comprehended what she'd said to him when the playful demeanor fell away and he hung his head. Steph stood, brushed the straw off herself and then pulled his bridle and saddle off. I grabbed my kit and worked on brushing him out with her help and then we settled him in for the night.

CHAPTER FOUR

KAI'S STORY

WITH PROPHECY in for the duration of the storm and realizing I was still in need of some unwinding, I headed for my quarters. Beyond spending time with the horse, I'd found naps a great way to relax and get my mind off of things. Not to mention the fact I could have probably dropped and fallen asleep right where I was standing. I said goodbye to Steph and hauled myself into the small space I called home. After kicking off my boots and once again changing into dry clothes I dropped a few more logs on the fire.

I settled onto my makeshift bed on the floor of my room after propping the door open so the smell of the rain still coming down outside could filter into the space. My hands folded behind my head I stared up at the ceiling, the new fire burning in the corner casting shapes across the surface. My mind wandered as I stared at the morphing shadows, picking out familiar things. A dog, a pony, a butterfly, a bird, all present in the shifting grays and blacks above me. They grabbed my mind even though I had been ready to fall over less than an hour earlier.

I gave up on the idea of sleep as the light outside faded into darkness and the rain slowed then stopped. Bradley and his group would be back with our captives soon enough and I would be questioning them. I rolled off the bed, stood up and left my room, not bothering to douse the fire or close the door. I wandered the area for a bit, thinking too hard and making my head hurt. I needed a distraction and as soon as the thought entered my head, I knew exactly where to go.

I took a sharp right and cut between two buildings, coming to a small house, nothing more than a larger version of the room I lived in. The buildings we used were what was left of this part of the city. Most of the metropolis had been blown to hell except a few undamaged panic rooms which had held up. There had been this one corner however, this single bastion of civilization amidst the devastation which had leveled the rest of the city. It had once been a retreat of sorts with sprawling fields, houses, barns, stables and meditation areas. Now they served as our saving grace, giving us places to sleep which kept the rain out and were mostly fire proof.

The residence I stepped up to had been a reinforced house once, owned by a particularly paranoid man who had been very right to be so prepared. The family living in it now were his descendants and had kept the place up wonderfully. Well, wonderfully considering how long it had been since we'd seen anything like decent cleaning supplies. I grinned as I took the five front steps then crossed the wraparound porch to the front door. The sounds of the children laughing inside made me smile as I pushed the massive wooden door open and walked in.

"Kai! Kai!" I had made it three steps into the room when my knees and shins were assaulted by a tight hug from the rambunctious child chanting my name excitedly.

"Hey, Michael! What are you doing up so late?" I squatted to scoop the seven-year-old boy up into my arms. The silky waves of his long golden locks fell down the back of my shoulder as he leaned his head on it.

"I couldn't sleep without a story but mommy said she was too busy tonight. Can you tell us one?"

A pang tightened my stomach at the mention of Keira being too busy for her family since I knew it was my fault. She was one of my top guards and I knew for a fact she'd be out on patrol tonight with the threat of Purists being so close. I'd have to make sure she and Luke were given time to spend with their younger kids when this all ended.

"I don't know, would anyone else want to hear one of my stories?"

I glanced across the room, one of Michael's two brothers and both sister's smiling at me. The eldest of the group still living at home, Brandon, glared in my direction. I chuckled at him as I remembered being thirteen and thinking I was far too cool for pretty much everything.

"Please, Kai?"

I turned my gaze down to the green ringed blue eyes looking up at me and nodded.

"Yay!!" The shout came out with a hefty wiggle which forced me to put the boy down before he fell. I watched him bound across the room to his bed and crawl in then joined the group as the younger ones all did the same. Brandon folded his arms across his chest and continued to glare at me.

"Alright you lot, what kind of story do you want to hear?"

"Tell us about when you were little like me!"

I grinned down at the little blonde I'd been holding a minute ago. As the youngest of the siblings he was generally the most excitable.

"Little like you? Well I don't remember much from when I was seven! But I do remember when I was about Brandon's age." I received another glare and a trademark Brandon eye-roll for my comment. "I also remember stories I heard and things I learned from adults when I was younger."

"Oooh, tell us some of those!"

I ruffled Michael's hair and thought hard for a minute, letting my mind wander to the days when kids still attended schools and read books, back when books existed. These days something like half of the members of my compound could read. Not because we didn't care, no I was very interested in having all my people be able to read. It was because the materials needed to practice at a young enough age to learn properly simply weren't available any longer.

"Well, I remember something I learned. Once, long before I was born, the world was split into these things called countries. Each country had its own leader, government and even religions, sometimes more than one. Back then, people used to fight each other all the time."

"They fought each other? Like we do now?" I turned a sad smile down at Michael.

"Yeah, like we do now. Only lots more people from all different parts of the world. Well, after years and years and years of fighting each other and getting nowhere about it, people finally came together and seemed to work out their differences. We finally had peace. A world government was put in place and several people were picked to lead it. Diseases were healed, technology advanced and everything seemed to be going right."

"If everything was going so right, how did we end up here, like this?" The sharp tone ripped my gaze to Brandon and I had to take a deep breath, releasing it slowly before I replied.

"Well, Brandon, not everything goes the way we plan every time. Sometimes, things just happen, they go wrong and we can't fix it. We had a new way of producing energy, something more efficient that seemed better for the planet at the time. It produced some minor radioactive waste but people had managed to find a way to deal with that. Don't ask me how, I never did understand any of it, they didn't teach us about it other than how well it worked for supplying us with electricity."

"What's electricity?" The innocent question made my heart tighten as I realized for at least the thousandth time since I was in my twenties these new generations might never know electricity, running water or things as taken for granted as a microwave oven.

"Electricity was what we used to have for lights when it was dark."

"Like fire?" I hadn't ever explained electricity to someone and it dawned on me how difficult it could be.

"Kind of like fire. But without the flames, so things didn't get burned. And you didn't need to stay with it and add wood to make sure it didn't go out. You just flipped this thing called a switch and it came on and then stayed on until you turned it off." The little boys' eyes went wide and when I looked up at the rest of them they all had the same look. Except for Brandon who still wore his glare.

"Sounds great. So why don't we have that now?"

Oh how annoying and trying teenage attitude and angst could be. I wondered how his parents put up with it. Every time I visited the group I gathered a new level of admiration for Luke and his wife.

"Well, see, we should have it now. There were these things called fail safes in place, they were supposed to protect us."

"Seems like they worked fabulously." The sarcasm dripping from his tone hit me like a solid punch in the stomach but he wasn't exactly wrong.

"The problem with fail safes is that they are created by people and, well, we're flawed. Something went very wrong and all the protections the scientists had in place failed. The system broke down and the devices started to explode. It was like a ripple after you toss a stone in a lake. Some, the ones closest to the main operating zone, went off in seconds and no one near them survived, some had several hours' notice. Those zones had people who survived, who managed to hide like we did here. Even then, people found out pretty fast that they fell into one of three types. The first couldn't fight the radiation, it got into their systems, created disease. They didn't make it long, five or ten years.

The second group caught on to their differences about twelve years after the explosions. That was when they realized that, well, they weren't affected at all. It seemed like the radiation just rolled off of them and left them completely human."

"The Purists."

My eyes met Brandon's and I nodded.

"Yeah, the Purists. The third group didn't actually know they were a separate group until about five years after the Purists figured out their immunity. Most of the first generation just thought they were Purists, that they were completely unaffected. It wasn't until some started showing weird effects and others began having children that they figured out how wrong they were. That group, well, they were special. The radiation did affect them but it didn't kill them. They mutated but in a way that allowed them to survive, to use the toxins rather than being killed by them. These traits showed in the strongest of them within just a few years as their genes mutated. The rest picked it up as they had kids, the signs allowed them to be identified."

"That's us!"

"Yeah, Michael. That's us." I chuckled at the little boy's enthusiasm. "Our bodies use the radiation to constantly regenerate our cells."

"Is that why the Purists call us 'Regens'?"

"Right on the dot, Brandon. Well, the world fell into chaos after that. Not much had survived the explosions then the fallout afterward and at first, everyone seemed to be working together and making a go at survival. Then the first true Regens were discovered, the first Level Ones and the Purists went off the deep end. Somewhere along the way they took on this belief that God saved them, chose them for something. They believe they have a calling, a higher purpose. That would have been just fine with the rest of us, if they hadn't decided we must be the enemy."

"Why would they decide that? At first, we were just like them so, why turn on us?"

I thought about it before I answered Hannah's question, knowing that she, at eleven, and Brandon were capable of handling whatever response I threw at them but the little ones might need easing into it all.

"The thing about them is they believe that with good, there must be evil. If God saved them to help bring the world back into His light, then there must be a darkness for them to fight. That meant us since we're pretty much their exact opposites. To them, if they fight for the light, we fight for the darkness and so we must be evil."

"But that's insane. We're not bad, we just reacted differently. Different isn't evil."

"We know that, Brandon. They don't, or if they do, they don't care. Soon after they realized that we existed, they started rounding us up and finding ways to get rid of us."

"Kill us you mean."

I shot the teenager a look, the story was depressing and terrible but it didn't need to scare the younger kids too much.

"What? It's the truth isn't it?"

"Yes, it's the truth. What they did was classify us, give us rankings so they would be able to tell the ones they thought were dangerous from those they deemed less of a threat."

"Mom and dad told us about those. We're Ones!"

I smirked and pulled nine-year-old Jesse onto my lap as I nodded.

"Yes, Jesse. Most of you are Level Ones. Brandon is a Level Two though."

"Oh, what's the difference?" The innocence staring up at me from the little girl's blue eyes made me smile.

"Well, there are four levels. You, your mom and dad and most of your brothers and sisters are all Level One. That means that unless someone is looking really hard, you could pass for human. You live a little longer, maybe twenty or so years more than they do, and you have a little tiny bright green ring right around the edge of your iris. Other than that, no difference. Level Twos, like Brandon, have a little extra green in their eyes, another ring around the pupil, and some have light green streaks in their hair. With good planning, they could still pass as human but they do live longer, an extra forty years or so."

"Wow! What about three and four?" I motioned at Michael to

settle down into his bed and moved to put Jesse in hers before I continued.

"Level Threes can't pass for human anymore. They usually have green eyes and at least one really bright green stripe in their hair though some with darker hair never get that. They can live sixty or seventy years longer than regular humans do. Then there are Level Fours."

"Like you."

I caught Brandon's eye and smiled when I saw his smirk.

"Yeah. I'm a Level Four."

"One of only four we know for sure are still around. That's what dad says." His smirk faded with his words as if he understood that Level Fours had been thinning in numbers and we didn't know how to recover.

"As far as I know, yes, there are four of us. There used to be more but, they figured out pretty quick that we can still die and they hunted us down."

"Why?"

The genuine need to understand I saw etched into his features tugged at my heart and I had to take a deep breath to steady myself, I would not cry.

"Because we scare them. Level Fours can't even pretend to be human. Bright green eyes that glow in the dark and brilliant green streaks in our hair start the problems." I reached up and ran a hand through my own brightly-streaked shoulder-length hair, the strands between the brilliant green a deep ebony. "We also have an ability to use the latent radiation hanging in the air and on the ground around us as a weapon."

"Dad told me about that. How?"

A look of intrigue had crept over his features and he couldn't hide his curiosity on the matter. I looked around at the other kids and caught them all staring at me intently, hanging on every word I said. *Lovely.*

"Well, I can pull it in and channel it then focus it. While the radiation hanging around us doesn't affect the Purists, a solid hit from a radioactive beam can sometimes do some damage."

I wasn't about to elaborate on it too much. We knew a bit more about the things our abilities could do than we generally let on. The four of us left had discovered decades earlier we could use our gift as a powerful weapon. It could kill. There was a cost however, and we often needed anywhere from several minutes to days of energy recovery after a hit to feel normal again. The use of the ability drained us rapidly and a handful of early Level Fours had actually died from overtaxing themselves.

Rather than telling them any of those things I stated, "It knocks them off their feet and puts a quick stop to whatever they were doing. That terrifies them."

"That's kinda cool." I could tell from the grin he attempted to hide he thought it was more than cool. He pressed on before I could call him on it though. "You live longer too, right?"

"Yeah, quite a bit longer."

"How long can you live, Kai?"

I turned my gaze down toward Michael as the same question ran through my mind.

"Good question. You remember that day I was talking about, when everything went bad and the explosions happened?"

"Yeah." All five children nodded as Michael answered.

"I remember that day, I was there. Actually, I was here. We used to call this city Dallas." Four curious expressions and one cloaked in doubt met my gaze as I glanced at the children.

"That was over two hundred years ago." I settled my focus on Brandon to give him a knowing look and his face drained, going a little pale, his expression turning to one of shock.

"Two hundred and twenty to be exact. I was fifteen. I'm still here so, we don't know how long we can live. So far the number stands at two hundred and fifty-five years since the oldest Level Four still alive was thirty-five when the explosions happened."

"Wow."

The single word was all the teen could manage to utter and I don't think I could have expressed it better myself. Wow was about right. I left the story telling there, deciding to leave out the fact a Level Four hadn't been born since the event. We had all been alive when it happened and the similarities between us didn't end there. We were all female as well, something which had been true even before the Purists had killed off the others who had existed.

There had been more than a few males who had begun the transformation and we believed they would join us as Level Fours. In the end, none of them had survived the mutation for more than a handful of years. My mentor had made it the longest of the group, almost twenty-five years but he had paid for the struggle with his sight. He spent the last fifteen years of his life totally blind. We had other problems keeping more Level Fours from coming into existence. From what we knew, we were all also sterile, unable to reproduce. We could only hope that we would survive to see the people left on the planet reunite, after that happened, and any extra years on our lifespans were a bonus.

CHAPTER FIVE

CAPTIVES

KAI'S JOURNAL - *Summer Cycle, 2606 – 220 years after the event:*
So much happens around this place in the summer. Kids are running around playing, enjoying the warm weather while it lasts and our crops are faring well after all the rain we got over the spring. Bradley and his scouting team have been out in the wilds for a while now and I'm hoping they'll be back soon. The news that the Purists seem to have Regens working for them has my Captains unsettled and I'll admit I'm right there with them. There's not much we can do about the phenomenon until we know how frequently they use them and why they're venturing into such weird territory to begin with. This could take months to figure out, longer if we can't catch someone from their side willing to talk. For the time being, I'm giving myself a headache so I need to force myself to get some sleep.

Shouted curses pulled me from a light, dreamless sleep and left me confused. As everything focused I recognized Bradley's voice drifting through the area and bolted from my bed. I tugged on my boots, pulled a shirt over my head and pushed out of my door in a matter of seconds to find out what was going on. Following the shouts and sounds of a gathering crowd I found my first scouting team with two well-restrained men in tow. I grinned as I watched them fight their captors appreciating their spirit. When Claire, one of my soldiers, stepped in and cracked the louder of the two men in the side of the head with her bow I jumped into action.

"Enough!"

The tone of my voice caused everyone present to start and several pairs of eyes turned in my direction, Claire's narrowed defiantly. She and I had come to verbal blows about her heavy-handed approach more than once and it appeared she hadn't learned.

"He was getting out of hand."

"Was he? Because to me it looked like he was just shouting at everyone."

"I couldn't let him..."

"Let him what? Be angry that he's been tied up and hauled into an enemy compound against his will? I think he has every right to be pissed off. Don't you?" Her response was a hard tensing of her jaw and an angry furrow of her brow. "Claire?"

"What?"

"Answer me, soldier!"

"Yes."

"Yes?"

"Yes ma'am. He has a right to be pissed."

"You need to back up right now."

The woman nodded and backed away from the two men, one now bleeding from his temple and the other glaring daggers at her for the blow she'd landed on his friend. I stepped in closer and moved to help the injured man up off the ground since he couldn't get himself to his feet with his hands tied.

"Don't fucking touch me, freak!"

His shout was followed closely by a leg sweep which knocked my feet out from under me. I hit the dirt hard, the force of the fall pushing the air from my lungs and leaving me gasping for breath. I willed air into my body and pushed myself off the ground right as Claire decided to forget my orders. She lunged at the man and I did a quick sidestep to put myself between them, my elbow coming up to meet her nose. The two body parts contacted hard and she cried out in pain as blood streamed from her nose.

"What the hell, Kai?" I ignored her and turned on the injured man again, my expression less than friendly.

"That was a cheap shot, and you won't get another chance at it so I hope you enjoyed it."

"I did, bitch."

He spat on my shoes and I shook my head as I waved Bradley

in to get him up off the ground. He was heaved to his feet and then I was in his face.

"Look, I get that you're pissed off. You have every right, but I'm doing my best to be as friendly as possible given the circumstances. I'd chill out if I were you, before I get angry and stop trying to be civil."

"I'd listen, man, the last thing you want is to see this one angry."

Something in the way Bradley said the words or maybe the look in my eyes as I stared the man down made his brain kick in. His expression shifted and I could swear fear trickled into his eyes. His anger wavered and he nodded as I took his elbow and turned him toward our holding area. We'd managed to piece together an old style jail system from keyed doors found in the aftermath. They weren't super secure by our old standards, but were perfect for this new world where nothing was electric and all a prisoner had was a pair of hands to break himself out. It made life easier on those doing the jailing.

I left the two men in the care of Bradley and sent Luke to help him then turned my attention to Claire. She had a bad habit of crossing me and disobeying my orders and it had reached the point where I'd had enough of it. She glared up at me from the dirt, even when I'd knocked her flat on her ass she was being a shit. I shook my head and offered her my hand, pulling her to her feet when she took it. I tugged her close so our noses were only two or three inches apart, hers already healing.

"Listen and listen close, Claire. I've had it with your shit. I'm sick of your disobedience and violence. That..." I indicated the man being led off to his cell, a trickle of blood still visible though I noticed that the wound on his temple had vanished. "Is not how we behave here."

"Kai, I was only trying to..."

"Shut up."

She listened for once and snapped her mouth closed before anything else could slip out.

"Good. I don't care what you were trying to do. I gave you an order and you took it upon yourself to disobey it. I want you out of my compound by sunset tomorrow. Gather whatever you need, say your goodbyes and get out."

The defiance which always tinted her green haloed gaze melted away, replaced by fear. Level Threes, like we Level Fours, didn't show fear often so the sight of it quickened my pulse against my wishes.

"K... Kai. Wh... Where am I supposed to go?"

"I'll send a runner to Thea, you'll report to her."

"Thea?" The color drained from her face and she swallowed hard, Thea had a reputation and it wasn't good. "But she's..."

"She's what?"

"Brutal."

"You seem to prefer brutality over following my orders. You should fit in just fine there. Now go, you have a lot of preparing to do. Remember, you have until sunset. If you're still here after dark, I promise you your fear of Thea will pale in comparison with your new fear of me."

She nodded slowly and then backed away several feet before bolting for her quarters to gather her things.

With Claire handled I made my way toward our small jail, catching the attention of Ingrid, one of our caretakers on the way. While it had looked like the wound on the one man had healed, other head injuries were always a possibility and I would prefer he be checked out. She followed me into the dimly-lit area, only the sun filtering through the tiny windows lending any form of light to the cramped room. I sent the two guards who had been left to watch our prisoners to handle other tasks. Once they vacated I asked Ingrid to tend to the previously-injured man. My focus settled on the one who didn't carry the probability of a concussion.

"I know this is a crap situation for you and your friend but I need some answers out of you."

"Screw off."

"Well that's pleasant. Aren't you a charmer?"

"I'm not telling you anything so you might as well give up now."

I hadn't expected anything other than what he kept throwing at me but knowing it was coming didn't make it less annoying. I closed my eyes and centered myself, needing to keep calm. Blowing up at either of them wouldn't do any good and could hinder progress. I had two choices, stay civil and hope to wear them down with patience or flip the switch and turn to beating it out of them. I cringed at the mere idea of running my base like we'd all heard Thea did and discarded the second option. In my company it would be a last resort and I would do everything I could to keep from going down that particular road.

"Okay. I'll leave you be then. We'll have someone check on your buddy every couple hours to make sure he doesn't have any serious brain injuries. She clocked him pretty good."

I shifted my attention to the man having his pupil dilation and reaction times checked by our caretaker. "I'm sorry about that by the way."

"Sure you are." I bit back the snappy retort I wanted to let slip out.

"I am. Despite what you may think of my people I don't typically allow them to stoop to beating our..."

"Prisoners?"

I thought about arguing but he had a point, they were our prisoners and no fancy label would change it.

"Yeah, our prisoners. She's been handled, she's being relocated. She won't give you any more trouble. I promise."

He studied me hard and I could see the skepticism in his eyes. After the day he'd had I couldn't say I would feel any differently if I were in his shoes.

"Thank you."

His voice was barely more than a whisper but the two simple words were still strong enough to make my chest tighten. Maybe there was a chance at getting something out of them without resorting to painful tactics after all. I replied with a quick nod and then excused myself from the room, I needed some air and a chance to check if anyone had heard from our second scouting team. I made my way across the space between our jail and the living quarters, running into Bradley before reaching the first larger building.

"Just the two?"

"Yeah, the other two didn't make it through the storm. Apparently the wolves got them."

Wolves were always a threat when anyone happened to be out in the wilds of the ruins. They were particularly nasty at night since their vision, enhanced by the radiation they had absorbed, peaked in the dark.

"It happens. At least you managed to grab these two. With any luck we can get some useful information out of them."

He glanced in the direction of the jail and heaved out a sigh as he said, "Yeah, though after that show from Claire, it might take a while."

"Oh, I expect it to. I wouldn't be interested in talking after what she pulled either. We'll give them some time and see what happens. You can go back to what you were doing; we'll do a full team briefing in a few days after I have a chance to talk to them a bit more."

"Sounds good, boss. C'ya."

I flashed him a smile and waved as he walked away then tried to decide what my next step was. I had been heading to find Steph and see if she had heard from the other team and while I figured she would have told me already if she had, I didn't have anything better to do.

"Steph!" I typically called for her the minute I hit her front door, not ever quite in the mood to go searching for her in the house her family shared.

"Coming!" I leaned in the doorway as I waited and only had to recline for a minute before she appeared. "What's up?"

"Any news from the second scouting team I sent out?"

"Not even a whisper. Sorry."

"It's fine. I didn't figure you'd heard anything but I was bored." She laughed at me and nodded toward the door.

"Come on, let's take a walk." I followed her out the door and we walked in silence for a few minutes before she broke it. "Kai, are you happy?"

The question threw me and I couldn't think of anything to say to her so I stopped walking and stared in her direction. When my brain processed the question and formed words, I spoke.

"I guess I am. Sort of. Maybe not. It's hard to be too happy in our situation."

"I get that, but I meant are you happy alone?"

Steph had been like my little sister when she was growing up and I'd always treated her as such. Sometimes she took the connection we had to places like this one. I knew she worried but I couldn't ever decide what to tell her.

"Am I happy alone? No. Not really. I get by and I'm not falling apart or anything. I'm okay."

"You're okay. Wow, great to hear."

I leveled a glare at her for the sarcasm, something I could do without today.

"When are you gonna let yourself feel something again?"

I narrowed my eyes further and picked up walking again, not liking where she had steered the conversation.

"Wait, Kai. Please just… Wait." I slowed and let her catch up to me, sighing as she looped her arm through mine. "You know I'm only worrying about you. I hate that you deal with all of this on your own. You used to be so happy."

"That was a long time ago. I haven't had a reason to be happy lately." I stared at my boots, my hands buried in my pockets as I walked.

"It was Laney who made you happy."

The mention of her name halted my forward progress instantly and the sudden pressure on my heart could have made a vice jealous. Just the sound of it made my entire being ache and I bit the inside of my cheek in a very physical attempt to bite back tears.

"Don't go there, Stephanie."

She looked at me like she was about to say something else but I threw a hand up to stop her. I gave her a hard look, shook my head and then turned and walked away. I couldn't handle the conversation she wanted to have, the one she had been trying to have for the last several years. I needed to put some space between her and myself and not think about it. I increased my pace and headed back toward the center of the compound.

I stepped into the open space near the center of the whole operation and heard someone call my name. I turned to find Bradley rushing in my direction and let out a heavy sigh. I really didn't think I could handle any more issues in a single day. I hoped whatever he had to say might be good news. My luck wasn't quite on the right side of good for happy things to happen but I tried to stay positive, sometimes.

"Kai, the second team is back."

"They are?" He nodded and my eyebrows raised a bit, imploring him to give me more information.

"I… You should just come see for yourself."

It was never good when he used such phrasing and my hands tightened into fists at my sides as I nodded to him. He turned and led the way toward the front of the compound with me on his heels. The minute we got close enough to see the second scouting group, I understood why he had wanted me to see for myself. The four of them were standing there with several Purist captives bound and looking a bit frantic. Not one of them had the look of a soldier or scout about them. My eyes narrowed as I approached the scene, turning my glare on Greer and watching confusion color her expression.

"What the hell is this?" She opened her mouth to reply, got nothing out, closed it to clear her throat and then tried again.

"This is the Purist groups we picked up and detained."

"How long have you been on my scouting team, Greer?"

"Ma'am?"

"How long?" I hated when I had to resort to shouting at her but she had to know what she had done was over the line.

"Almost five years."

"And in five years, how many times have you been walked through our rules of detainment?"

"Several, ma'am."

"Then why is it that I'm standing here looking at a bunch of women and children rather than soldiers or scouts?"

"I... Um... Ma'am I just..."

I cut her off by holding up one finger and then hefted out a harsh sigh as I tried to decide what to do with them.

"Look, normally we don't detain and question anyone not considered a threat but we definitely can't let them leave now that they've seen where we are."

I couldn't have them going back and leading their soldiers to us. I turned to Bradley and nodded over to the small group of three women and four children.

"Take them over to the jail and get them set up, I'll figure out what to do with them later."

He nodded and waved at the team to follow him with the prisoners but I stopped Greer with a hand on her shoulder and tugged her over to sit down with me.

"Ma'am, I'm really sorry I..."

"Stop, Greer, I don't blame you, I blame myself for not verifying your comprehension of the rules before sending you out on your own. However, I can't let you back out for a while. You'll go back through training so I can make sure you have a full grasp on the rules. Understood?"

She gave me a slow nod and I waved her off to return to the barracks while I tried to figure out what to do with our new captives. I pushed up off the stump I'd been sitting on and started toward the jail yet again. I had to wonder when I'd catch some kind of break and get a full day to be bored rather than an hour here and there. I chuckled to myself at the idea and shook my head at the sheer ridiculousness of it as I walked.

"Hey boss, they're all set up as far away from the scouts we brought in as I could get them. The kids are really shaken up."

"Yeah well, I'd be more worried if they weren't. I would be too. Poor things." I patted Bradley on the shoulder and nodded toward the door then waited for him to exit before I moved over to the cells. I felt around the small table in the area and managed to light the two lamps sitting atop it, casting an eerie yellow light around the enclosed area. I stood there looking into the two large cells, my heart aching a bit as I listened to the two younger children crying.

"What do you want?"

I focused my attention on the woman who had spoken and raised an eyebrow at her.

"What I want I don't need you to get."

"Then why are we in here?"

The defiance in her tone made me step forward and to the right so the lamps could illuminate her and give me a better look. She stood about my height with pale blonde hair and brilliant blue eyes. Once I was looking it took me a minute to get my thoughts together and speak again.

"You're in here because my scouts made a mistake. We don't advocate detaining innocent women and children here."

"Sure you don't."

She had some venom in her and it made me grin as I shook my head at the tone.

"Whatever you may think, this isn't my way. Unfortunately, now you know where we are and I can't take the chance that you'll lead your soldiers back here. For the meantime, you're stuck here. We'll do the best we can to make you as comfortable as possible."

She rolled her eyes at me as she leaned against the back wall and crossed her arms over her chest. It was pretty obvious that she didn't believe me, I probably wouldn't believe me either if I were her. I sighed and leaned against the bars of the cell, my hands in my pockets.

"Look, I'm sorry that they hauled you in here, I really am. I'm Kai, what are your names?"

I got a glare in response and all I could do was chuckle. If I could actually get her to loosen up she might be fun to chat with.

"I'm not telling you anything. You might as well just walk away."

I was about to give up on even trying with her and move on to attempting to get a name from one of the other women when the choice was made for me.

"I'm Julia."

The words were barely audible over the sniffles of the small child in the woman's lap but were enough to get my attention and pull my gaze to one of the other two.

"Julia?" She nodded and I responded in kind as I shifted to the other cell and squatted down to get down to eye level with her. "Hi Julia. Look, I'm sorry about this and I'll do everything I can to figure out a way to get you some place other than this cell. Okay?" She gave me another nod and kissed the mop of dark-brown hair. "And who is this?"

"Nathan, my son."

"Hi there Nathan. I know you're scared but don't worry, no one is going to hurt you. I'll make sure of that." He turned deep brown eyes toward me and my heart broke as I looked at his tear stained cheeks. He didn't look like he really believed me but his mother did, which counted for something. I straightened up and turned back to the woman in the other cell, finding her still glaring at me.

"Still nothing?"

She shook her head and I sighed before shrugging and taking my leave of the room, leaving one of the two lamps burning when I exited. She'd crack eventually, or I'd start calling her something so obnoxious she'd give me her name to make it stop.

CHAPTER SIX

WHAT'S IN A NAME?

KAI'S JOURNAL - *Summer Cycle, 2606 – 220 years after the event:*
Every time I think I've finally got myself pulled together Steph has to pop up and make waves. I don't understand why she can't leave it alone. How long I take to get over my past and move on with that part of my life has nothing to do with her. I may not be perfectly happy but I'm functioning and it isn't like I'm sitting around depressed and ruining everyone's days. To top off my best friend rooting into my personal life I had to deal with one of my scouts, Greer, bringing in a set of prisoners I wouldn't have normally allowed. I'm really not sure what I'm supposed to do with these women and I feel terrible having children locked up in cells. I'll have to do whatever I can to make sure they have somewhere else to go though I have no clue where. I'll admit that one caught my attention, she's got an attitude and I have the feeling she'd be a riot if she'd relax and realize I'm not interested in hurting them. The thing that makes me wary is how she's been making me feel. All twisted up around myself with this weird flutter in my stomach. I'm scared of what it might mean so I'm doing my best to ignore it. I guess I'll just have to see how things pan out.

Over the course of the next ten weeks I managed to get names from the third woman and the other three children. Miss-Attitude still refused to comply and give me hers but I had stopped asking for it. I had taken to calling her Sweetness and it seemed to irritate her quite a bit but not enough for her to give me something else to call her. Several of our builders and I had locked down one of the older houses and moved the group into it. They were more comfortable but still under lock and key.

The two captured men hadn't said a word we found useful and I put out an order to keep the women from being questioned. I visited them daily and had even managed to develop some kind of trust with the woman named Julia and her son. I unlocked the front door and stepped into the house-shaped cell, shutting and locking the door behind me. I made sure the keys were tucked away into one of my pockets before moving further into the space. After taking the stairs two at a time I rapped lightly on the first door before opening it and leaning against the frame.

"What do you want?"

"Well hello to you too, Sweetness."

"I've told you to stop calling me that." She shot a heated glare in my direction and I grinned back at her.

"And I've told you that I will when you give me a name to use instead."

"Go away."

"Such anger, Sweetness, you should really lighten up, that kind of pissed off isn't good for you."

She rolled her eyes at me and I chuckled as I turned and started down the hall to check on Julia, Patricia and the kids. I could play this game forever, probably rather literally and I figured she would break at some point.

"Hayley." I froze at the sound of the word tossed my way and then turned to look at her, my head cocked slightly to one side.

"What did you say?"

"My name, it's Hayley."

The glare still sat on her face but it had softened a bit and I smiled at her as I stepped back over to the door and leaned against the frame again. I crossed my arms over my chest and studied her for several seconds, trying to decide if she was telling me the truth.

"Well, Hayley, thank you. See, that wasn't so bad."

She offered up another eye roll but I caught her fighting a grin as she did it. As much as she wanted to hate me, we seemed to be making some kind of progress.

"Yeah, so far. Now will you *please* stop calling me Sweetness?"

I let out a laugh as I nodded to her.

"Yeah, I'll stop calling you sweetness. It was really starting to stick and feel right though, I'll miss it."

"Ha! I sure won't." After another laugh I turned and started down the hallway again, pausing halfway and looking at her over my shoulder.

"I know this situation isn't ideal, but I'm trying." Without giving her a chance to reply I continued on my previous path and knocked on the door at the other end of the hall. It swung open and Julia offered me a small smile which I returned.

"Hey."

"Hey Julia. How are you holding up?"

She shrugged and I knew given their current circumstances it was a completely ridiculous question to ask. They might all be housed in a decent living space with warm beds and food but they were still prisoners. I crossed the room and sat on the smaller bed, my chin resting on my hand as I scanned the room.

"Now where on earth could Nathan be? I could have sworn he was here this morning."

I heard the soft giggle the little boy tried to suppress coming from under the bed but pretended I'd heard nothing. I pushed off the bed and moved to the closet, pulling the door open with an 'aha!' and then turning to be sure he would see the dramatic pout I put on. I tapped my chin with my index finger and made a face, looking like I was thinking hard then said, "I know!" I moved over to Julia's bed, turned my back toward his smaller one and dropped to the floor. After scanning the vacant space underneath thoroughly I stood, put my hands on my hips and let out a heavy huff I knew he would hear.

"Well I just don't know where he could be. Oh well, I guess Brynn will get his sweets then." I winked at Julia and she covered her mouth to keep from laughing as I turned toward the door.

"I'm right here!" I whirled to look at the smaller bed as he crawled out from under it, a completely fake look of shock painted on my face.

"So you are. What a good hider you are! I never would have found you under there."

He giggled as he ran over and wrapped his arms around my legs. I reached in my pocket, pulled out a piece of folded fabric and unwrapped it before I picked him up. I rested the somewhat small four-year-old on my hip and raised the piece of dried fruit where he could see it. We had taken to boiling down various berries then soaking apples in the juice before letting them dry. They were the closest thing to candy we had in this forsaken world.

A high pitched squeal emanated from the child as he wiggled around trying to get the fruit. I laughed then moved it closer so he could grab it off the fabric. He nibbled at it as I glanced over to find Hayley leaning in the doorway. I caught the smile on her face a second before it slipped off and she looked away. She cleared her throat as she brushed some hair behind her right ear and I kept quiet, allowing her to have whatever moment she needed to compose herself.

She must have decided she didn't want to say anything and after a minute she turned and went back to her room. I raised an eyebrow at her door as it closed then shook my head. She could be frustrating but every small step was one I would gladly take. I turned my attention back to Nathan who had finished his fruit and was trying to wiggle his way out of my grip. I grinned as I put him down and made my way over to sit across from Julia as he dropped to the floor to play. She watched her son for a few long seconds before she turned to me with a sad look in her eyes.

"I'm really sorry you're stuck here. I know it's hard on you both."

"Actually," she began as the hint of a smile began on her lips, "it may sound strange but this is the happiest he's been in months." Confused, I cocked my head to the left at the comment. "Our situation back where we came from was, well let's just say less than ideal and leave it there for now. He was scared so often I'd forgotten what his laugh sounded like." She glanced over at her son again where he sat pushing around a little wooden boat I'd carved for him the week before.

"You looked so sad for a second there though. Isn't hearing him laugh a good thing?"

"Oh definitely. What made me sad was thinking that it took being captured and imprisoned by the very people I've always been taught would kill us on sight to make him this happy. This entire experience has been a little surreal."

"I can understand that. I've always wondered what the leadership on your side teaches you about us. It seems every time I have to detain someone they assume I'm just going to kill them."

"Sadly that's exactly what they teach us you'll do. They tell us from the time we're old enough to understand it that Regens are evil, that you hate us and want us all dead. They tell us that you teach all your children to ride and shoot a bow as soon as they can walk so they can go wipe out our people."

My eyes widened as she spoke, I couldn't believe what I was hearing. Nothing she'd said was anything close to the truth. Less than half of the population of my compound had ever been on a horse and even fewer were proficient with a bow to any degree. I shook my head and blew out a long sigh, understanding more every day they were with us how bad things were.

"None of it is true, is it, Kai?"

"Not here. I can't speak for the other Generals, obviously, but we don't operate that way here."

"I knew that the moment you scolded your woman for detaining children. Even if there are some out there who are like we were taught, I know you aren't. You've been nothing but kind to us since we were brought here. I know we're captives but even knowing that I still feel more at home here than I did in my old home."

A combination of pride and sadness swelled in my chest as I fought to keep from tearing up at her words. While I was thrilled Nathan was happy and she felt settled with my people, I couldn't help wondering what she'd come from to have captivity feel homey. I managed to get my emotions under control, ran my fingers through my hair to allow some breathing time then smiled at her. She returned the gesture and the expression was so genuine I almost lost it again but pulled myself back under control.

"Well, I'm glad he's dealing with all of this well. Can I ask you something?"

"Of course."

"Purely out of curiosity... If you could stay here, permanently. Have Nathan learn with our kids his age, go out and spend time with the residents here and maybe learn one of the skills my people pick up to help around the compound... Would you want to?"

She seemed to be thinking the idea over as she watched Nathan play for a couple minutes. She turned back to me with a small nod as she rested her chin on her palm. She offered me a grin as she said, "Yes, I think I would. I've been pleasantly surprised by you, Kai. You haven't been what I expected of a Resistance General at all. You've made sure we're healthy, the kids are happy, we're well fed and even when you could have left us rotting in that jail forever, you didn't. I can't honestly imagine we'd be any happier where we were headed than we would be here."

"Well give me some time. I might be able to make that happen."

The brilliant smile she gave me made my heart ache as I hoped I could find a way to assimilate the small group into our population. I would do everything I could to make sure they could get out of this house shaped jail they'd been living in as soon as I could manage. The children needed fresh air and other kids to play with. Being cooped up wasn't good for them. The only hitch in the plan lived down the hall since I couldn't imagine letting Julia, Patricia and the kids out while leaving Hayley locked up. I stared at the door, letting out a huff which made Julia reach over and put a hand on mine.

"You okay?"

I turned to look at her and the concern I saw in her eyes sealed the deal, she cared how I felt. I couldn't let her stay in here much longer.

"Me? I'm fine. I think."

"Seems reassuring." She let out a gentle chuckle and I smiled at her with a shake of my head.

"That's what my best friend is always saying. Look, I need to go check on Patricia and the other kids but I'll be back."

"I know you will. Nathan," the little boy turned when he heard his name and looked at his mother who continued by saying, "Come say goodbye. Kai is leaving."

He was off the floor in a flash as I stood from the bed, still gripping the little boat in one hand as he threw himself at my legs. I grinned and reached down to ruffle his hair as he looked up at me, grinning from ear to ear.

"Bye, Kai!"

"Bye buddy. I'll come see you again soon okay?"

"'kay!"

"You go play, I'm gonna go visit everyone else." He gave me a big nod before he went back to his place on the floor, picking up right where he'd left off.

Julia walked me to the door then watched as I headed toward Patricia's rooms, closing her door as I knocked on the one in front of me. It was answered ten seconds later by her daughter Brynn who smiled at me, revealing two missing teeth. I smiled back as she stepped out of the way then waved to her mother as she approached.

"Hey, Kai."

"Hi, Patricia. I see Brynn finally lost that other tooth." She laughed as the seven-year-old flashed her gapped grin at me again and I mirrored the sound.

"That she did. You see Julia and Nathan already?"

"Mmhmm. How are you holding up over here?"

"We're okay. I think Jamie is coming down with a cold but it should pass pretty quickly."

My brow furrowed at the news of her two-year-old possibly being sick.

"I'll get Ingrid over here later to check on him. No sense in waiting to see if it's something worse. She knows some good herbal remedies for sickness."

"Oh thank you. I wouldn't have asked."

"I know you wouldn't. I'll make sure she stops in tonight. So Jamie might be sick, Brynn lost another tooth, how is Gregory holding up?" At the mention of his name the eleven-year-old stepped around to look out the door. He grinned when he saw me, his emerald eyes lighting up under his unruly mop of curly red hair.

"Hi."

"Hi there. How have you been feeling?"

"I'm fine, just bored."

"I'll bet. I'm working on that, okay?" He gave me a nod then turned and moved into the adjoining room to go check on his younger brother. I turned toward Patricia as I said, "I can't stay too long but I wanted to check in."

"We appreciate it. I heard Hayley give you her name earlier."

The mention of the spirited woman down the hallway made things in my body which hadn't reacted in longer than I liked to admit tighten. I cleared my throat to keep the groan attempting to break free from coming out and nodded.

"Yeah, finally."

"Give her time. She's stubborn as the day is long but she'll come around. She just doesn't trust easily."

"I know the feeling. I have to go; I'll check in again soon." She offered me a nod and a smile in response before closing the door as I walked away. I made it down the stairs and almost to the door before a voice stopped me in my tracks.

"Kai, wait." I turned to find Hayley standing at the bottom of the stairs, she slowed as she came closer and then looked at her feet. "I'm sorry."

I was floored to hear her apologizing but rather than showing it I asked, "For?" She sighed and looked up at me before answering.

"Being so stubborn. It was just my name. It wasn't like you

were asking for the location of the compound or something."

"True. But I understand why you didn't want to talk to me. Don't worry about it, I'm a big girl, I'll survive the distrust."

She rolled her eyes but smiled at the same time before nodding and turning to head back upstairs. If nothing else we were making baby steps of progress, I would work with it and could only hope it would continue.

Chapter Seven

Chatting with Captives

I LEFT the house with more on my mind than I cared to deal with, things had gotten all varieties of mixed up for me recently. I couldn't help the ways I had been reacting to Hayley, the things she was causing me to think. Even worse sometimes were the reactions she caused in my body, the physical manifestations I had been trying to ignore. It had been years, decades since anyone had affected me the way she was and I couldn't make heads or tails of it. I'd spent so many years avoiding feeling what she was so easily bringing out and it scared the hell out of me.

I wasn't sure how to manage the situation since I didn't think there was a way to make it stop. I also wasn't in the mood to analyze it so I was glad when I heard my name being shouted from somewhere behind me. I turned to see who needed me and what for, the smile falling off my face when I caught sight of Steph. I'd been avoiding her the last few weeks since she had taken it upon herself to continue hounding me about my personal life. My emotions and lack of a love life were not subjects I was interested in discussing with anyone, even her.

The fact there was suddenly something to discuss and I was actively keeping from her wasn't helping much. I wasn't the most open and honest of people by any means but if there was one person in my life I told almost everything, it would be Steph. Lately I felt like I'd stumbled into a weird alternate universe where I couldn't tell her anything. I knew if I told her the things I'd been feeling, and thinking about Hayley she'd flip out. I let loose a sigh as she trotted up to me, a huge grin on her face.

"Glad to see you at least stopped."

"Yeah well, I didn't realize it was you calling me or I probably would have kept walking."

"Ouch. Okay, so maybe I deserve that."

"Maybe?"

"All right, definitely. Look, I know you hate it when I dig and get into your business but I'm your best friend Kai. I worry about you."

"I know you do and I appreciate it but that doesn't mean I want to discuss it. It's just not a topic I wanna get into." Her hands came up in front of her, palms turned out.

"Okay, fine. I'll drop it."

"Thank you."

"For now."

I glared at her and she responded with a bright smile which managed to make me roll my eyes before I turned around to walk away. "Anyway, I came to find you with some actual news. If you care."

"Of course I do. What is it?"

"We got word from Trista."

"Oh?"

I hadn't expected to hear anything from her so quickly, I'd only sent the runner asking her for a meeting nine weeks earlier. He would have spent at least four of those getting to her, if the weather had stayed pleasant all the way. I had expected another two to three weeks of her usual indecision before she made up her mind and sent one of hers with an answer.

"Mmhmm."

I stopped walking and turned toward her, one eyebrow raised in inquiry. She stuck her tongue out at me and for a moment I wondered what I had been thinking when I made this woman an officer.

"Well are you gonna tell me or am I beating it out of you?"

"So violent, sheesh. Okay, she's on her way, should be here in a couple weeks."

"Glad to hear it."

"And her communication said Lila was in her area already so she's coming too."

"Perfect! Makes it easier that I won't have to meet with them separately."

"We do all know how much you hate repeating yourself."

She smirked as I grumbled at her and walked away again. She might be my best friend but she could be the most annoying person in my entire group. Hundreds of people and she alone had the power to crawl under my skin and irritate me on a deep, personal level. I was relieved when I heard her footsteps heading in the opposite direction. Somewhere buried under the surface layer of aggravation I knew she had a point, I was miserable alone. The knowledge she might be right, justified in pressing me about the issue served to fuel my irritation.

I ducked behind one of the outlying buildings we used for teaching our younger scouts archery and took a dozen deep breaths. Once my temper had cooled I decided it was time to visit our prisoners again. They had continued in their adamant refusal to speak to me but I was holding out some hope they might crack. I hadn't tried in days so with the knowledge Trista and Lila were on their way, it was time to give it one last shot. I wasn't sure if anything they knew would be useful after so many weeks, but it was worth trying.

I stepped into the dimly-lit jail and gave my eyes the few seconds they needed to adjust. Once they had I stepped over and grabbed one of the battered chairs pushed up to the grungy table against the wall. I dragged it over toward the cell holding the two men, set it near the cell out of arms reach and dropped into it. I used the toe of my boot to kick the door of the cell, rattling it hard and the sound of metal screeching against metal woke the two men. The first sat bolt upright like he'd been jolted from a nightmare while the other simply rolled over and looked at me.

"General."

I nodded to the second man as he sat up and rubbed at his eyes, his sleep tousled hair sticking out in every direction. Over the weeks they'd been in our custody I'd only managed to get two pieces of information out of them, their names.

"Gabriel. Sorry to wake you but I thought maybe we could have a chat."

"Of course you did... Is it even daylight out?" I crossed my arms over my chest as I leaned back in the chair and grinned at the second, larger man.

"It is, Raphael."

I gave them the time they needed to yawn, stretch out their stiff muscles and relocate to the small table we'd set up for them. Gabriel pushed his chair back some, leaned against the backrest and kicked his feet up on the table as he looked at me.

"What can we do for you today, General?"

"Well Gabriel, I was hoping maybe you boys were up to talking today." A loud bark of laughter followed my comment and I turned my grin on Raphael, quirking a brow at him as I did. "Something funny?"

"Oh, just you. We haven't said anything useful the entire time you've had us locked in here. Now you think we'll just change our minds."

Raphael's deep baritone reminded me so much of Luke it had sent shivers up my spine the first few times he'd spoken. I'd managed to get used to it over the weeks though and now it was nothing but another voice.

"I was hoping so, yeah."

"And why would we do that?"

"Well Raph," I watched him flinch at the nickname, I knew he hated it when I called him anything other than his name but I felt like being a pain in the ass today. "I have some visitors on the way."

"Why would we care about that?"

He growled the words at me and despite the dim interior of the space I could see the laughter shining in Gabriel's eyes. For some reason he rather enjoyed it when I got his cohort all amped up. I could only conclude these two were not friends, merely soldiers in the same unit who were stuck working together.

"Oh well, see these are some very special friends." He grunted as if I wasn't getting any closer to convincing him and I probably wasn't. The next bombshell might change his tune though, I couldn't wait to find out. "Names are Trista and Lila." Still not impressed he raised one dark black, bushy eyebrow at me. "Oh sorry, I guess you know them as Famine and War."

His eyes widened and the color drained from his features. The dim light in the room left him looking a sickly pale yellow.

"You're bringing War here?" I turned to look at Gabriel when he spoke, nodding in response to his question. "Why?"

"We need information; you have it but you're refusing to give it to me. I had to find another way." The faint movement of a repressed shudder rippled through the big blonde man. His pale blue eyes focused hard on me.

"It's a horrifying thought but, we still won't tell you."

"Suit yourself. See you in a few days boys." I stood up, grabbed the back of the chair I'd been using and dragged it over to its former place.

I was reaching for the handle on the door when Raphael spoke again, his low, "Do you know why they call you Conquest, General?" catching my attention.

I dropped my hand and turned back toward the two men, my gaze locked on Raphael.

"I don't actually."

The nicknames given to the four of us ranked as Generals had been well known for more than two centuries. News of them had traveled through the resistance at astonishing speeds and we had each embraced our new name. We'd never known the terms under which the Purists had given them to us however. All we knew was each one of us represented one of the four horsemen of the apocalypse, fitting if you asked any of us.

"They say there is a General in the resistance, one of the forgotten, the damned, who never loses. They say she can ride into any battle, no matter the length of engagement or who is faltering and arise victorious. She is the one who can conquer any obstacle and when she is present, all is lost."

I raised an eyebrow at him and fought back the grin attempting to steal across my face. I'd never known how I'd been blessed with Conquest but now that I'd heard the reason, I liked it even more.

"I say it's a load of crap," Raphael said.

"Do you?"

"I do. No one wins every time. It isn't possible."

"Is that right?" I was baiting him, trying to get him worked up so maybe he would slip and reveal something.

"Yeah, that's right. No one is that good. There's just no way to get so much experience. Besides, my grandmother tells stories about you that her mother told her."

"So what?"

"So no one lives that long. I'm thinking you're the third or maybe fourth Conquest we've dealt with."

I couldn't help myself, I broke out in a fit of laughter. It was apparent the Purist leaders didn't tell their followers everything they knew about us.

"That's really what you think? Do you have any idea how old I am? Have your leaders never told you?"

"I would wager you're around thirty."

"Awww, shucks, thanks for the compliment Raph. I'm over two hundred." Two pairs of eyes widened at the information and while Gabriel maintained the look of total shock Raphael quickly assumed an expression of disbelief.

"No, not a chance. Father Rivers would have told us if..."

He snapped his mouth shut abruptly, cutting himself off before finishing his sentence. The glare Gabriel turned on him told me he'd just made a slip of biblical proportions.

"Father Rivers, huh? And who is he?"

"No one. Forget I said it, I'm not telling you anything else."

I shrugged, dropped my arms to my sides and turned to leave the room. I didn't need him to tell me anything else, I was somehow confident if I went to Julia with a name she would feel comfortable telling me all about this man.

CHAPTER EIGHT

THE SINS OF THE FATHER

FIFTEEN MINUTES after walking out of the jail I was standing at Julia's door, my hand raised to announce myself. I pulled in a deep breath, held it and rapped out a soft knock on the door. I blew the air I'd inhaled out in a steady stream as the door opened and the slim brunette smiled at me. I flashed her my own in response and she backed up, waving me into the room. After stepping in I settled on Nathan's bed which prompted him to crawl into my lap.

"Hadn't expected to see you again so soon."

"I know and I wish I was here under other circumstances but..."

I paused, all at once not sure if I could ask her to reveal the information I sought but knowing I had no other choice. Besides, if I backed out now I would look more than a little ridiculous. If there was one thing I hated, it was making a fool out of myself when I could easily avoid it.

"But?"

"I need information Julia. I have a name but I need to know who this guy is. Since the scouts I've been chatting with aren't exactly the friendly sharing type I was hoping maybe you could help me."

I studied her features as several emotions played across them, hurt, panic, fear and finally acceptance as she nodded and said, "Okay I won't lie, I'm scared to start handing out information about the inner workings of that whole crazy scene. They don't take well to their people giving away secrets and they tend to go a bit, well, overboard on the punishments. However, I'm not planning on ever going back there so give me the name and I'll tell you what I can, if I know anything."

"Father Rivers."

Her sharp intake of breath followed by a sudden push off the bed she'd been sitting on across from me made me lean away from her. She grabbed Nathan off my lap, pulling him into her arms and I worried for a moment I'd irritated her enough she'd ask me to leave. She crossed the room, set the little boy down and opened the door to the hallway.

"Nathan, go down and ask Patricia if you can play with Brynn. I need to talk to Kai alone for a little bit."

I was glad to hear she was going to talk to me. The fact she was sending Nathan to play with the other children meant whatever she planned on saying could be over the top. I wondered how bad things on the other side could really be then decided I might not want to know. I returned my attention to the pair when Nathan offered her his exuberant response.

"Okay, mommy!"

He chirped at her before he bounced off down the hallway, knocked on the door and asked whoever answered it his question. He must have received an affirmative response since he vanished into the room and the door closed. Julia shut her own, closing off the room and crossed back to where I was seated, settling herself in across from me once more.

"Father Rivers is..." She paused as if she was trying to pick her words carefully, or possibly unsure of how to phrase what she wanted to say. She finally blew out a heavy breath and shook her head, "He's their leader."

"So a General, like me?"

"No. We have Generals as well. He's more like... Well I guess a bit like a King. The leader of all our leaders."

"Oh, well then." This was news to me, I'd never heard of him, or his position before.

"He's not a very nice man. Most of our people don't follow his word because they love him or even like him." I raised a brow at her in question and she let out a sigh as she shook her head, her eyes landing on her shoes. "They follow because he terrifies them."

"That's not good."

She lifted her gaze to meet mine again and offered me a forced smile as she said, "No, it's not good at all. I've never met him so I couldn't tell you how true it actually is but I do know that from what I've heard I had no desire to find out if it was true. I'm glad I never met the man."

"And in spite of all of that no one has tried to get rid of him?"

"Several people have. They always fail, though. The general consensus is that he was chosen by God to lead us and therefor only God can remove him, not men. At least that what he's led us to believe and no one is really in any position to argue with him. At least, not if they value walking around free."

"Well that doesn't sound completely crazy at all." I rolled my eyes to punctuate my sarcasm and she laughed as she nodded.

"In his case it is crazy. I fully believe in a lot of the teachings and I follow the word but there's only so far I'm willing to take it. I think he's using what we believe to keep himself on this pedestal."

"Understandable. How bad is he?"

"Very bad. His decrees keep everyone in check. Children are expected to be able to recite his laws by the age of five."

"Oh that's just silly."

"Maybe so but it's the way we live with him in charge. We're expected to follow his teachings on your kind whether we believe what he tells us or not. Obviously we've reached the point where most of us just believe him. There aren't enough of us who have had any real contact with the Regens so we have no real information to argue with."

"I've gathered as much. I admit as weird as it sounds it's good to know we're being targeted because some crazy man is telling lies. It beats being killed off because we're actually that terrible."

"I can imagine that helps a bit in a weird kind of way. Add to those things that parents are often forced to punish their children for major misbehavior by beating them publicly."

The comment halted me not only because of what she had said but because of the calm, off-hand way she had said it. As if such behavior was completely normal and nothing to be worried about. "He what? Were you ever forced to? With Nathan I mean?"

"Me? Oh lord no. Thankfully Nathan is not only young but a good kid. He never did anything he needed severe punishment for."

"I'm glad to hear that." I couldn't imagine anyone forcing her to actually hurt her son, he was such a sweet child. "Please tell me that's all?"

"I wish… He also refuses to allow women to choose their own husbands, we're traded off to the men our fathers prefer we marry whether we like them or not."

"You've got to be kidding me?" The look on my face must have been one of complete disgust because she was quick to look down at her hands.

"Not even a little. He follows the scripture with a very strict hand. He believes this is how it was done then and it is how it should be done now."

"I'd have left too. Ick."

A sneer pulled up the left side of my upper lip, I couldn't imagine being forced to marry someone I didn't like. I couldn't even imagine being forced to marry a man, talk about a total departure from my usual lifestyle.

"He's pretty well known for having those speaking against him and anyone refuting his teachings whipped and locked up. I've heard talk of a handful dying in his jails the last few years of starvation."

"That's awful. What a horrid man."

My brain had begun throwing around images and ideas of the things I'd like to do to him if I ever got my hands on him. I pushed them aside after I decided I didn't have it in me to do the things I'd thought anyway.

"There are even rumors that he killed his first wife after she gave birth to his oldest child. No one can give a reason why but the whispers are there." My eyes went wide and my jaw dropped at the news as I wondered how he could have made it so long without being picked off by someone. He must have some seriously tight security. It had to be because short of actually being chosen by some higher power I couldn't see any other way he'd stayed alive.

"That's… Wow."

"Yeah. Wow is about all there is to say about it."

I nodded and then sat there staring at the wall over her shoulder as the seconds ticked by in silence. I turned my focus back to the woman seated across from me and offered her a smile which she returned.

"Thank you Julia. I know I put you in a strange position by asking you to give me this information but I needed to know."

"I already told you I plan on staying here with Nathan. I can't fear speaking out against him anymore. As far as I'm concerned, he isn't my leader any longer. You are. I have to trust that I'm safe here."

A distinct tug tweaked my heart at her words and I couldn't resist reaching over and pulling her into a hug. She returned the friendly embrace with a tight squeeze before we parted and I hefted out a sigh. I was glad she felt she could trust me and was comfortable enough with me and my methods to want to stay with her son. I stood, giving her shoulder a gentle squeeze before I turned and headed for the door.

"I'll be back as soon as I can but we have two of the other Generals on their way so I may be busy for a few days."

She nodded her understanding, stood and followed me to the door as I opened it and stepped into the hallway. She kept in step with me until we reached Patricia's doorway when she stopped and knocked. I continued on as I heard her ask Nathan if he wanted to return to their room or keep playing with Brynn. His exuberant expression of wanting to continue playing made Julia, Patricia and myself laugh. The sound of a fourth chuckle made me glance over at Hayley's doorway where I found her standing, a smile on her face.

"Hi, Hayley."

"Hey, Kai. Not hanging around today?"

"Unfortunately, no. I have a lot to get done in the next couple days."

"Oh, okay." Maybe it was wishful thinking or even the reappearance of the sudden tightening in my belly but I thought she sounded sad I wasn't staying longer. I shook the thoughts off, cleared my throat and managed to smile at her.

"I'll stop by after our guests leave in a few days. Maybe we can find a way to get you out of here for an hour or so by then."

The smile she flashed me set off an intense flutter in my stomach. Weird, I couldn't remember swallowing a colony of butterflies. I forced myself to turn and descend the stairs, leaving the house and almost forgetting to lock it up again before heading toward the stable. I needed to visit Prophecy and get my mind off of the irritating woman I'd walked away from. Irritating but absolutely gorgeous with a smile I would swear to anyone asking could light up a room.

I released a shuddering breath as I attempted to push the thoughts aside. The last thing I needed was to develop a crush on a Purist we were holding captive. If Trista and Lila caught on I'd never hear the end of it. The mere idea of such information ever getting back to Thea stopped me dead in my tracks and sent a shiver racing through me. No. I definitely needed to get myself under control before whatever this was I'd begun to feel became noticeable.

CHAPTER NINE

CONQUEST, FAMINE AND WAR

KAI'S JOURNAL - *Summer Cycle, 2606 – 220 years after the event:*

The information Julia gave me about Father Rivers was worrying to say the least. I'm not sure how I feel about this man. I keep bouncing between the urge to throw up over his rules and demands and really wanting to meet him and punch him in the face. I can't believe he treats his people the way she says and then labels us the evil ones. It makes me sick and pissed off all at the same time. Setting aside being unable to imagine treating any group of people like he does, the idea of anyone doing those horrible things to Julia is heartbreaking. I've become closer with her and Nathan which leaves me with a knot in my stomach over the things they must have gone through. On the upside of things, I finally got the crabby woman's name. Hayley. I keep catching myself whispering it into my empty room and then smiling. As much as I know I should try to keep my distance from her because of these weird things she makes me feel, I can't deny how right her name sounds coming out of my mouth. I've got to get myself under control before these reactions I'm having to her become noticeable. Thankfully Trista and Lila are on their way which should give me plenty to focus on and keep my attention diverted away from Hayley.

I had so much to do the next week to prepare for Trista and Lila to arrive I barely had a spare moment to think about anything else. While I was glad for the reprieve from my mind whirling with thoughts of Hayley I was about ready to rip my hair out. I did find I got so busy at one point the last five days passed in a flash. Everything was set and ready for their arrival, at least I was hoping it was since I'd had to delegate several tasks out to my Captains. I was forcing myself to believe they'd finished everything I'd asked them to do so I wouldn't waste more time checking.

By the time the other two Generals and their entourage arrived I was worn out and ready to drop. I'd slept less than usual in the past few days with my usual barely enough to run on. I was dragging and not ready to sit down and discuss planning and tactics with the other two women. These meetings didn't happen often and when they did we always had trouble agreeing on much. However, since I didn't have much choice I found myself walking into the meeting area as a huge yawn hit me.

"Been here five minutes and we're already boring you, huh?" I allowed the yawn to run its course and then shot a grin at Trista as I pulled my right shoulder up in a half shrug.

"Can't help it, you're just so void of excitement you make me wanna take a nap."

I burst out in laughter when her glove hit me in the head a breath later then stuck my tongue out at her. Two hundred years old or not when Trista and I were in the same room we were prone to acting like big kids. I held the belief it was part of our charm while almost everyone else around us said it was immature and annoying. What the hell did they know?

"Okay you two. Enough. We have actual issues to discuss. You know, serious things?" I pulled a face as Lila spoke, one which was frequently used by our resident teens when they thought their parents were being ridiculous. The expression fell away when Lila's palm connected with my forehead in a solid slap.

"Hey!"

"Act like a teenager and I'll treat you like one. Now get it together and let's do what we're here to do." She raised both brows at me as if challenging me to act up again but rather than push her I walked over and took my place atop the stump I always perched on. "Thank you. Now, have you managed to get anything else out of those prisoners since you sent your runner to us?"

"Actually, yes. Not that they meant to talk but I managed to tweak one of them enough that he slipped." I grinned as Trista rolled her eyes, muttering 'of course you did' under her breath and giving me no real choice but to wink at her in response.

"Do tell."

Lila had apparently chosen to ignore our exchange in favor of new information so I soldiered on, repeating what had happened in the jail. Trista found my method of riling up the prisoners interesting but Lila only wanted the information. I gave in to the older woman's demands and began telling her what the man had slipped and said. Then I elaborated on information with the details Julia had given me. Once I was done I noticed Lila smiling and Trista was rubbing her hands together as if preparing to do something nefarious.

"Oh great god, what are you two cooking up over there?"

"Well," Trista started before she looked to Lila who nodded, giving her the go ahead to continue her train of thought first. "What if we make ourselves a bit of a thorn in big papa's side?"

"Go on." Lila leaned forward as she urged Trista on, her elbows braced on her knees as she listened.

"If we go on a mass scout, hunt, and capture run we might piss him off enough that he'll leave his throne or wherever he hides himself."

The idea had some merit so I nodded my initial agreement with it before I leaned in closer to join the plotting.

"Okay, that could work. But how many captures are we talking?"

"Not sure, why?" I glanced at Lila as I did a mental walk-through of my small jail before returning my focus to Trista.

"Well, I'm not sure about you two but I can only house something like ten or twelve men comfortably."

"How about uncomfortably?"

I shot a glare in Lila's direction for her comment, not sure she was serious.

"Uncomfortably? Well, I suppose somewhere around twenty but I'm not really okay with that."

"Why not?" I turned a look I was sure would say 'are you kidding me?' on Trista before shaking my head when I realized she wasn't kidding at all.

"Because I'm not interested in torturing these people."

"Oh come on, Kai. We're not talking about torture, just some uncomfortable overcrowding. Maybe if they have to live on top of each other for a few days they'll be more willing to talk."

I drew a deep breath as Lila finished speaking, doing everything I could think of to keep my temper under control. As far as I was concerned she had known me long enough by now to know I wasn't going to be okay with the suggestion. It showed how little we really interacted and how well we didn't know each other.

"Look, I'm fine with capturing and detaining groups for questioning but I refuse to pile them on top of each other like animals." I leaned back, arms crossed over my chest in a clear indication to the other two I was serious and refused to budge on the matter. My heart was racing and a red tinge had clouded my thoughts, readying me to fight them tooth and nail on the matter.

"Why? Isn't that exactly how they treat us? Like animals?"

My gaze moved to Trista, my calm returning as the red haze cleared from my mind and my pulse slowed to a more normal rate. I could argue with her and not lose my temper if she was willing to simply question me. Once she started demanding things it could get ugly and turn into a fight but for now, we could discuss calmly.

"Yes. That's exactly how they treat us." A smug smile stretched across her face and I was sure she thought she'd won the round, until I continued. "But aren't we always touting how we refuse to stoop to their level? We demand to be treated as more than what they see us as. We claim to be better, more evolved. How can we claim that if we treat them exactly as they treat us? Or worse even? We have to take the higher ground here. Capture? Yes. Detain? Definitely. Question? Absolutely. But torture, abuse or mistreat? No, never. I refuse."

Trista dropped the smug look as her hand came up to rub at her temples and I knew I was frazzling her nerves. As far as I was concerned if doing the right things caused her stress then we had bigger problems than this Purist King. Lila stood from the place she'd been seated and paced the length of the space three times from end to end before she stopped and faced me.

"You're right, Kai. We do need to be careful how we handle these situations lest we become exactly what we claim to despise."

"Exactly. Thank you."

"Can you convert any other spaces into housing for prisoners?" I took a deep breath at her question, my gaze flickering from her to Trista and back again. I knew I needed to say what was sitting in the back of my mind but admitting it would be difficult.

"I have a house set up with lockdown measures in place. It could comfortably house another sixteen men if we slept them four to a room."

"So use it."

I locked eyes with Lila as she said the words and bit my lower lip.

"I will but, I'll have to clear it first."

"Clear it?"

"Yes. I currently have three women and four children living in it. A detail of my younger scouts detained them against my rules and I refused to leave them in the jail."

Trista's brows furrowed but other than a quick flicker of my gaze in her direction I refused to look at her.

"What do you propose to do with these women and children?"

"I intend to assimilate them into my population."

"What?" Trista exploded from her seat with the exclamation and I flinched an inch or so with the sudden movement. "You have got to be kidding me!"

"What makes you think they'd be safe to release to wander freely?"

I was thankful Lila had kept her cool at least, it made me pull my pride back in order and believe I'd had the right idea.

"Julia, the one who gave me the information about Father Rivers, has told me she intends to stay. Her son is already happier here than he was where they came from. I'm sure Patricia and her children would be more than happy to carry on here as well."

"And the third woman you spoke of?" I grimaced when Trista brought up Hayley since I couldn't be sure she'd stay put if not under lock and key.

"I honestly don't know. But she could easily be put under guard until we know for sure. One woman is easier to keep guards on than three, not to mention all four kids."

"And none of the children are hers?" I shook my head in response to Lila's question and waited while she considered the idea for a few seconds which seemed to never end. "I don't see why that wouldn't work."

"Have you both lost your damn minds?" Lila waved off Trista's outburst and continued with her thought.

"There have been defectors from both sides before. They typically relocate themselves into smaller colonies away from the central bases but I don't see why resettling with you here would be out of the question. Would Julia speak with me?"

"I can ask her but I don't see why not."

"Do it, I'd like to chat with her and see how intent she really is on staying here with you."

I nodded and stood, making my way over to Lila as we both ignored Trista. She was glaring daggers at us both but she would have to get over her reasons for rejecting the idea. No matter how detrimental it might seem, I trusted Julia and I knew deep down she had an honest desire to stay. If nothing else she had a need to see her son safe and happy which to me was enough of a reason to trust her desires. She'd proven to me it didn't matter what she wanted or needed, it mattered what was best for Nathan and for the moment staying in my compound was best for the boy.

Chapter Ten

Departures and Releases

I ARRANGED for Lila to meet Julia and their conversation went as well as I had hoped. After meeting with Patricia, the children, and Hayley, my fellow General was quick to agree with my assessment of the situation. Trista continued to fume through the end of their visit but by the time they packed up to leave she had cooled off. Julia, Patricia and the children were all out of lockdown and we were preparing a plan to get Hayley out of the place as well. As the other two women mounted their horses near the gate I stepped up and patted Lila's cherry chestnut, Blood, on the neck.

"Have a good journey home, be safe."

"Thank you. Keep an eye on Hayley, that one has some fire in her."

"And don't I know it!" We laughed together as Trista walked her giant of a black stallion, Plague, up beside Blood.

"I'm sorry I lost it with you, Kai. You know my temper."

"I do and don't worry about it. I knew you'd come around after you met them. You be safe heading home as well."

"I will. Take care."

I nodded as two of my guards pulled the gate to our compound open then watched Trista and Lila heel their mounts into a trot. Once they were through both turned to wave and I returned the gesture as the guards pushed the heavy gates back into place. I stood staring at the huge wooden constructs after they'd departed, allowing five minutes to pass before I turned and headed off into the compound. I had an idea to run by Hayley and I'd been putting off talking to her for two days. It was time to get over my weird reactions to her and get it over with.

I decided to let those reactions run through my mind as I covered the ground between the gate and the house. I'd been avoiding thinking about them, analyzing them or even admitting they were happening but doing so was getting harder every time they occurred. It had been the hardest thing I'd ever put myself through to keep myself in check around her when Lila and Trista had been there as witnesses. I'd exhausted the last bit of energy I had keeping my mind on track and forcing my body to not betray me. I sighed as I crossed the porch, unlocked the door and pushed it open.

I stepped inside and made my way up the stairs, not bothering to lock the door behind me. She hadn't made any attempts at running and I trusted she would believe the doors locked even if they weren't. I paused outside her door and filled my lungs as much as I could, holding the air for a count of fifteen before letting it out slowly. After rocking my head from side to side to pop my neck I raised a hand and knocked on the door. It swung open two seconds later and the smile sitting on the face staring back at me ripped every thought I'd been going over out of my mind.

I knew I'd come here for a reason. I had things to say and I needed to go over some planning I'd been doing with the woman standing in front of me. The sight of her stalled it all and her smile effectively shot all the plans I'd made right to hell and ripped them from my head. I couldn't get anything I'd been thinking to surface again and it threatened to flare my temper. I needed to stop letting this happen but since I wasn't sure why it happened in the first place I didn't have the slightest idea how to make it cease.

"Kai? You okay?"

I shook my head when she spoke, realizing I'd been standing there staring at her for a lot longer than I'd meant to. I needed to kick my brain into gear again so I could remember why I'd come to see her in the first place. My reactions to her were growing more awkward every day I saw her and I felt like a damned teenager again. I remembered why I was there but began questioning what I was about to propose, no longer sure it was a good idea after the way I'd responded to her when she answered the door.

"Um, yeah. Sorry, lost my train of thought. I wanted to run something by you."

"All right."

I shoved the part of my brain questioning how bright this idea I was about to present to her was aside and locked it up. I couldn't start second guessing myself with her, it wasn't like me and I needed to stop letting it happen. The thought in mind I decided to quit being worried about how it might end and let it begin in the first place.

"I know it's probably awkward being left in this house after I let Julia, Patricia and the kids out."

She shrugged as she said, "Somewhat. But I get it. They've both expressed an interest in staying here. I've done nothing but give you trouble."

"Well, what if we tried to fix the situation?"

"And how would we do that?" She crossed her arms over her chest and leaned against the door frame as she spoke. I fought to keep my eyes on hers rather than letting them roam like every fiber of my being wanted them to.

"Wha," I had to pause and clear my throat which widened her smile a fraction and I would swear I saw her fighting back a giggle. I waited a three count and tried again. "What I thought was we could start spending afternoons outside this building."

"We?"

"Yes, we. You and I."

My gut roiled, my heart raced and my mind screamed at me that I was making a giant mistake. I ignored it all since I'd put the idea and the words out there. No taking it back now, it would only disappoint her. I found the idea of disappointing her upset me and the fact it upset me confused me. I pushed all of those things aside as well.

"Uh huh. And what would we do during these afternoons?" One pale eyebrow arched with the question and my gaze followed its feathery curve before returning to her eyes. The question and my reaction had given me the time I needed to process the words and formulate an actual response.

"Walking, talking, we could visit the stables. Anything to get you outside these walls and give me a chance to get to know you better. Once I feel like I can trust you I won't feel like I need to keep you in here." She nodded as she followed my thought process and then beamed at me as she pushed off the frame.

"Sounds like a plan. Shall we start now?"

I was startled she would want to get right into spending any kind of time alone with me. Then again, she had to be bored cooped up in the house all day with nowhere to go and no one left to talk to.

"Uh, sure. Come on."

I led the way down the stairs and out the front door onto the porch, stopping at the edge and glancing over at her. She stood beside me and stared out at the open area over the wall at the bottom of the hill the house was perched on. Her shoulders rose then fell again as she took a deep breath and I could imagine the fresh air must be nice after so many weeks trapped inside. She looked in my direction and I offered her a smile as I ignored the flutter in my stomach. The particular reaction happened a lot around her, usually when she dared to turn that brilliant smile on me.

I shivered, glad there was the mild bite of a chill in the air I could blame the action on. I shook it all off, the feeling in my stomach, the knot in my throat which was forming and the shiver she'd given me. I needed to be clear and thinking if this was going to happen since I would be solely responsible for her. I took a cleansing breath and cleared my throat before I nodded toward the path and started walking. She followed, keeping closer than I thought she needed to since her arm brushed mine every few steps.

CHAPTER ELEVEN

REACTIVITY

KAI'S JOURNAL - *Summer Cycle, 2606 – 220 years after the event:*

After a little arguing and disagreement Trista, Lila and myself managed to work out some kind of plan we hope will work. I'm not sure how effective it will be but I'm not above trying it and seeing what happens. I'm happy they seem to agree with me about Julia and Patricia. It means the women and those poor kids can finally get the hell out of that damn house they've been locked up in. I am worried Trista noticed my reactions to Hayley though and that's a bit worrying. If she did I'm not sure what it might mean or what she might say to Lila on the way back toward their territories. I suppose I'll just have to hope I wasn't too obvious and focus on other things. Now that they left though, I feel the need to do whatever I can to get Hayley out of that house too. I can't bring myself to leave her in there for too long all alone now that the rest of her group has been moved. I thought I had an idea and I took the first step yesterday. Now that I've had the chance to think about it I'll be the first to admit it might end up being the biggest mistake of my life. However, I think I just need to take a leap of faith and follow through with it, see what happens.

I showed up at the house the next afternoon right after lunch but hesitated when I went to knock on the door. I was questioning the sanity of the choice I'd made for what had to be the thousandth time since the night before. I knew I'd committed to this thing so I would follow through with it no matter what I had to do to make it happen. Keeping said commitment didn't mean I had to feel entirely okay about the things I was allowing myself to be exposed to. I was a mess emotionally and still hadn't figured out how to either stop it or allow myself to accept it.

I huffed, rolled my shoulders then leaned my head from side to side popping my neck out of habit. Whatever it was Hayley made me feel I was all knotted up about it, inside and out. I had an idea what it all was but I hesitated in putting a label on it since doing so would make it a real thing. I briefly considered turning around and walking away, telling her later I got caught up doing something important. She would be upset but would understand, I was a General and had things to do, people who needed my time and input.

The mere idea of lying to her made me queasy though and I had to let the idea fade into the background. With my heart driving against my ribs in a recently familiar cadence of mild panic and my stomach knotted and fluttering I opened the door. I had to get over this feeling or at the very least ignore it long enough to make some strides in assimilating her into the community of the compound. It was the only way she could get out of this imprisonment I'd thrown her into. She deserved a chance at some type of freedom again.

I closed the door, leaning my forehead against the cool wood with my back to the room in an attempt to ease the trepidation I was feeling. I knew I couldn't will it away or even reason with it, nothing I'd been dealing with was rational. At the lowest level it was a deep, intense reaction which left me light headed and fighting to do even simple things like breathing. Above the intensity was a crisscrossed tartan of longing, I could even begin to admit a kind of desire. Over this was the doubt, the belief I couldn't ever be enough for anyone ever again in my condition, after the things I'd been through.

Layered over those things was a level of sheer, animalistic panic which locked me up. It prevented me from allowing the other emotions to surface, be seen. This layer though was beginning to fracture slowly, a piece at a time. More and more of the layers beneath were showing through and it made me worry. I couldn't let myself give in to it all, not if I had any chance at maintaining not only my sanity but my grip on the compound and its residents. If they knew what I'd been feeling, what I was considering allowing myself to do, they would never trust me again.

"Kai?"

The sound of Hayley's voice from a few short feet behind me made me jump, letting out a sharp yelp as I turned to face her. My heart raced as my vision swam, the intensity of the sudden reaction overwhelming me. I remembered how to breathe, drew in a deep, shuddering lungful of air then bent at the waist, hands on my knees and blew it out in a steady stream. Once my vision cleared and my head stopped throbbing I straightened and looked at the other woman. The concern in her expression made another small sliver of my resolve break away.

"You scared the hell out of me."

"Sorry, I didn't mean to. Are you okay?" I caught a flicker of emotion behind her eyes and it made my stomach flutter. God help me, she actually cared.

"Yeah I think so. Just thinking too hard."

"What about?"

I waved her off as I said, "Just some things bouncing around in my head. Nothing you need to worry about." The last thing I wanted was to get into it all since letting her know how I'd been reacting to her terrified me

"Okay." She didn't seem to believe me but she did seem to drop the subject as she asked, "Well are you still up to this today? Or do you need some time to deal with things? I mean, we can push this back if you need to."

There it was, my out. While the deepest parts of my brain screamed at me to jump on it, take the chance to bail out I found my heart overriding my head. Before I had the chance to think it through too much I heard myself say, "No, of course not. I'll be fine I think I just need some time out in the fresh air. Maybe we can go to the river and take a walk."

She brightened at my words, nodded then joined me by the door. When she flashed me a genuine smile my stomach did its usual annoying flutter as I momentarily forgot how to breathe again.

"Sure, shall we?"

Her hand found my elbow as she spoke and I took every ounce of willpower I had to keep from pulling away at the jolt the touch sent through me.

"Uh, yeah, sounds good. Come on."

I yanked the door open and stepped out into the afternoon sun. I was glad for the deep draw of fresh air, not to mention the space. Hayley stepped out after me, shut the door and we started off toward the river. We had remained silent for most of the previous day's outing and it appeared the trend was to continue. I was fine with the development since I didn't trust myself to carry on a conversation at the moment. It would be my luck to say something embarrassing or worse, give myself away.

My first two afternoons spent out in Hayley's company went better than I expected, with the exception of the lack of conversation. By the third we started a kind of awkward back and forth, getting to know each other a bit better. Within the week we were carrying on short but decent conversations and by the beginning of week two were becoming more comfortable with each other. I was still reacting to her more intensely than I liked but I wasn't as worried about showing it. Either I hid it better than I thought, she didn't notice, or she chose not to comment.

Whichever it was, I would take it and pretend everything between us was normal, nothing more than two people becoming friends. Lying to myself proved to be much easier than I had expected so I continued on with it as the days went by. By the time we'd made it through a full four weeks of daily outings and were moving into the second month we had graduated to long, intense conversations. We talked about our likes, dislikes, hobbies, childhood accidents and things of the sort. We remained well clear of any true depth, keeping emotional situations clear of our time together.

The downside of the extended contact with her seemed to be an intensifying of the already confusing things I'd been feeling. My stomach, not to mention my nerves, was a total mess and the little sleep I'd been getting seemed to be shot all to hell. Somehow I managed to keep everyone but Steph from noticing, though she could have spotted a two-hour gap in my sleep after only a night. Hiding anything from her was a total wash and I knew it. She'd been on my case about why I was so out of sorts, I'd been giving her the runaround but it wasn't working and she was prying more and more.

When two months had passed since the first day of this experiment of mine I was forced to admit it seemed to be going well. Hayley seemed much more relaxed in my company though we still didn't talk about anything of real importance. At the very least she'd been smiling which she hadn't done much of the first few weeks, with good reason. I'd also managed to get her laughing a few times in the last couple weeks and I would do anything I could to keep hearing the sound of it. Every time she laughed, giggled or even stifled a little chuckle it sent a flutter of nervous excitement through me.

I dragged myself wearily into my quarters one night after spending the entire day out gathering firewood, Hayley at my side. She'd been my almost constant companion the last eight weeks and I wondered again at the intelligence of my choice as I fell into my bed. I had reached the point where I'd crossed the line into exhaustion and passed out for half a day more than once in the last few weeks. I felt I was close to the line again and probably would be several more times in the coming months. All I knew for sure was cutting her out of my daily routine wasn't an option, even considering it made my chest ache.

With a huff I turned onto my side and closed my eyes, willing sleep to find me even though it didn't seem to be listening. After tossing and turning for longer than I cared to admit I crawled out from under my blankets and yanked on my boots. I tugged on a sweater to combat the chill in the air then stepped outside with every intention of walking off my nervous energy. I set my eyes on my boots and started walking, not caring where I ended up. The idiocy of the move dawned on me when I stopped and looked up several minutes later.

I rolled my eyes when I realized I'd ended up in front of the house Hayley was still calling home. I'd spent every day of the last eight weeks with her, but I'd never shown up to see her in the middle of the night. Deep down I wanted to go inside and see if she was up to talking for a while even though I knew this was crossing a very clear line I'd made sure to maintain. I knew she was awake because I could see the light of a lantern flickering in the window. I pulled in a deep breath which stung my lungs and made my chest ache then nodded to myself, choice made.

I walked up the steps, unlocked the door and stepped inside, I'd given up on locking it behind me weeks ago. I started up the stairs toward her room, pausing halfway to bolster my courage and tell myself I wasn't doing something completely idiotic. She must have heard the door open because she had the bedroom door open and was standing in the hallway wearing a smirk when I reached the top step. I had the decency to blush before I smiled at her and cleared my throat. I'd known what I was going to say when I made the choice to come inside but now the words seemed to have fled me. Instead I reached up to scratch the back of my neck and uttered the lamest single word greeting in history.

"Hey."

Yeah, I was feeling really smooth and intelligent now and I was imagining her laughing at me when I looked up and saw only the smile still on her face.

"Hey yourself. Everything okay?" Well, if she wasn't going to think I was weird then I wouldn't bother to think it either.

"Yeah, why?"

"Because it's the middle of the night and you're standing here with me instead of sleeping."

"Oh, that." Wow, I was really on a roll with this conversation thing tonight. "I uh, was having trouble sleeping. Got up to work off some energy and found myself here so I thought I'd see if you were up for a walk or something."

"Sure. Let me grab my boots."

"Okay. You probably need something with longer sleeves too, it's a bit cold out there." She nodded as she pushed her feet into her boots and laced them up then snatched a sweater off the end of the bed.

"Let's go."

She was still smiling as we made our way downstairs and it took every bit of self-control I had to keep from watching her right back as she studied me. We left the house and walked in silence for what felt like years but was something closer to five minutes. Things between us hadn't been this awkward in weeks and I wondered if I was setting her on edge with my strange nighttime visit. When we paused near the southern edge of the compound I looked up into the sky.

The night was clear and since it was a new moon every star was visible overhead. It was stunning.

"There was a point a while back when you asked me why we were out alone when we were caught. Three women and four children trekking without guards." Her voice pulled me from my reverie of the star-scape overhead so I turned my attention, and my gaze toward her.

"That I did."

"Julia was running from her father. She actually got pretty lucky as far as her personal life goes. Her husband was a decent man and she really loved him. After Nathan was born he joined their local scouts to train. He did well and was on a team within the year.

A few months ago he was sent out on a mission... He never made it back."

"She's never mentioned that." My heart tightened as I imagined Julia, the sweetest person I'd ever met mourning the loss of someone she loved.

"I know. She doesn't like to talk about it. Her father was pushing to find her a new husband and when she told him she wasn't ready he threatened to hand her over to the jail guards. He said if she wouldn't submit to being a proper wife and mother she didn't deserve to be treated like one. She was terrified but she was still mourning her husband. It had only been a little over four months."

"No wonder she ran. I would too." She nodded as she crossed her arms over her chest and looked up into the sky. "What about Patricia?"

"Her husband was one of the bad ones. He was horrible to her but she put up with it because she didn't have any other choice. A few months ago he started escalating and he hit Brynn. She decided she'd had enough and when she found out Julia was attempting to run, she jumped at helping she and Nathan get away. I decided to escort them."

"Are you related to one of them?"

"Nope." I raised a brow at her as I tried to figure out why she would risk so much trouble when she hadn't said she herself had any reason to leave.

"So you just helped because you could?"

"Something like that. At least we'll call it that for now. I wasn't thrilled with the idea of staying anyway." I'd always had a gift for being able to tell when people were lying to me and something about what she'd said was off. It wasn't a total lie but it wasn't exactly the whole truth either.

"There's more, I can tell."

"Yeah, there is."

I allowed the smallest of grins to tweak up the corner of my lips, glad I hadn't lost my touch.

"And? Care to share it?"

She shook her head as her brow drew down and she walked a few feet away, her eyes still turned up toward the stars. I had the burning feeling I shouldn't push her on the matter so I decided to listen to my gut and dropped the subject. "Are you feeling less like a captive these days?" My heart stammered in my chest when she lowered her eyes to focus on me and her expression softened.

"I really am. I know I'm still locked in at night but being able to get out and interact with people during the day helps."

"Glad I'm doing something right."

"More than you know." There was a flicker of something I couldn't identify in her eyes before she closed them and turned her face into the gust of wind kicking up around us. She breathed in deeply and I watched the rise and fall of her shoulders as I tried to decide what it was I'd seen in her gaze. By the time she turned to look at me again I'd given up and whatever it was had faded.

She said, "I'm freezing and I think I might actually be able to sleep now."

I agreed with her comment so I responded with, "Let's head back, then."

She nodded and we turned to head back the way we'd come, walking in silence once again. We made it back to the house and I walked her inside. When she stopped me from leaving by placing a hand on top of mine on the doorknob my stomach twisted itself into knots. My heart attempted to break free of my ribs and my lungs refused the air I was trying to pull into them. My mind was a racing, raw bundle of chaos as she took a step closer and leaned in.

In the span of a single, breath-stealing heartbeat everything stilled. My stomach relaxed, my mind went blessedly blank and I would have sworn to anyone standing nearby my heart skipped several beats. By the time I registered that she was kissing me the moment had passed. She took a step back and at the loss of contact, the departure of her body heat my brain kicked on again. Then I actually did panic, causing a knee jerk reaction.

I ripped the door open and bolted, only pausing long enough to lock it behind me. I ran all the way back to my quarters, slamming the door behind me after skidding to a stop inside. I was breathing hard, my heart pounding as I tried to process what had happened. As my physical condition returned to normal and everything settled back into its usual rhythm it dawned on me what I'd done.

Hayley had validated everything I'd been feeling, all the nervous, chaotic emotions I'd been fighting the last few months and I'd rewarded her boldness by running away.

CHAPTER TWELVE

WORDS OF ADVICE

KAI'S JOURNAL - *Autumn Cycle, 2606 – 220 years after the event:*

I can't believe after spending so much time getting Hayley to trust me, not to mention having her on my mind for months I spooked the minute she did something about it. I'm not really sure what scared me more, the fact she kissed me at all or that it made me actually feel something. I wanted to kiss her back with everything in me but something inside wouldn't let me. Somehow I feel like I'd be betraying Laney if I allow this to happen. Even though I know deep down I wouldn't be doing any such thing, I'm having trouble convincing my heart of that. Maybe I should try talking to someone, after all, there's at least one person around here who knows me well enough to give me some real advice.

As much as I didn't want to do what I'd set my mind to, I knew it had to be done. I knocked on the door looming in front of me before I could change my mind and waited for an answer. When it was pulled open I realized I must look like ten different kinds of death since the expression which crossed Steph's face was pure concern. She waved me out of the way before she stepped out, closing the door behind her then grabbed my arm. I followed her, not having the energy to fight after being up all night.

"You look like hell on the edge of death."

"Thanks." I glared at my boots as she let out a loud sigh and squeezed my arm.

"Spill. What's going on?"

"I haven't slept in two days. I'm a mess."

"I can see that much. Why?"

"Hayley."

Her name was all I could manage before all the chain reactions began again ending with an inability to breathe properly. The single word stopped Steph dead in her tracks and she turned to face me, the concern in her expression tinged with the edges of her temper.

"What about her?"

"She kissed me."

"She did what?" Her tone took on a unique screeching quality which I'd discovered only she could manage.

"Calm down, Steph. I didn't tell you so you could freak out or get all judgmental on me."

"I would never!" The look I threw at her said 'yeah, sure you wouldn't' so she huffed and shook her head. "Okay maybe I would but I can refrain this time. Why are you telling me?"

"Because I may have allowed myself to have the worst reaction possible when someone kisses you."

"Oh crap, you threw up on her didn't you?"

"Ew, no! I... Ran."

"Ran? As in away?" I nodded and she grimaced, lending a face to what I was feeling right then. "That's not good. Why?"

"Why did I run?"

"No, why didn't you take up knitting? Yes, why did you run?"

"Okay enough with the sarcasm. I don't know why I ran. I just kinda panicked. I wasn't expecting it."

"Fair enough. What if you had been?"

"Had been what?"

"If you had been expecting it. Like, if she had told you she wanted to do it instead of just springing it on you like she did. What would you have done? How would you have reacted?" Her question made me pull in a sharp breath and walk a few yards away, my arms folded across my chest. She followed, putting herself right beside me and staring me down until I caved and responded to her.

"I would have let her, and probably kissed her back."

"I figured as much." I turned a questioning look on her and cocked my head to one side. "I kept hoping I was just paranoid and misreading you. You've been awkward and nervous around that girl for weeks, Kai."

Damn, I'd been hoping no one else could tell I was waging an internal war with my feelings but I should have known Steph would catch it.

"What do I do now, Steph? She probably hates me after the way I reacted."

"Go find out."

"Do what crazy thing now?"

She chuckled at me and shook her head, no doubt wondering how I'd managed to lead hundreds of people into battle with an attitude like the one I was currently displaying. At the moment, war sounded easier than this craziness my best friend was expecting from me. Facing down an army of Purist soldiers somehow seemed less daunting a task than speaking to this one woman.

"Look, I'm assuming this reaction had something to do with past events, and people she couldn't possibly know about?"

I let out a resigned sigh since denying the validity of Steph's words was pointless, she knew the weird place my head had been since Laney. Instead of attempting to argue I said, "Yeah, it did. We haven't exactly been talking deep inner truths and past experiences. None of it has come out."

"Well then, you have no clue how she'll react once she knows the truth about it all."

"So you think I need to pour my heart out to fix this?"

"I do. Go back over there, talk to her, explain what happened and see what she says. Never know, maybe she'll understand how you and that crazy little mind work."

"I can't believe you, of all people are suggesting this. Shouldn't you be telling me to be careful? To not be so quick to think about trusting her? To guard my heart better?"

"Sounds to me like you already told yourself all of those things. Why waste my time and breath repeating them?" She smiled as I shook my head then turned my gaze out to the horizon with a thoughtful sigh. "Besides, you have been keeping yourself in check for weeks. I'm actually a little impressed it was her that made the first move and not you."

I shot her a small glare but when she grinned at me I returned the expression before I mumbled out, "I'll think about it. Might be best if I just keep my distance for a while though."

"Up to you, I won't push."

I nodded and kept my eyes on the wisps of clouds in the distance.

She patted me on the shoulder and headed back toward her house, leaving me to work out the details on my own.

I stood there and let the fresh air filter out some of the panic I was still feeling about the entire situation. After watching the sun edge closer toward setting, I turned and started back toward my pitiful room. I shuffled the whole way, taking my time and stepped into the space only minutes after the sun had disappeared and left the deep purple of the night sky behind.

I needed some clarity on the situation but I had the feeling I wouldn't find it no matter how hard I looked. Somehow I knew the answers I needed would only surface after I found the guts to approach Hayley. Not wanting to consider visiting her in the near future I got up, started a fire and occupied myself tending it for a few long minutes. Once it was going I returned to my bed, crawled in and turned toward the wall to follow the flickering of my shadow on the wall. I studied the dark lines but found no further answers.

CHAPTER THIRTEEN

CONFRONTATION AND CLARITY

HOURS LATER, I was back to staring up at the ceiling of my small room as I tried to calm my thoughts. I needed to get them onto a topic other than the proud, stubborn blonde. My brain had been running full steam since I'd run after her kiss and showed no signs of stopping. Sleep was far from my mind despite the fact I needed it more and more with each night I missed. I groaned as a sharp pain stabbed its way through my left temple in the beginnings of what I was sure would be a massive headache. While I couldn't recall ever being sick I did have frequent headaches which were capable of rendering me useless for a day or more.

I was forced to give up on sleep when the throbbing in my head drove me out of bed and into the darkness outside. There was a bite in the air, the frequent gusts of wind whipping by cutting into every inch of skin I'd left exposed. In a moment of much needed decisiveness brought on by the autumn cold, lack of sleep or maybe both, I turned and headed for the house Hayley was still locked in. After reaching it I hesitated for a split second before unlocking the door, pushing inside and swinging it closed behind me. I charged up the stairs, on a mission and intent on forcing myself to face her despite the nausea sweeping over me.

I opened the door without knocking and had to remind myself

to breathe when she looked away from the window and met my eyes. For a precious moment in time I thought maybe she wasn't mad about the way I'd reacted, then a glare worked over her features and she snapped out, "What the hell do you want?"

"I wanted to talk to you."

"Oh now you can handle being around me?"

"Look Hayley, I just wanted to..."

"Glad to know I'm at the mercy of what you want." She snapped the words and I couldn't stop the flinch of reaction it caused.

"Please let me talk."

"Fine. What did you want to talk about *oh great and powerful master?*" Ouch, I'd never realized how much words could sting until the sarcastic emphasis she'd put on the statement hit me full force.

"I, uh, know I didn't have the best reaction the other night and you're mad at me but..."

"No you didn't. In fact, you had what I would classify as one of the top three worst reactions." She turned her eyes back to the window as she spoke but I didn't miss the hurt flashing through her expression.

"Can you give me a chance to explain?"

The glare returned as she flicked her gaze to me once more. "Explain what? How you've spent weeks doing everything in your power to be nice to me. To make sure I was comfortable and happy and even going out of your way to make me laugh. Making me think you might actually care about me and not the information I could give you only to make it apparent you don't see me as anything but your captive? Your prisoner? Well I got the information loud and clear, *General.*" The word was like a slap in the face, it sure as hell stung as much.

"I..."

"If you don't mind I'd like to be alone." Her eyes settled in the window again as she cut me off. Damn, this was not going the way I'd planned when I'd walked through the door.

"Hayley, please."

"Go. Away."

"No."

I made the single word as forceful as I could manage given the ache in my chest and the panic settling in my stomach. Her glare hit me full force and I winced as I reached up and ran my hand through my hair, eyes adjusting to the wall behind her.

"Look, you're pissed, I get it and I won't tell you that you shouldn't be. Actually, you should be because you're right about a lot of what you said. Except I don't just see you as a source of information, or my prisoner or even my captive anymore."

She may have started out as my prisoner but my feelings toward her had evolved rapidly into something deeper, more profound.

"Sure you don't."

"I don't. Do you even care why I ran? Why I panicked?"

"Panic? What the hell was there to panic about?" She shot off the bed and stood a few feet in front of me. Her hands were balled into fists and the muscles in her jaw were twitching. She was more upset about how I'd reacted than I'd thought she would be. Was it possible she did have deeper feelings for me and the action hadn't been simply a fleeting, one time lapse in judgment?

"Everything! Let's set aside for a minute that you're supposed to be the enemy and the fact that since you got here you've refused to tell me almost anything personal about yourself and focus on my side. The fact is that I haven't been kissed by anyone in years, Hayley." I paused to draw a deep breath, fighting off the tears threatening to fall at the things I was about to admit.

"I've been alone for a while and it isn't always easy to deal with everything on my own. When you leave yourself open you get hurt and I got tired of ending up hurt so I locked everyone out. I've been closed off and shut down since my wife died twenty years ago." The comment seemed to get her attention and the glare slipped away, replaced by sheer shock.

"Your... Wife?"

"Yeah, my wife. I was married for a very long time Hayley. She was the only person who ever really knew me. I have a best friend, she's like a sister but even she doesn't know everything. Laney did. She was my world. Then I lost her and everything fell apart. I threw myself into this, into being General, becoming Conquest. It was all that made sense anymore."

"I still don't understand why that would make you panic? It's been twenty years, you said. You can't still feel... I don't know, like you're betraying her or something. Can you?"

"No, it isn't that. Well, actually sometimes I do still feel like that but I know it's crazy. The issue is that it's been so long since I've felt this way. I never thought I'd care this deeply about anyone after her and I definitely didn't expect to find myself falling for a

Purist. Is that enough to panic about for you?"

I watched the last of the anger edge out of her expression as she processed my words. A few seconds later her arms dropped to her sides and she let out a sigh with a shake of her head.

"I had no idea, Kai."

Oh thank whatever God was listening, she was using my name again. I had never liked the sound of General anyway but the way she'd said it was had ripped through my system. It had hurt.

"I know you didn't because I haven't exactly been in the sharing mood about the personal stuff either. I can't change how awkward and scary this is for me or the fact that I freaked out. Please try to stop being mad at me for it and don't hold it against me."

I must have gotten through to her since she took a halting step toward me, paused and seemed to be considering her options for a beat. I had to guess she made up her mind from one moment to the next when she took the plunge and covered the last few feet between us. She all but collapsed against me and my immediate reaction was to wrap my arms around her. It sure as hell beat the one she'd gotten out of me a couple nights earlier. I closed my eyes and breathed a sigh of relief over the situation, hoping her current position meant she understood.

"I hate to interrupt this moment but..." I paused, I really didn't want her to move, I was happy with her wrapped right where she was but I knew we needed to talk. "We need to sit down and really talk. We've been skirting everything personal and it's made this all so much more difficult."

With a sigh she nodded and then leaned away from me. My entire body screamed at me for allowing her to break the contact but I told it to shut up. If we had any chance of things going anywhere, we had a lot to get out in the open.

We made our way downstairs, deciding the old living room would be the best place to sit and talk since it had a fireplace. The drop in temperature had the inside of the house bordering on frigid. I popped outside long enough to grab another armload of wood, knowing we'd need it. I slipped back in and dropped it beside the stack already present beside the stone fireplace. Once I had a decent fire going I moved to sit in front of Hayley, close enough to reach out and touch her if I'd wanted to.

It felt nice to be so close, even though I knew what was coming. I'd been keeping her at a distance, arms-length or more when we'd been out together. Every day I spent around her intensified my reactions to her and heightened my awareness. I'd tried to keep exactly what had happened from happening. She had been the one to cross the line and while I'd done everything possible to maintain the distance, I'd failed. With the barrier breached, I felt keeping her from getting close was pointless so I didn't bother to move away.

I found myself wanting to be close, wanting to keep her near me and I decided I wasn't going to feel bad about it.

CHAPTER FOURTEEN

UNEXPECTED INFORMATION

"BEFORE YOU tell me anything else, I have a confession to make."

Hayley's words ripped me from my thoughts and sent ice water flooding through my veins. The serenity I'd found in my decision to remain close to her a moment before was stripped away. It took every ounce of willpower I possessed to repress the shudder the comment attempted to cause.

"Okay." The single word wasn't long enough to carry the panic her statement elicited down in the core of my being. Honesty may be best but it was rarely pretty so I was left feeling nervous and jittery all over again.

"When you asked me why I was with Julia and Patricia and I skirted the question... I was terrified of telling you the truth. I still don't want to tell you. It might change everything and there's a decent chance you'll never trust me after tonight. Not once I tell you this. But you deserve it and if I have any chance of actually having this... Whatever this is between us work out, you need to know the truth."

"Which is?" She had piqued my curiosity which in turn bled away the nerves leaving me with a blessedly close to calm demeanor.

"Well, at the risk of having you run again... I was the only woman in our area well trained enough to accompany them and keep them safe. Asking any of the men to be their guards would have raised suspicion and we couldn't have that."

"Trained? As what?"

"A soldier. Well, actually..." She locked eyes with me and worry crawled its way up my spine over what she might say next. "I'm a Captain... In the White Guard."

The world dropped out from under me at the statement. The White Guard were the Purists most elite soldiers were trained in stealth, hand-to-hand combat, tracking and archery. They worked alone, often carrying out special missions and they were deadly. We'd learned they existed a mere fifty years earlier when we discovered in every instance of one of our Generals being assassinated by the Purists it had been the work of a White Guard. I levered myself up off the floor and paced over to the fireplace, it wasn't much distance but I needed every inch of it right then.

I leaned against the mantle, heart pounding, breathing ragged until I could pull myself back under control. Then I dropped my arms and whirled to focus on her as I let loose an accusatory, "Are you kidding me?"

She flinched and somewhere deep down, under the fear and new panic I hated having caused it, but there were more pressing matters at hand. "I wish I was. Unfortunately, it gets worse." Worse? How the hell could anything she said after the bomb she'd dropped on me seconds earlier be worse?

"I have a hard time believing there's worse than that."

"There is... I heard you talking to Julia a while back."

"When?" I had a sinking feeling I knew which conversation she was referring to but I'd been in the place so often visiting there was no telling what she'd overheard.

"About Father Rivers." I hated being right sometimes but I still wasn't sure why she was bringing up such a specific conversation. Unless she knew something Julia hadn't known or hadn't told me.

"I wasn't exactly being covert about the conversation." I hadn't been either; I'd wanted the information but I hadn't cared if the other women overheard us talking.

"I know. But Julia didn't tell you everything she knew."

"She lied to me?"

"No, not lied. She withheld, to protect me." Now I was bordering on confused and my brows knit down as I tried to follow the path she was taking me down. "I was sent with them. But not to help them relocate. They were a decoy; the whole thing was a trap." My heart stuttered in the middle of its rapid rampage and I couldn't breathe for a minute as I tried to grasp what she was telling me.

"What kind of trap?"

"I was sent in the hopes we'd be detained. I was supposed to allow myself to be brought into the compound and then…" I didn't want to hear what she was about to say but I couldn't bring myself to stop her. "I was supposed to kill you."

The information hit me like a hammer and I would have sworn a lead weight had been dropped into my stomach. The world spun and I suddenly had the urge to relieve my stomach of its contents but I managed to fight the reaction back. Once everything righted itself again and the room stopped spinning I took a chance on speaking, I needed to know more, mainly the why of it all. I dropped into one of the basic chairs I kept into the room and shook my head as I looked over at her.

"Why you?"

"Because I was the only one he felt he could trust with the mission."

"You mean Father Rivers?"

"Yes."

"Why would he trust you?"

"Because Lee Rivers is my father."

Those six words dropped my heart and spun my entire world upside down. I couldn't stop the violent reaction my body had to the news this time. It was all I could do to shoot to my feet and falter my way out of the room before I doubled over. I found myself thankful I hadn't been able to eat for the last two days since it meant all I did was end up shaking. I didn't want to process what had happened, what she'd told me. The news meant the woman I'd confessed I was falling in love with less than five minutes earlier had been sent to murder me. For all I knew getting close to me like this was all part of the plan. And I had fallen right into it with open arms.

I started for the door, feeling the intense need to run from her for the second time in as many meetings. She positioned herself between me and the door, refusing to move so I could leave. Her hands held up in front of her as if trying to show me she meant me no harm she eased her way closer. For every foot she gained toward me I took a step or two back into the living room. The space which had felt warm, inviting and comforting a minute earlier was now stifling.

"Kai, please. You have to believe me when I tell you I have no intention of following through with that now."

"Believe you? Are you kidding me? I can't believe a word you say, Hayley. How am I supposed to trust you, trust that this isn't all just part of your plan?" Hurt flashed onto her features as her arms dropped to her sides and the first glimmer of unshed tears flickered in her eyes.

"I've had more than enough chances if that was my plan, Kai. Or have you forgotten the days I've spent wandering this place with you? Seems to me you forgot who you were with several times. Would you like me to recount the times I remember you having your back to me and your guard down?"

I hated it but she was right, I'd allowed myself to relax in her company over the last couple months. The fact she'd been able to kiss me was proof enough of that. "I wasn't supposed to get close to you. He didn't want me getting to know you, I was supposed to get in and the minute you tried to question me, take you out."

"But how am I supposed to believe that?"

Rather than replying she took a long, deep breath then stepped over closer. Since I had managed to back up against the wall I was trapped and she closed the distance between us in a few steps.

"Do you trust yourself? Do you believe that if someone was trying to make you think they cared you'd be able to tell?"

"I would hope so. But now..."

I was beginning to have some serious doubts about my gut instinct since it seemed to have lost its shine. I was about to say as much when she leaned in and in a repeat of two nights earlier, kissed me. This time when I froze she didn't pull away but leaned against me, slid her arms around my waist and held me closer. As much as my brain was telling me to fight, to get away, my heart and my body betrayed me. My resolved melted into a puddle at my feet and I let the kiss happen, returning it with abandon.

My hands came up to her hips and with a sudden ripple, clarity washed over me. This wasn't a woman attempting to get close so she could kill me. This was a woman turning her back on everything she knew because she felt something for me. I forced myself to lean away, breaking the contact but not bothering to attempt getting away from her. As it stood, if she wanted to kill me then she had her moment, and I wouldn't fight my feelings any longer, I couldn't.

"Even if you believe this was my plan all along, do you really believe I could fake that?"

I had no doubt about there being people who could fake intensity and passion to reach and end goal. I did doubt Hayley had it in her to be one of them. Over the months I'd spent getting to know her she'd proven herself to be proud, to the point of being stubborn and cocky. Not the type who would lower herself to pretending she cared for someone and allowing them to see her soul. I had to believe what we were sharing was real, if not for her state of mind then for my own sanity.

The twitch of a small grin turned up the left corner of my lips as I sighed, giving her a barely perceptible shake of my head. I caught myself thinking about what I would do if I was wrong, if she was still trying to get close and complete her mission.

I decided if I was meant to die in such a way after so many years being careful, bordering on paranoid, so be it. With any luck I'd get to experience the feeling of being cared about again for a little while first. When my eyes met hers again, the doubt, the questions, all of it was swept away and all I saw was the woman I'd fallen for.

"You win."

I assumed I'd given her the answer she wanted when she pulled me back in, ending any chance at further conversation in the blink of an eye.

CHAPTER FIFTEEN

FRESH BLOOD

KAI'S JOURNAL - *Autumn Cycle, 2606 – 220 years after the event:*

Steph talked sense into me and I went and had a chat with Hayley. A chat during which she dropped a bomb on me. The crazy leader of the Purists being her father isn't something I'm finding easy to swallow. I tried to push my feelings away, lock them up and pretend I could walk away from them, and her. In the end I gave in, apparently since I'm adding this entry from her bed. I can't remember the last time I had a night like this. The last time I felt this way about someone was Laney and now I know for sure, she would want me to follow through with this. Now I'm putting this away, wrapping myself around the gorgeous girl sleeping beside me and letting the world slip away for a few hours.

The sound of birds singing outside the window coaxed me from the peaceful sleep I'd been enjoying the next morning. Still half asleep I stretched, pointing my toes and expecting to meet the wall the end of my bed rested against. Instead I met open air, my brows knitting as my brain frantically attempted to remember where I'd fallen asleep. I willed my eyes open and the panic which had been setting in faded as I glanced to my right and found Hayley sound asleep beside me. A smile spread across my face as I relaxed, shifting onto my side.

I propped my head on my hand, my elbow against the

threadbare, handmade mattress so I could look down at her, watching the steady rise and fall of her chest as she breathed. I could hear the sounds of the compound waking up to start the day and knew I needed to get moving. I had two options and after considering them for a minute I decided I didn't have it in me to wake her. I leaned in and brushed a light kiss across her forehead before I eased out of the bed. After finding my clothes and pulling them all back into place I tugged on my boots and slipped out of the house silently.

I had my quarters in sight when Steph caught up with me, nudging me with her shoulder as she said, "So, imagine my surprise when I came over to check on you and found your room empty." I shifted my gaze down onto my boots as the telltale heat of a blush crept over my face. The flush was accompanied by its old pal the grin which settled onto my features without asking permission. "I take it things went well with Hayley?"

"Pretty good, yeah."

"Pretty good? You're getting back to your own quarters well after sunrise. You're blushing. Not to mention you have that damn goofy grin on your face and all you can manage is *pretty* good? Come on, Kai."

"Okay, it went great." A bright smile took over my face, replacing the grin as I looked up at my best friend, beaming as I remembered the previous night. "She understood once she let me talk and she even opened up and told me a few personal things."

"Oh good! What kinds of personal things?" I shook my head, unwilling to divulge the things she had shared with me. While I wasn't interested in sharing Hayley's secrets I was also reluctant to tell Steph anything I'd learned. I knew her reaction to the information wouldn't be a good one. "Okay I get it, don't want to share things that aren't yours to share. I can take the hint."

"Thanks. So, why were you checking in on me?" I let the smile fall into a tiny smirk at her before turning my attention toward the drill yard where half a dozen scouting recruits were being put through target practice.

"I was worried. But since you seem to be just dandy, I suppose I can dive right in to giving you an update."

"Update?" The question was aimed in her direction but my focus was still on the newest recruits. I had hand-picked each of them a month earlier. They were in the early stages of training but a couple of them showed promise.

"Mmhmm, Bradley and his team are back." The comment snapped my focus back to the head runner as a wicked little grin worked its way across her face.

"Are you gonna make me drag it out of you?"

With a chuckle she shook her head and told me, "No, they had three Purist scouts in tow. Luke was getting them settled in a cell while I came to find you."

"Well why are we standing here chatting? Let's get over there and see what we've got." She nodded and we made our way past the yard and toward the jail. As we approached one of the younger runners darted up to us, skidding to a halt a few feet to our left.

"Sorry to interrupt your plans ma'am but there's a runner here from Thea."

I rolled my eyes at the news, not as interested in hearing Thea's excuses for not coming to our gathering as I was in seeing these new scouts. I glanced over at Steph who glared at me, grumbled something under her breath and then waved at the young man to lead the way. I watched them as they walked away, waiting until they turned to go around one of the buildings to step inside our jail. Once inside I allowed my vision to adjust which didn't take long thanks to my level of mutation. Within seconds I could see clearly again.

I easily made out Luke leaning against the wall across from the cell Julia and Nathan had once been housed in. I stepped over, leaned beside him and turned my gaze toward the cell. The three new men were inside, each looking irate and ready to explode but no worse for wear. I stood there, silently evaluating them, letting the seconds and then the minutes tick by. You could tell so much about someone by how long it took them to lose their temper. Whichever one of these three became irritated with me first would be my best bet for slip-ups.

"Are you just gonna stand there and stare at us all day or do you intend to say something?"

Without moving anything but my eyes I shifted my gaze onto the man who had spoken. He was the smallest of the three, I estimated about an inch taller than myself. Some of his chocolate brown hair had fallen loose of the leather tie holding it out of his face giving him a haphazard, disheveled look. His jaw was set in a hard line, the muscles tense, ticking with the flicker of a twitch every few seconds. He was ticked off and it showed, it would be far too easy to provoke him. I decided to do nothing, let him think he was being ignored.

"Hello? Are you listening?" I kept quiet and Luke followed suit, becoming an almost inanimate version of himself against the wall. The man pushed off the patch of dirt he'd been sitting on and approached the bars of the cell. His left hand gripped one of the bars as he leaned forward, his forehead resting against the rust-tainted metal. His eyes narrowed as he studied us and I wondered what could be running through his mind as his gaze flickered from me to Luke and back again.

The man said, "Huh. We were told you weren't nearly as smart as us but I didn't expect to discover you were incapable of even speaking. Guess you're even dumber than we thought."

When neither of us reacted the man huffed and reached up with his other hand, gripping another bar three over from the first he'd grabbed hold of. After leaning back to take his head away from the bars he tightened his grip and shook them violently. It took everything I had to keep from bursting into laughter at his outburst. I'd always gotten a kick out of seeing grown men throw tantrums like small children. He had just become the most entertaining moment of my life.

After three minutes one of the other men in the cell apparently tired of his comrade's outburst. The huge blond stood, crossed over to the confrontational man and slapped him in the back of the head. The rattling ceased as the smaller man reached up with a loud 'ow!' and grabbed the back of his head. He rounded on his assailant, appearing unaffected by the six inches of height the fairer man had on him. With one finger in the middle of the larger man's chest he glared up at him as he shouted.

"What the hell? Why did you do that?"

"Because you were acting like a child." He was right of course, though I wasn't about to open my mouth and agree with him.

"And? I'm allowed to act as I please. Last I checked, you weren't in charge here!" The muscles in the bigger man's jaw twitched and I repressed a grin. We'd now learned that the wall of man standing before us wasn't in command. I'd also be willing to bet from the scowl he was now wearing he wasn't very happy about the fact.

"No, I'm not. But being in command doesn't give someone the right to act like a spoiled brat and cause a scene."

Oh good, now we knew the smaller man probably was in charge. The things one could learn by simply keeping quiet and observing. My gaze shifted enough to lock eyes with Luke who flashed me the hint of a smirk before returning to his emotionless mask. He'd caught the same thing I had and now had the information filed away for later use. I could always count on Luke to remember everything he heard, it made him an amazing asset.

"What did you just say to me?"

Even in the dimly lit space I could see the flush of red crawling up the back of the smaller man's neck. He was losing his temper and wasn't doing anything to try and hide or slow the reaction. Someone had made a grave mistake by putting this man in charge of anything. I gave a quick glance at the third man in the cell, the one who had remained silent and unmoving through it all. I found him staring right at me, his dark brown eyes in contrast with his pale skin and almost white hair.

He must have realized I was looking at him because a slow grin pulled at his lips and the look was far from friendly. The menace the expression held chilled me through to my core but I fought back the shiver trying to ripple through me. Even as a small voice at the back of my head screamed at me to look away, I refused to tear my gaze from his. I wouldn't be the first to falter and I had the feeling I could outstare him with ease. At least, I should be able to since I'd worked for decades to perfect my stare down technique.

The heated conversation between the two other men raged on in the background but I had tuned it out. Luke would catch it and let me know if I'd missed anything important, I had other things to deal with. The pale man finally looked away but not before winking at me, sending a shiver up my spine I had no hope of containing. His attention was refocused on his arguing cohorts who he distracted with a sudden, sharp whistle. It took all the willpower I had to keep from flinching as the shrill sound echoed through the space.

The pair turned to look at him, the larger seeming far calmer than he should after catching a look at his counterpart. The smaller man was bright red, sweat forming on his forehead and neck and the rapid rise and fall of his shoulders showed he was flustered and out of breath. The smirk the third man had been wearing fell away, replaced by a scowl which caused the bigger of the other two to look away from him. An interesting development if I had to say so. The smaller man continued to stare him down, defiance in every inch of his stance and the set of his shoulders.

"What do you two think you're doing?" His voice was calm,

collected and not as deep as I would have expected it to be but it held a ripple of power which made me hold my breath.

"If you were paying attention Phillip, you'd know we were arguing. But since you were too busy making flirty eyes with the girl over there you apparently missed it." One nearly white brow arched up as the flushed man spoke to his comrade, venom in his tone. With shocking grace, the pale man who we now knew was Phillip rose and moved over to where the smaller man was standing.

"And if you had even half the amount of sense as you have pride you would have realized you were probably giving them everything they wanted to know Jacob."

From the expression which crossed Jacob's face I assumed he managed to process what Phillip said and turned on Luke and me. He glared at me for a minute before apparently deciding he should address Luke. His focus settled on the massive man on my left as I bit back a laugh choosing instead to shake my head. Purists we captured often assumed they should address Luke, Bradley or really any of the other men in my presence once we had them detained. I had to assume after my conversations with Julia it was a societal thing, they'd been taught all their lives that women were beneath them.

"Why were we detained? What are we doing here? All we were attempting to do was find places to resupply. There was no need to haul us in here." Luke remained silent, choosing to refrain from addressing Phillip which seemed to frustrate him. "Are you incapable of processing a simple question? Why are we here?" Luke glanced at me, receiving a nod in response to his unspoken question and then replied to the man.

"Why are you asking me?" The humor his deep voice held made me grin and I tilted my chin toward my chest, ducking my head to hide it.

"Because I want answers."

"And you think I have them."

"Yes. Of course." The man was barely more than half Luke's weight but he had some serious boldness.

"Why would you think that? There are two people present after all."

The smaller man glanced at me then turned to look at his two cellmates, holding their attention for several long seconds. When he finally turned back to us his brow was furrowed and he appeared confused as he said, "Why would I bother addressing *her?*"

I guessed Luke found the comment entertaining when he laughed outright, not a chuckle or a stifled sound in the least but a full, echoing guffaw. I looked over to find him shaking his head as if the comment from Phillip were the most ridiculous thing he'd ever heard. The reaction to what I had to believe was a very serious inquiry from the captured scout man him fume. His glare deepened as the set of his jaw muscles intensified. He looked as if he was about to explode and I had a mental image of smoke coming out his ears.

Luke looked in my direction as I pushed away from the wall and crossed over to the cell, deciding it was time to speak. I stopped close enough to be out of the light and give them a closer look at my eyes, knowing they would be glowing faintly in the darkness of the room. "Because I'm in charge here. Name is Kai, but you can call me General or, if you prefer, Conquest."

Shock worked its way across the face of the small man as he took a step back, nearly colliding with the one he had called Jacob. I shook my head as I turned and walked back toward Luke, rolling my shoulders to work the tension out of them. I'd slept well but not long and I was beginning to feel the effects of all the lack of sleep I'd been subjecting myself to. I reached up and put a hand on Luke's shoulder, drawing his attention down to me.

"Get whatever you can out of them, I'm exhausted. I'll come back and work with them myself sometime after I get in something like decent sleep."

He nodded his understanding and without another word spoken between us I turned and left him alone with the three men. I knew he wouldn't hurt them; Luke wasn't the type to resort to violence unless all other options had been excluded. He would however, scare the living hell out of them.

CHAPTER SIXTEEN

MISUNDERSTANDINGS

I SET out from the jail intent on going back to my quarters and catching up on some sleep but changed my mind halfway there. With a quick course alteration, I headed back out to the house I had left a short three hours earlier. Despite my reluctance to admit how I felt about Hayley over the past months I found myself drawn to her now that I'd actually said it out loud. A smile worked its way across my face as I hopped up the steps onto the front porch and pushed through the front door. I laughed to myself when I registered finding it unlocked, realizing I'd left it wide open when I'd left earlier.

With the knowledge I was beginning to trust this new woman in my life I took the stairs to the second floor two at a time. I knocked on the door but was met with total silence. My brow furrowed as I tried again only to meet with the same result. I decided to try one more time and as soon as the third knock died away a response came as I heard her shout, "Go away!" through the door.

Not understanding the reaction, I decided to check on her and opened the door, finding the room dark, a thick woven throw hung over the window. My eyes adjusted to the dim interior as I shut the door and I saw Hayley curled up sitting on the corner of the bed.

Her back was pressed against the wall and her head was down, her face hidden against her arms atop her knees. Confusion settled over me as I crossed the room and sat beside her, reaching out to brush her hair back from the side of her face. The light contact of my fingertips against her neck made her flinch and lean away from me as far as she could get.

"Hayley, what's wrong?"

Worry began overtaking the confusion as it became clear she was upset about something. I had no clue what could have possibly happened in the last couple hours since I'd left to make her so testy. I had every intention of finding out if I could get her to at least look up at me. I waited, my impatience building in a steady wave and was about to press further when she looked up. The harsh glare she leveled on me sent me into a tailspin as I wondered what I could have done to upset her, again.

"What's wrong? *You* are what's wrong."

"What did I do?"

"Seriously? I open up and pour my heart out to you. I tell you the truth knowing it'll only make things between us more difficult and then after you seem to accept my explanation, you spend the night with me... Then when I wake up, you're gone. You ran. Again. So much for believing me." I was stunned and as she finished speaking I realized how my departure while she was still sleeping must have looked to her.

"Oh Hayley, no. It wasn't like that at all. I had things to get done this morning and when I thought about waking you up I just... I couldn't. You looked so peaceful laying there that I decided to let you sleep and come see you later."

She studied me hard as I began counting to ten, only making it to five before I realized she'd been crying. I reached over and brushed a thumb across her cheek, wiping away the rogue tears still breaking free. The gentle contact seemed to do the trick and I watched her entire body relax as she leaned over to wrap her arms around me. I mentally kicked myself for making such a stupid mistake and knew I would have to be more careful. I held her as she squeezed me hard and let her hang on as long as she needed.

When she leaned back and offered me a sheepish smile I knew we would be fine. We would have to work on trusting each other but I knew we could manage it. I swept a few stray strands of hair back behind her ear and returned her smile before I leaned over and pressed a kiss to her forehead. I caught her eyes, holding her gaze in the near darkness as I considered my next words carefully. I knew what I wanted to say, the offer I wanted to make to her but I also knew what might happen if she agreed.

"Hayley, we need to get you out of this house. There's really no reason to keep you here alone anymore."

"I have to admit that would be great. I've been lonely here, not that having days out with you hasn't been amazing but..." She seemed nervous as she spoke, like she was worried about insinuating she didn't like spending time with me. I chuckled which seemed to ease some of the tension in her shoulders.

"I know, there's only so many nights you can spend cooped up here by yourself. I figured we'll get you settled in somewhere else today."

"I can't wait. Where did you have in mind? Near Julia or Patricia?"

"No... Not close to either of them at all actually." She gave me a curious look and I knew she had to be wondering what kind of people I would be housing her with if not her friends. "I was thinking you might be most comfortable staying with me."

Shock widened her eyes and her mouth fell open an inch or so as a thick silence fell over the room. I decided to keep my mouth shut and let her process the idea. She would speak when she was ready and all I might manage to do would be to stick my foot in my mouth. I eyed her closely as she seemed to pull herself together and cleared her throat.

"Are you sure, Kai?"

"I am."

"And what will your soldiers think?"

"Whatever they want to think. I can't stop them from thinking it's weird or wrong but I can decide to not let what they think bother me or dictate how I behave. We've made some major steps and I honestly think I can trust you."

"You can."

"Then I don't see why we shouldn't take this leap. I mean, let's be honest with ourselves here. If I put you staying with Julia or Patricia after last night, what would happen?" She grinned at me and I saw a light flush creep across her cheeks.

"I'd probably end up slipping into your quarters most nights anyway." The flush darkened into a full blush and expanded to cover the bridge of her nose.

"Exactly, so why even bother."

"You make a valid point. Okay, let's do it."

I nodded, slipped off the edge of the bed and gathered her clothes from where we had dropped them all the night before. After handing them to her I went on a hunt for her boots as she pulled the layers back on. I located both boots, handed them over and waited while she stuffed her feet into them. Once she completed the task and straightened up again I reached out, offering her my hand. She beamed at the offering, took it and followed me down the stairs to the door. She picked up the sweater she'd left thrown over the railing as we descended the stairs.

When we reached the path outside the house she paused and I caught her trying to pull her hand back. I gripped it harder and shook my head at her. I knew what she was trying to do, what she must be thinking but I had my own ideas. I was intent on making sure any and all rumors and whispering were quelled before having the chance to begin. Being with Hayley was my choice and one I hadn't made lightly. My people would either accept it or choose to leave and join one of the other Generals but I wouldn't hide her like I was ashamed.

CHAPTER SEVENTEEN

CONFRONTATION

KAI'S JOURNAL - *Autumn Cycle, 2606 – 220 years after the event:*

I'm having to get myself back into the habit of this relationship thing. It's been a while and the last time was quite a bit easier since Laney and I started on the same side. With Hayley coming from a place of not trusting me to where we are now means we have some issues to work around. I need to make sure I think things through before running off and doing them. Something as innocent as leaving her sleeping after our night together because she looked so sweet laying there could be taken the wrong way. At least for the first few months. I'm hoping we can learn to open up to each other and communicate better. It's the only way this thing will work. In the meantime, I'm glad I made the decision to get her out of that house. Being with her this way and knowing I'm still treating her like a prisoner is too hard for my heart to handle. With any luck the reaction from the residents of the compound won't become a mass exodus into another territory.

The news of Hayley's relocation swept through the compound at a startling rate. Most of the residents, while confused by the choice I'd made, accepted it and let it be. The few who had a problem with it seemed to be deciding what their options were. No one had dared to confront me about the situation but if they did I would calmly let them know it was my business, not theirs. I had no doubt someone would approach me about it at some point.

What I hadn't been expecting was the first one to speak out to be someone close to me. When it turned out to be three someone's close to me I couldn't help feeling a bit betrayed. Not to mention cornered. Luke, Bradley and Steph sought me out the same afternoon, only hours after I'd decided to move Hayley. The two of us were in the stable, looking over the horses and letting them meet the newest member of our population when my best friend came in.

"Kai... Can we talk?"

"Hey Steph, sure." I dropped the brush I'd been working over the dusty coat of one of our mares and wiped my hands on my pants. Steph's gaze flickered over to Hayley and then back to me before she ran her fingers through her hair.

"Uh, alone?" My eyes narrowed slightly as I tried to figure out why she would want to talk to me alone, knowing it couldn't be anything good. When Luke and Bradley stepped in behind her it only confirmed my suspicion.

"Whatever you think you need to say to me, just say it."

"Kai, I can leave if you need to..." I shook my head as Hayley spoke, reaching out and putting a hand on her shoulder to keep her from leaving.

"No Hayley. If this is going to work between us we have to learn to trust each other. That means you hear everything I do. No secrets." She didn't reply but the smile she gave me in response spoke volumes, I'd made a huge step in the right direction in her eyes.

"Fine. Let her stay. We're worried about you." I cocked my head at Steph's words, feigning stupidity at why they would be worried. I knew what she meant but I was going to make her say it. "Don't play stupid, Kai. You know exactly what I mean." I crossed my arms over my chest, shrugged and shook my head, refusing to let her get the upper hand in this little game we were playing. "Okay, act dumb, I'll lay it out for you. It's not safe for her to be out wandering around the compound and it definitely isn't safe for her to be staying in your quarters."

"Isn't safe according to who?"

"We all think it's a bad idea." I glanced over her shoulder at Bradley when he spoke up and narrowed my eyes at him. I couldn't believe these three, of all people, were second guessing me.

"But why? I'm hearing that you don't think it's safe, that you think it's a bad idea but I'm not getting any reasons. Fill in the blanks for me guys."

Luke decided to speak and added, "Because we don't know

why she's here. We've gotten the why from the other two. We know they left trying to escape bad situations. We don't know anything about her, Kai. She's an unknown and you know how much I hate those unknowns."

"I do know Luke, but trust me, she's fine. I know why she's here and I'm perfectly comfortable with the situation."

"Care to share the situation with us?" I shook my head at his request, knowing he was looking out for me but not about to give them any further ammunition against Hayley.

"No. I'm the only one who needs to know."

"Kai..." Steph was about to argue with me, I could see it in her eyes and the set of her shoulders. I had to end this immediately before they stepped too far out of line.

"Enough. All of you. Look, I said I know the details and I'm fine with it all. That should be all you need to know. All I'll tell you is that if I'm wrong, the only person who really pays for the decision will be me." I turned my attention toward Hayley, my brows raised as I asked her, "Right?"

"Yes. But you aren't wrong. I swear on my life." I could see the truth of the words in her eyes and it warmed me through to my core. I turned back to the three, leveling a look on them which said very clearly I was finished with their verbal attack.

"Are we done here? We were about to saddle up and head out for a ride." Steph looked as if she might be about to argue but Luke's hand on her shoulder stopped her.

"Leave it Steph, she's right. She's in charge here and she's never done anything to put us in harm's way. I doubt she would change that now. We just have to trust that she knows what she's doing." Steph relented, nodding her agreement as Bradley did the same. I knew they were still worried but they would let it go, for now.

CHAPTER EIGHTEEN

A NEW FRIEND

ONCE MY three Captains cleared out, leaving Hayley and I alone again, I turned back to her and shook my head. She stepped over and slipped her hand into mine, squeezing gently as she gave me a smile.

"Sorry about that."

"Don't be, wasn't your fault and they have every right to worry. You know everything but they don't. They're just looking out for you. Seems like they care about you."

"They do. Sometimes I think they care too much though." I chuckled and she smirked before she pulled me over and silenced the noise by kissing me. When she pulled away I had to take a moment and let my lungs remember how to work. I sucked in a deep breath and flashed a giddy grin at her before reminding myself why we were in the stable. "Right, so..."

I cleared my throat as I pulled away, putting a little distance between us but still feeling overheated. I peeked over my shoulder to find her following me, that sly smirk still settled firmly on her lips. *What a brat. Sexy, beautiful, funny as hell, but a brat...* I thought as I returned my attention to the line of stalls in front of me.

"I'll admit, I hadn't expected such a strong connection between you and your Captains." I looked at her over my shoulder, shooting her a questioning look.

"Oh?"

"Yeah, I mean, I was a Captain for the Purists, my father is their leader and even he and I weren't ever as close as you are to yours. They come to you with things, feel comfortable warning you when they think your judgement might be clouded. No one would ever approach my father that way. They'd be terrified they'd end up behind bars, or worse."

I saw the shudder ripple through her and agreed completely with it. The idea of being so scared of someone you trusted to lead you was horrifying. I couldn't imagine my people afraid of me. They knew better than to step too far out of line, but they didn't worry I might hurt them, only that I might be angry. They all seemed to understand I had their best interests, and safety, at heart.

"Well, these aren't just my people, simply the residents of my compound. They're my family."

"I can see that."

I smiled at her then turned my attention back to what I'd been in the process of starting before I'd been ambushed. I ran through a mental list of the unclaimed horses housed with us, trying to decide which would be a good match for Hayley. We had a handful, just over a half dozen who were unclaimed and had the training I insisted they go through before being paired. Of those seven only two came to mind so I started down the aisle. I was headed toward the first even though I was terrified of the two meeting.

The horse was a good mare, at least as old as Prophecy and she had been with us for a very long time. I had trained her myself so I knew she was settled into our ways properly. The problem was in the fact she had been impossible to pair since she'd lost her former rider. She was picky, like me and we'd discovered giving her a new person was easier said than done. She'd thrown, kicked, bitten and displayed every other manner of nasty behavior with everyone we'd tried. Even Steph had ended up with a broken arm compliments of the moody mare.

My being now flooded with apprehension I approached the stall, took a deep breath and exhaled sharply. I had to find out if there was a chance, if she would accept Hayley as a possibility for her new companion. The idea had flickered in and out of my head several times in the last few weeks but I had dismissed it more than a dozen times. The last thing I wanted was for Hayley to get hurt. Now as we stood here in the stable, the stall only feet away, I knew my first thoughts had been right. I had to try, even if the idea failed, at least I'd know.

"Hayley, this is Genesis."

I split my focus between Hayley and the mare as human approached horse for the first time. Genesis had come to us right after I'd decided to settle in our current location almost a hundred and fifty years earlier. She'd charged into the compound in our early years, wild and on a rampage. In the end, it was Prophecy who had managed to calm her after she took a shine to him. They had been attached to each other ever since. She had been Laney's horse before she died and I knew that was what made it so hard for me to attempt this bonding between she and the new woman in my life.

I held my breath, my heart in my throat as the mare poked her head out of the stall, her bright green eyes settling on Hayley. She eyed the new human in her space as Hayley raised a hand toward her, the movement slow and steady. When her palm connected with the deep chestnut forehead and Genesis responded with a soft, happy chuffing noise, a wall I'd erected crumbled. Without warning I found myself crying and had to turn away from the scene playing out before me. I'd never considered how I might feel when my departed wife's horse finally chose someone new.

Hayley realized I had walked away a short minute later and followed me back to the doors, catching up with me as I stepped out into the cool afternoon air. She stepped up behind me when I stopped walking and her hand rested on my shoulder. The light contact shattered the last of my resolve and a wave of emotions I hadn't realized I was holding back flooded me. I'd never taken the chance to break down after I lost Laney, feeling I needed to stay strong for the people who followed me, counted on me. Now all of the things I'd refused letting myself feel overpowered me and my legs gave out.

As I collapsed to my knees in the dirt, Hayley lowered herself beside me, her arm coming up to wrap around my shoulders. I leaned against her and let it all go, needing to get it out now that I'd let it begin. She held me while I cried and when the tears slowed then stopped she leaned back and brushed my hair out of my face.

"Are you okay?"

"I think so." My voice was shaky and I'd gone a bit hoarse from the sobbing but I realized I'd let go of so much pain I felt a hundred pounds lighter.

"What happened? If I did something that..."

"No." I cut her off before she could continue blaming herself for something she couldn't have seen coming. "It had nothing to do with you. Genesis... She was Laney's horse. Ever since she died that mare has been hell on hooves. She won't let anyone but me near her and every attempt I've made to give her a new rider has ended in disaster and injury."

"And you wanted me to meet her? Why?"

"I had to know." She gave me a funny look so I decided to elaborate. "I'd always wondered if she would be able to tell. If she would react differently to someone if I ever..."

"Ever?"

"Moved on. Fell in love again. I swear they know, somehow they just do. Prophecy wouldn't leave me alone for the first month after she passed. He was my shadow. I think he knew I was hurting even when I was refusing to show it."

"So what's the consensus?"

"She has to know. Even Steph, my best friend, can't touch her."

"At all?" She seemed unable to believe it but anyone who had ever watched Steph try and groom her would know it was true.

"Not anymore. I attempted to let Steph ride her a handful of years ago, Genesis threw her, busted her arm up pretty good. The last time Steph tried to groom her, Genesis bit her." I watched as she fought to hold back a laugh but failed, a small giggle breaking free. "It's okay to laugh about it, I did. But it has been hard watching her just sort of... Be. She hasn't connected with anyone else since Laney. Until today."

"Wow... I'm shocked. And if I'm being totally honest really confused but... Honored. Thank you."

"Wanna saddle her up and try going for a ride?" Her eyes went wide and I saw panic flow into them which made me laugh. "Oh come on, if she starts any of her usual antics we'll stop and try another horse. How does that sound?"

"Okay. I can live with that."

"Good. Come on." She nodded then helped me off the ground, pausing long enough to pull me into a tight hug. After giving me a squeeze she took my hand and we made our way back inside to get the two horses geared up so we could get out on the trails.

Three hours later we stopped to let the horses get a drink from a nearby stream and graze a bit while we hunted down something to eat. Dinner caught, gutted and skinned the rabbits we'd snared were settled over the fire I'd started while we sat nearby chatting.

"So, no desire to ditch me here and head back home?" My question received a glare as a response which faded away when I laughed.

"No, none at all."

"Glad to hear it."

"With any luck I'll eventually get you to believe that I'm happy here with you. I know things have been touch and go the last few days but I can't imagine going back now." I studied her as she looked out into the trees across the clearing, realizing how relaxed she looked. It was hard to believe she'd been sent to dispose of me a few short months earlier. Strange how a little attraction could alter the course of a life so much. "What are you thinking about so hard over there?"

I jumped at the sound of her voice and had to think for a minute to process her words, not having realized she'd returned her attention to me while I'd been lost in thought. "Just musing about how something as simple as chemistry, an attraction, can change things so drastically."

"Simple? If this process has been what you call simple, I really don't want to visit with difficult." I laughed at her comment and shook my head as I reached over to check if our dinner was cooked through. Deciding the critters needed a little longer I returned them to their place over the fire and leaned back, arms stretched behind me to prop myself up on my hands.

"Okay, maybe simple was the wrong word. But you have to admit that both our lives have been completely changed because of something we, and probably no one else, ever considered."

"I can definitely agree to that. But unexpected doesn't mean it wasn't a good development." I glanced over at her after the statement and returned the smile she gave me. I wouldn't argue the point; I was thrilled with the way things had developed even if I was still working on trusting her. I knew trust came with time and she was more than likely still building hers for me as well. We would simply have to navigate the path there together. I had turned my gaze toward the fire and zoned out again so the gentle contact of her hand covering mine made me jump. "Relax a little. You're so jumpy."

"I know; I can't help it. I'm always jumpy when I'm outside the compound, comes with the territory."

"I guess it would have to. You have a lot of people to consider." I nodded and she turned to stare into the fire as I stole a glance at her in my peripheral vision.

"Those should be ready."

I sat up as I nodded toward the rabbits cooking over the fire and dusted my hands off. We pulled our dinner from the heat and ate in silence. I had found my way back to the strange place we'd been in at the beginning when it came to keeping a conversation with her going. At least she seemed to be in the same awkward boat so I had company in the weird silence. We finished eating and then decided to pack up, kill the fire and head back before it got too dark for her to see.

I loaded up the few things we'd packed into the bags hanging from our saddles and then helped her mount up. She settled in on Genesis and smiled down at me but before I had the chance to return the gesture a noise from the woods behind me caught my attention. I turned and stared into the unrelenting darkness, not seeing anything but hearing movement from behind the trees. Prophecy and Genesis began shifting from foot to foot, huffing and tossing their heads and I knew they'd caught something moving in the woods as well.

"Kai?"

"Shhh." I stopped her from saying anything else, still unsure of what was stalking us from the darkness. I caught a flash of something between some bushes and while I couldn't be sure what I'd seen, I was a better safe than sorry type of person. I turned and looked up at Hayley, catching her concerned expression before I held a finger to my lips to tell her to keep it down. She nodded and then glanced toward the trees before looking back to me. "Head back toward the compound, Genesis knows the way. Just kick her into a gallop, give her the reins and hold on tight."

Her eyes widened at my whispered words and she shook her head, about to speak when I put a hand on her knee and stopped her. "Hayley, I'll be right behind you. Please, go." We locked eyes and whatever she saw in mine convinced her. She placed her hand on top of mine, gave a gentle squeeze then turned Genesis and gave her a solid kick to get her running. I watched until they were barely more than a cloud of dust on the trail toward the compound before I turned back to the trees. I took a deep breath, shrugged off my sweater and tossed it over Prophecy's saddle.

"Whoever is in there, you might as well come out. I already know you're there."

I scanned the tree line for movement, zeroing in on a rustle in the bushes off to my right. I shifted my stance and adjusted my position so I was facing the sound. In the world we lived in, anything could be a threat and it was best to assume the worst and come across as paranoid than end up dead. Tension spread through my body as the rustling grew more intense. I was ready to spring into action when a figure broke through the greenery then lost its footing and landed sprawled in the dirt at my feet.

It took a handful of stuttered heartbeats and ten ragged breaths to get my mind to settle. When I could think straight again I furrowed my brow as I asked, "What the hell happened to you?"

I stared down at the broken figure of a young wolf panting heavily, nose almost touching my boots. I took a slow, deliberate step back, eased down onto one knee and reached one hand out to the massive animal. She was already almost twice the size of a normal wolf but I could tell she was one of the mutations by the bright green stripes gracing her fur. Given the piece of information I would guess she was more than likely only a few years old. The beasts could continue growing at a crawling pace until well into their lifespans and I'd seen several bigger than this one.

I had begun considering how I'd managed to come across a somewhat young animal displaying Level Four mutation since breeding was out of the question when a noise pulled me back. The whine which slipped from the animal made my heart break as I looked her over, trying to assess what might be wrong. I circled her in a slow, intent movement, looking for any signs of injury. She seemed to be down and out but I'd learned the hard way decades ago not to trust initial judgements. Better to know for sure if your opponent was out of commission than end up missing an arm or leg.

As I circled to her hind end I came across a huge, jagged and very angry looking gash on her left side beginning at the back of her ribcage and extending to her knee. It was red, raw and ragged, not something I would guess had been done by another wolf. The flesh between the two edges had been removed, slowing her healing process. The muscles below the surface layer were already beginning to stitch together but the pain of healing the massive gap in her skin could kill her without some help. My mind made up I summoned my strength, not to mention my nerve and worked my arms under the huge animal.

She growled and yelped in pain as I moved her but then fell silent and I assumed shock had taken hold. Probably for the best if I planned on getting her back to the compound. I hauled her over to Prophecy who eyed me as if I'd lost my mind but stood still while I heaved the giant wolf onto his back. I secured her atop the horse so if she came around she wouldn't hurt herself then grabbed hold of the reins.

I'd have to keep a steady pace if I didn't want to hurt the wolf more but it meant I'd be back to base after nightfall.

"Come on boy." I said with a sigh before clucking at Prophecy with my tongue and heading toward home. "We have a nice long walk ahead of us." He huffed and when his nose brushed my shoulder I knew he understood.

CHAPTER NINETEEN

RELIEF

AS IF wanting to add to my already amazing luck for the day a driving rain kicked up with almost two hours left to the compound. I yanked my sweater back on, knowing it wouldn't help much in the chilled downpour but thankful for anything between my skin and the pelting water. The wolf remained unconscious across my saddle despite the soaking the rain was delivering. The brilliant green of the streaks in her fur seemed to give off a faint glow in the light from the full moon rising overhead. I was forced to tear my gaze away from the large canine when I stepped in a waterlogged hole and nearly fell on my face.

I corrected quick enough to stay on my feet but made sure to keep my eyes trained on the path in front of me after the slip. The final trudge to the compound was wet, muddy, cold and miserable but I managed to slog through it. I arrived well after the sun had set to find the place in a frenzy, a group of ten scouts gathered near the gates as Luke barked out orders. I grumbled as a shiver ripped through me and shook the water from my hair as I stepped under the makeshift roof over the gathering space inside the gate. Luke turned as I sneezed, caught sight of me and went wide eyed as he rushed over shouting an order to hold.

"Kai! We've been worried sick about you! When you didn't

come back we started to panic."

My brain kicked in through the chill as I remembered sending Hayley ahead alone and realized he hadn't mentioned her. My own panic surged through my system, heating me through to my core and causing my head to snap up, my eyes meeting the green ringed chocolate gaze of my second.

"Luke, where's Hayley?"

"I don't know. Last I saw her she was taking Genesis back to the stable. You might check there."

"I need to get Prophecy over there and dried off anyway. Stay here, get these horses out of this tack and back in their stalls. There's no need to go running out in this weather. I'm fine."

"I see this. Okay, I'll have them settled back in for the night. But you should let one of us handle Prophecy. You need to get yourself into bed."

"No, I need to check on Hayley."

"Kai..." I shook my head and pushed past him, dropping Prophecy's reins since I knew he would follow.

"Don't Luke. I know you don't think I should care but I do. Did you happen to see if she was hurt or anything when she came in?"

"Uh..."

"I didn't think so. Regardless of whether you think I should or not, I care about her. I'm going to find her and make sure she's okay. After I do that, I'll get myself dry and into bed."

He sighed, the sound resigned as he nodded at me and waved toward the stable. "Okay. Go do what you need to do. I'll handle this."

I nodded to him, gave a small whistle in Prophecy's direction and started the trek to the stables. I caught Luke eyeing the wolf strapped to my saddle as the horse passed him. Thankfully he seemed to sense my urgency and let whatever question he had about the animal wait until later. I hustled toward the large building across the compound and pushed open the door. I ducked under the cascade of water sheeting off the roof to get inside then shook as much of the water from myself as possible.

"Hayley?" My voice could barely be heard in the space over the racket the rain was making on the roof of the building. I was worried she wasn't in the stable when I got no answer after a few seconds but then a familiar head popped out of a stall down the aisle.

"Kai! Thank god!" She barreled down the wide hallway toward me and threw herself into my arms. I wrapped her in a tight embrace, neither of us seeming to care about the chilled water soaking me from head to toe. I heard her sniffle as her fingertips dug into my lower back and I turned my face into her neck in an attempt to comfort her. "I was so worried about you. When you didn't make it back by dark I tried to go out after you but they wouldn't let me leave."

"Good. If they had and something had happened to you I'd have to seriously consider killing whoever allowed you to go." She laughed at the comment and I smiled against her shoulder, glad she was laughing instead of doing more crying. "Relax, I'm fine. It wasn't anything Earth shattering. Look." I leaned away from her, taking her hand and leading her over to where I'd left Prophecy standing. She stopped dead in her tracks when she saw the wolf, refusing to go any further.

"What the hell, Kai? Is that a wolf?"

"Yeah, she's hurt pretty bad. Come see for yourself. Don't worry, she's out cold, I think the pain got to her."

She approached slowly, keeping her eyes on the head of the huge creature as she came around to where I was standing. She gasped when she saw the wound in the wolf's side and shook her head. Apparently getting over her initial fright at seeing the animal she reached out and ran her fingers through the dark fur along her shoulder. I placed my hand over hers, feeling a combination of her heartbeat and that of the she wolf. After a minute I pulled my hand away and moved to untie the wolf.

"Where are you going to put her?"

"There's a set of fully enclosed stalls at the end we use for new horses during training. She'll be fine in there, won't be able to get loose and hurt anyone but she can heal without anything attacking her."

She nodded and helped me finish untying the beast then spotted me while I carried her into the stall. I added some extra grass to the floor and then found a spare knit blanket we used for the horses and draped it over her. She whined in her sleep and I saw Hayley bite her lower lip at the sound. I figured she was feeling the same thing I was, sympathy for the poor animal. I made my way over to the other woman, slid the stall door closed and latched it as I wrapped my arm around her.

"Is she gonna be okay?"

"I hope so. Come on, help me get Prophecy settled in for the night then we can get back to the room, get a fire going and get warm."

She nodded and we moved to get the large white horse clean, dry and bedded down for the night. Once he had been fed and we'd dropped some grass in with Genesis we left the stable. We were soaked by the time we made it back to the quarters which had once been mine and we would now be sharing. I couldn't explain or express the nervous twitching which had begun in my fingers. I was also trying to ignore the fluttering in my stomach she still seemed so good at producing.

"You're shivering."

I turned my attention to her when she spoke, registering her words several seconds after she said them. She was right, I was shivering but I wasn't about to tell her it wasn't because I was cold. She walked over to me, shaking her head as she reached out and took hold of the bottom of my sweater. It was heavy, weighted down with rainwater but she pulled it over my head and draped it over the chair by the fire. After helping me out of my boots and kicking off her own she tugged me over closer to the heat of the blaze.

She pulled me in close and wrapped her arms around me, her cheek rested on my shoulder, forehead pressed against my neck. With a sigh she squeezed me hard once then dropped her arms and took a step back. She proceeded to relieve us both of the rest of our clothing though she took her time doing so, not in any rush it seemed. Out of the soaked garments she pressed in close again this time pulling my face down to hers and kissing me. I didn't fight it, didn't panic and didn't bother to question if I might be making a mistake, those days and insecurities were long gone.

I was already head over heels for this woman and I would take whatever consequences came my way because of it. I kissed her back with everything I had, not giving her any hesitation. She backed us the few feet to my bed and dropped onto it, dragging me down with her. I settled in where she tugged me, my body half covering hers and dove right back into the kiss our movement had interrupted. It wasn't the first night I'd spent with her and I would make damn sure it wasn't the last.

CHAPTER TWENTY

UNCOMFORTABLE TRUTHS

KAI'S JOURNAL - *Autumn Cycle, 2606 – 220 years after the event:*
Here I lay again writing another entry in this thing while Hayley is out cold beside me. She mumbles in her sleep and I have to admit that it is all kinds of adorable, though none of it is recognizable as actual words. I had the best night of sleep I've managed to get in years wrapped up with her and I'm looking forward to another. Speaking of which, warmth and cuddling are calling to me so this one is staying short.

A shiver pulled me from a very peaceful sleep the next morning and I growled as I rolled over and snuggled into the form beside me. A smile pulled at my lips as the heat of Hayley's body chased the bitter cold from the space. I slipped an arm around her as I dropped a light kiss on her shoulder, moved to her collarbone, her neck, her jawline and then her cheek. She smiled, her eyes still closed as she stretched then curled around me, increasing the warmth. I wiggled further up the bed, putting me at eye level with her as I waited for her to open her eyes.

She took a deep breath, let out a happy sigh and found my lips without even fluttering an eyelid. I happily kissed her back, letting the contact linger, enjoying it more every time it happened. We parted after what I would have sworn was a few short seconds but was probably more like several minutes. She let out a happy sigh as she leaned down and nuzzled my neck. The action pulled a soft purr from me, my lids sliding down to block out the light filtering into the room.

When she nibbled and nipped at my jawline I whimpered and wondered if she would protest a push toward a more intimate encounter first thing in the morning. I opened my eyes and trailed my lips across her cheek, pausing at her lips to leave a gentle kiss there. I followed it with a second then a third before I nipped the tip of her nose. The action made her open her eyes, staring at the place I'd kissed cross-eyed for a few seconds. She giggled, uncrossed her eyes and looked up at me, giving me the first up close look I'd had of her eyes in daylight.

The sun streaming through the window across the room illuminated the space, casting a picture perfect set of highlights and shadows over her features. I caught her eyes and held them, smiling down at her as I took in every flicker of color. I paused, the smile dropping from my face and my brow furrowing as I caught sight of a far too familiar ring of color around her iris. What I was seeing registered and my heart began pounding as I struggled to breathe against the flash of brilliant green staring back at me. I pulled away from her and slipped out of the bed, gathering my clothes and getting into them.

"Kai? What's wrong?"

"Why didn't you tell me?"

I turned to face her as I shoved my right foot into my boot and adjusted the bottom of my now dry sweater. She shot me a confused look as she crawled out of the bed we'd shared and grabbed her pants from the chair near the door. I crossed my arms over my chest and stared her down, refusing to give in to whatever game she was playing. She had to know what I was talking about, which meant she'd kept it from me and I wanted to know why. I waited but she took her time getting into the rest of her clothes then stood there and looked at me.

"Kai... Tell you what? I honestly don't know what's going on."

"You expect me to believe that?"

"I thought you were finally starting to trust me."

"I am, but I'm having trouble believing this is something you didn't know about."

"What? I really don't know what you're talking about and you're starting to scare me. Please just tell me. What did I supposedly keep from you?"

"That you're a Level One Regen."

CHAPTER TWENTY-ONE

SHOCK AND AWE

HER EYES went wide as she stumbled back three steps, ending up sitting in the chair perched by the door. She leaned forward, her elbows on her knees, head in her hands as she fought to catch her breath. Taking her reaction into account I had no choice but to believe she hadn't known, no one could fake shock this well. I grabbed the chair near the fireplace and dragged it over to where she had sat down. After placing it beside the one she was seated in I settled down onto it and took a deep breath.

My least favorite part of jumping to the wrong conclusion was having to apologize for the accusation. I Ran my fingers through my hair and shook my head then reached over and put a hand on her shoulder. She looked up but not right at me, hurt evident in her expression but she didn't pull away, a good sign if even in the smallest measure. After blowing out a hard sigh I hooked the index finger of my free hand under her chin and turned her face so she was looking at me.

"I'm not, Kai. I can't be!"

"You are. You have the marker, it's hard to see in Level One's but it's definitely there, honey." Tears rolled down her cheeks and I did my best to wipe them away only to have them replaced with new ones by the time my hand moved to her chin.

"I swear I didn't know. I wouldn't have kept something like that from you. You have to believe me."

"I do." I'd been so ready to believe she'd lied to me less than two minutes earlier but seeing her in such a state had changed my mind. I knew I needed to learn to trust her without breakdowns and freak-outs or whatever this was developing between us would never survive. I also needed to get better at apologizing while I learned said trust if I expected her to stick around. "I'm so sorry Hayley."

"Don't be, I can understand how you might think I'd been hiding it from you. I'm so confused now though. I have so many questions. How could this happen? Does my father know? My mother would have had to be a Regen for me to be. Right?"

"If your father is human then I believe so, yes. We don't know everything about the mutations but it does seem to be hereditary."

"So my mother must have been but... He would have known. There's no way he wouldn't have. I mean, we've been together for all of a few days and you already caught it. There's no way she could have hidden it for years."

I nodded but kept my mouth shut. My brain might be a writhing mess of possible scenarios but I wasn't about to voice any of them until we had more information. There was an explanation. There had to be. I'd found there almost always was. I just had to dig around and find it. Until then I would keep my suspicions to myself rather than upset her with more accusations. It could all be nothing but my imagination.

I looked over at Hayley and saw the emotions playing across her features. A combination of hurt, confusion, panic and relief was visible. The relief was the one I couldn't seem to figure out, the others made perfect sense to me. I watched her for a few moments, allowing some silence as a buffer for her to process for a bit. The last thing she needed was for me to start bombarding her with questions or theories.

When it appeared she had calmed down and was breathing at a normal rate again I leaned over close, my shoulder to hers and whispered, "We'll figure this out."

"Thanks. It just doesn't make any sense. Then again, very few things my father has ever done make sense." She let out a sigh and shook her head before leaning it on my shoulder. I found myself wishing I knew how to take the confusion away and give her an explanation. All I wanted was to see her smiling again, hear her laugh.

"Yeah well, in the category of doing things that don't make sense... I carried home an unconscious, injured, mutated wolf the size of a small horse."

Her smile caused a light pull on the shoulder of my shirt a split second before her soft giggle reached my ears. I closed my eyes and soaked in the sound, a smile painted across my face as it wrapped itself around me.

"I'll admit, not the most stunningly brilliant of choices but I think I understand."

"You do?" Her comment stunned me since I wasn't even sure I understood my motives in bringing the animal to the compound. She nodded as she sat up straight and turned so she was facing me.

"If I had to take a stab in the dark I'd say you sympathize. You see something of yourself in her."

"I guess I do." She was a hurt being, alone, in pain and misunderstood. I could definitely relate to all of those things until the last few days.

"What do you think you'll do with her?" I shrugged in response since I didn't have the slightest clue what I'd end up doing with the canine as she began to heal. She would have to be released eventually, almost no question there but when was something I didn't know.

"Right now I'm just hoping she survives. The rest will have to wait until she's actually awake and moving."

"Good point. She can't heal properly if she can't eat and she can't eat if she's out cold."

"Mmhmm. Exactly."

"Great. So we can check on her later." She grinned at me and I quirked an eyebrow at her wording.

"We?"

"You seriously think I'm letting you out of my sight for the next few days after you forced me to leave you out there yesterday? Hell no. I thought you'd been caught... Or killed." I cringed at the thought of either of those things happening, though one was decidedly worse than the other.

"If one has to happen, I'll take killed thanks." She gave me a funny look and I knew she didn't understand why I would choose death over capture. "Let's just say your former people aren't very nice to us Level Four Generals when they catch us alive. Dead is much, much less painful."

Understanding filtered onto her features and she nodded as she leaned over, pressing a kiss to my forehead. I gave her knee a quick squeeze, pushed out of my chair and crossed the room to the fireplace. It was a cool morning and the chill hanging in the air had begun to creep its way into the room. I piled some wood into the brick enclosure on top of some dried grass, fought to get it lit then stepped back once it caught and let it get going. I made my way to where I'd left her sitting and dropped back into the chair I'd vacated a few minutes earlier.

We sat in silence for a few long minutes, staring into the fire, my mind running a hundred miles an hour. There were so many things I wished I had the answers to and knowing she didn't have any of them either was what kept my mouth shut. Badgering her about her mother when it was obvious she was even more lost about the whole ordeal than I was wouldn't do any good. If anything it might make her frustrated and cause her to distance herself from me. I definitely wanted to steer clear of anything which would drive a wedge between us.

"How about we head down and take the horses out? When we get back we can check on that walking nightmare you brought back yesterday." She winked at me and I chuckled as I stood up and stepped over to the door.

"Fine, but you're taking care of me if I get sick from leaving the comfort of this nice warm room to go parading around the woods with you."

"Fine with me. You don't get sick so my job sounds pretty easy."

I narrowed my eyes at her as she walked by, smirking since she knew she had me on that one. She stepped out of the room and I followed her, grumbling as I went but grinning all the same. We took our time getting to the stables, not in any hurry. I had to assume she was replaying the day before in her mind as we stepped inside. As we got the horses tacked up she confirmed my suspicion when she turned to face me and cleared her throat.

"So today, please try to refrain from forcing me to leave you alone out there." I stifled the laugh trying to break free but couldn't stop the smile which spread across my face.

"I'll do my best. Though if it's dangerous, I'll hang behind to protect you every time. It's in my nature."

"Awww, my hero." There was sarcasm dripping from her words but the small grin she flashed me said she really was a bit impressed.

I held back my curiosity about the wolf I'd brought back with me the previous night. If she had come to she was being quiet and not terrifying the horses. Best to leave her alone if we planned on being out for a while. I would check on her when we returned from our ride, see if she was awake and up to trying to eat something. We left the stable, stopped long enough to grab a few supplies and then headed out of the compound and into the sprawling landscape beyond.

CHAPTER TWENTY-TWO

SURRISES

OUR RIDE started out like every other one we'd taken together though I noticed she stuck closer to me than usual. Normally having someone worry about me so intensely would drive me insane but with her it sent a warmth through me I hadn't been expecting. I realized after pondering the thought for several minutes that I hadn't let anyone worry about me without getting onto them for it since Laney. The idea made me smile and Hayley chose the exact moment it spread across my face to glance over at me.

"What are you grinning about over there?"

"Hmm? Oh, just thinking. You know I usually get bent out of shape when people worry about me too much?"

"You? No! Never!" I shot her a glare and she burst out laughing, Genesis tossing her head in apparent agreement. Prophecy nickered his own thoughts on the matter and I attempted to feel betrayed but only felt light-hearted and truly happy for the first time in ages.

"All right enough out of you two. And you!" I leaned over Prophecy's neck, giving it a pinch which he flicked an ear at me. "You're a traitor." He responded with a huff and a sidestep which threatened to dismount me. I caught myself in time thanks to heightened reflexes. "You jerk!"

Hayley burst out laughing as Genesis pranced, adding her own amusement to the moment. Prophecy had the decency to pretend he was sorry for the action, but I knew him too well to fall for it. I rolled my eyes at the three of them, settled deeper into my saddle and proceeded to pout. The expression on my face made Hayley pull Genesis up beside me so she could reach over and take my hand.

"Hey, stop pouting. He was just having fun with you."

"I know, but I have to make him feel bad about it or he does it more often." I shot her the flicker of a grin and she bit back a giggle as she leaned forward and slapped Prophecy's ear.

"She's right you know? You are kind of a jerk."

Now it was his turn to pout, his head dropped and his ears went back which caused the two of us to burst into laughter again. We got our laughter under control and continued our ride, the entire thing proceeding without any catastrophes. I could tell Hayley was pleased to no end when we returned to the compound before nightfall, together. After we got the horses settled in for the night I decided to check on the wolf but a hand on my arm pulled me up short. I turned to face Hayley, not sure why she was stopping me from what I'd already planned to do.

When she tugged me closer and wrapped her arms around me, I melted against her, taking in every moment of the hug she offered up. I hugged her back, giving her a tight squeeze before we parted and I smiled at her.

"Everything okay?" She nodded, blew out a weighted sigh then met my eyes.

"Yeah. Just... Be careful. I know you had an easy time getting her back here but she was knocked out from the pain. If she's awake, well... Who knows what she'll do to you."

"Don't worry, I'll be fine. I'm not planning on walking in there and petting her or anything. I'm not crazy."

"Well..." She gave me a look, waffling her hand from side to side as if weighing the truth of my statement.

"You brat!" I swatted at her as she giggled, grabbed my hand and gave it a squeeze.

"I have to pick on you, keeps you on your toes."

"Oh does it?"

"Mmhmm, sure does. Can't let you get used to being looked up to and worshipped, someone needs to keep you grounded." A narrowing of her eyes and a shake of her finger in my direction accompanied the comment.

"And I'll bet you just *hate* the job don't you?"

"Oh, so much. It's hard for me, picking on you." She winked at me and I replied to the gesture with a smirk.

"Sure it is. Don't worry okay? I just wanna see how she's healing."

"Okay. But being serious, be careful."

She followed me to the stall I'd locked the wolf in the night before and when we looked inside I was hit with a solid wall of shock. She was awake and seemed to be healing fine but that wasn't what caught my attention first. My focus was held by four small, furry bodies huddled against her stomach. Each was small enough to cradle against my forearm, still bigger than any normal puppy I'd ever seen. I glanced at Hayley, finding her looking as stunned as I felt and I couldn't help but laugh.

The sound drew her attention as well as that of the mother wolf who looked up at me, held my gaze for a five count then laid her head back on her paws, closing her eyes. I couldn't believe what I was seeing, mostly because I hadn't had a clue the animal was even pregnant when I'd brought her into the stable. We'd been convinced the animals which mutated so fully carried the same mutations as we Level Four Regens and couldn't reproduce. It now appeared we'd been way off in the theory and it would have to be tossed out so we could begin again. I shook my head, backed away from the stall door and turned to Hayley with a grin.

"How about that?"

"Did you know?"

"That she was pregnant?" She nodded and I shook my head in reply as I said, "No, I didn't have a damn clue. Actually, we were convinced the animals who showed this level of mutation couldn't breed. I mean, we can't. At least..."

She raised a brow at me as she asked, "At least what?"

"Well, Thea, Trista, Lila and me. We've always assumed we can't reproduce but now that I think about it. I wouldn't know either way since my only relationship since the event was with Laney, another woman. I'm pretty sure Thea hasn't let anyone get that close to her and last I heard Trista and Lila have the same... Well, preferences I do." I grinned at her and she offered me a small chuckle in exchange for the look.

"So there's a chance you could, only none of you have ever been in the position to find out." I nodded as I glanced to the wolves again then turned and looked up the wide hallway of the stable.

"Come to think of it, I've always just assumed Prophecy and Genesis can't..." I paused, thinking on the things we thought we'd learned over the numerous decades since the event. I wondered how many of them were wrong, nothing more than what we believed without evidence to back them up.

"Hmmm. Thinking about giving them a romantic date now?" I chuckled at her, turning to look at her as she waggled her eyebrows at me then risked a glance directly at Prophecy. He had his head sticking over the door of his stall, listening to us. I knew he'd caught everything we said when he tossed his head and whinnied at me.

"Crap, he heard you. You have to watch what you say around that pain in the ass, he gets bad ideas." She gave me a funny look and it took me a minute to remember she didn't have the experience with Regen animals growing up that our children did. "Think of Prophecy and Genesis as teenagers who don't talk. They know what we're talking about, they'll answer us, throw fits and even show us when they're happy or sad. We just have to know what to look for."

"Really? I mean I've caught them reacting to things out on our rides but I thought it was just situational. Maybe tone of voice or something like that."

"Oh no, they are definitely listening, and understanding. Watch." I left her side, reminding myself to check in on the mother wolf and puppies later in the evening. As I walked up to Prophecy's stall I crossed my arms over my chest and tweaked a smile at him. "Hey buddy." He tossed his head and huffed in response as Hayley stepped up beside me. "What do you think Prophecy, you want some time out in the pen alone with Genesis?"

If the toss of his head he gave wasn't enough to answer the question the prancing he did immediately after would have. Hayley's eyebrows shot up on her forehead as she watched the horse closely. I reached out, gripped the slide lock on his stall door and pulled it free then slid the door open. I stepped aside to let him out and watched him trot his way down to the stall Genesis was housed in. He stopped in front of it and looked over his shoulder at me.

"You wanna let her out?" Another toss of his head made Hayley let out a soft giggle beside me, bringing a grin back to my face. "Well, go on then." With my approval he leaned down, gripped the slide in his teeth and pulled, freeing it from the lock.

With the task handled he used his nose to nudge the door open enough to let Genesis out and we watched as she pranced around him. "Get going, you can't linger in the aisle you brats. Training pen, right now." The pair started off toward the pen at a steady walk as I called after them, "And shut the door behind you!"

"That did not just happen."

"It did. And it gets better. Come on." I took her hand and led her down the aisle after the horses had vanished around the bend toward the pen. As we rounded the turn I stifled a laugh and pointed to the door they would have had to go through to get into the area. "There ya go, as instructed."

Hayley's eyes went wide as she took in the closed door of the pen, the two horses running and playing inside. I chuckled at her, gave her hand a squeeze and then tugged her over against my side as I said, "Come on." The movement seemed to break her stunned marveling at the two animals and she leaned into my embrace as I slipped my arm around her.

"Now that you pointed it out I'm remembering all the interactions and they do seem strange. Like we had mute people around rather than horses. I guess I just overlooked it, brushed it off before this."

"It's easy to tell yourself it's normal behavior, just coincidence or something of the sort until you see it in the kind of setting I just had play out. Plus, Purists don't really have interactions with animals, do they?"

"No, rarely and usually not by choice. Most animals left alive mutated to some degree so we stay clear of them. Actually, I had never eaten meat until I came here."

"Now that I didn't know. They won't even eat meat?"

She shook her head as she turned her eyes out onto the horizon, her voice sounding distant as she said, "They believe the animals are tainted with whatever evil your people carry. The general belief is that if they eat it, they'll become like you."

I scoffed at the idea as I rolled my eyes, it sounded ridiculous. Then again, if I'd grown up hearing it then I might believe the same thing. I let out a sigh, gave her shoulder a squeeze and felt her shiver against me. With the realization it was beginning to get cold I turned my gaze down to her and smiled saying, "Let's go find some food for the wolf then get back to our room and warm up."

"I like the sound of that." She smiled as she slipped her hand under the bottom of my sweater and began trailing patterns on my back with her fingertips.

"What? Warming up? Yeah, it was chilly out today."

"No. Our room. That's the first time you've called it that. I like it." She looked up at me again, beaming and the expression was infectious, taking over my face as I placed a kiss on the tip of her nose.

"Well get used to it, because it is ours now." She reached her free hand up, linking her fingers with mine where my hand sat on her shoulder. We headed for the supply houses in silence, not finding any further need to talk until we had settled in for the night.

CHAPTER TWENTY-THREE

FALLING INTO PLACE

KAI'S JOURNAL - *Autumn Cycle, 2606 – 220 years after the event:*

I was shocked enough to find an injured wolf in the woods then I apparently lost my sanity for a few hours when I brought it home with me. Imagine my shock when she had puppies in my stable! While I will be the first to admit they're adorable (well, maybe the second, Hayley thinks they're the cutest things she's ever seen) but that doesn't help me figure out what to do with them. Not to mention I have no clue how it's even possible, seems we were wrong about a lot of things. Makes me wonder about all the ideas we have about the Level Four mutation. How much of it could be wrong? I'll have to start doing some back tracking on some of our teachings and start over. Should be loads of fun!

When two weeks had managed to pass without any major catastrophes I felt like I could finally breathe a sigh of relief. I had picked up a habit of wandering out into the woods every couple days in the hopes of finding a counterpart for the wolf I'd rescued. Hayley accompanied me naturally since she'd been wary of letting me out of her sight since the night I'd found the poor ragged creature. The thought was if she had another adult of her species to keep her company it might speed her healing process. Physically she appeared back in full form but something was still off.

We had yet to decide what to do with her once she seemed

fully up to speed. We'd talked about returning her to the place I had found her that day but the idea had some flaws. First was the fact she had a litter of small puppies to care for. Well they were small for huge mutated wolves anyway. Next on the list was the very real possibility of whatever or whoever had torn her open in the first place still being in the area.

While I was aware of the fact she was a wild animal and shouldn't be caged up it seemed cruel to return her to the forest only to have her or the puppies killed in a matter of days. She seemed to be settled in fine for the moment and hadn't started clawing at the walls or attempting to massacre the horses. I had to believe she felt her little ones were safe and so she was behaving herself. Since the planning and prepping for figuring out what to do with her had gotten us nowhere, we took a day off. Hayley and I were worn out from all the searching and planned to do nothing but wander the compound for the day.

I stood leaning against the wall we'd erected around the training area watching the newest guard recruits practice their hand-to-hand. They weren't bad but they had a long way to go before I considered them ready to go out on missions. I was known for my intense training schedule and every group of new guard hopefuls was normally down to half numbers by the third month. I ran them ragged and let them beat the living hell out of each other. The Purists they would come up against out in the wilds of this world we lived in wouldn't go easy on them, so I wouldn't let them go easy on each other.

I was doing my best to keep my mind focused on what was happening in the arena but my thoughts kept wandering. In the forefront of my mind were my feelings for Hayley, these newly revived and recently accepted emotions I'd let free. They whirled around keeping a smile on my face almost nonstop. The other side of those was the doubt, this deep, nagging kernel of truth poking at me every time I let my mind settle for a few brief moments. Those thoughts, doubts kept reminding me she was barely more than human and one day I would lose her.

I did the best I could to ignore those thoughts, to keep them from weighing on me and ruining the time I did have with her. I'd known from the first day I'd met Laney she wouldn't be with me forever but I had never let it interfere with our interactions. Maybe those years I'd spent with my first love had tarnished things for me. I was more reluctant to simply let go and free fall into a future with this new woman. I glanced over at her as the pestering thoughts lingered again, poking at the back of my mind. I had to figure out a way to get my head past the inevitable and let our new relationship simply, be.

Sure she would be gone someday but how far in the future would it be? Another ninety years? A hundred? More? I couldn't be sure since lifespans had altered drastically since the event. Even before the fallout we were living longer, fuller, healthier lives. The average lifespan in the country when I was a teenager was well over one hundred years. Most people got to celebrate reaching one hundred and ten before succumbing to things which tended to make the body wear out over time.

I realized in a flash I hadn't ever asked how old Hayley was so I couldn't even begin to guess at a timeframe. The thought made me grin since there was the very real possibility she was well under thirty. She certainly looked it. I would have to remember to ask her when a conversation was struck up later on. For the moment I was content to stare at her and try pushing those pesky thoughts and concerns back into the box they belonged in. I stared a few moments longer then turned my attention back toward the arena, not really seeing anything transpiring between the recruits.

"Earth to Kai. You okay over there?"

"Huh? Oh, yeah sorry. I got lost in my head." My vision cleared of the haze which had taken over and I noticed the arena was clear, I must have been deeper in thought than I originally realized.

"You do that a lot. Everything all right?"

I shrugged in response since I wasn't sure how to answer her question. I wasn't ready to tell her I was contemplating her death when we'd only been in this happy place a few weeks. Instead, I tried to think of something else I could bring up. I needed something as far from the subject in my head as I could manage to focus on. I grasped at and released questions I knew she couldn't answer, half formed thoughts and ideas then grabbed hold of one I could run with.

"Can I ask you something?"

"Of course."

"How did you end up in the White Guard?" Her brows knitted as she cocked her head at me.

"What do you mean?"

"I mean, obviously you weren't born with the intent of placement there. Or were you?" The thought was a scary one but I had to be willing to entertain it or anything else really.

"Not that I know of. As far as I remember I was faster and more agile than the other kids. When my father realized I could outrun all the boys twice my age he put me in the program." The information made me nod as I let my eyes flicker from building to building. I was thinking rather than focusing on any one thing in particular.

"Okay. And the others in the White Guard?"

"What about them?"

"Did they end up there for the same reason?"

"As far as I know. The White Guard are my fathers' pride and joy. He used to say he only put his stars in because we were expected to be the best, better than his most well trained soldiers." Ideas were forming in my mind, new questions which might bring more information neither of us had realized she had.

"Makes sense. Did everyone who was put in the program finish it and become part of the White Guard?" My question didn't hold any of the excitement I was beginning to feel over the entire conversation. I was thankful I'd learned to school my features and keep the emotions from showing plainly. It often allowed me to gain further information without appearing as if it meant anything to me.

"No. Some washed out, didn't make the cut. They mostly ended up as scouting teams."

"Teams? Like, they were sent out in groups of these former White Guard candidates? Not just with other random scouts?" Her answer might give me the lead I'd been looking for, something to grip and run with.

"As far as I know. I never saw former candidates with regular scouts. Always in groups from the program. Why?" I was becoming more convinced my thought process was right by the second as she spoke.

"Hayley, what if your father was pinpointing Regens born into your group and training them to hunt us? What if those candidates didn't wash out but proved to be better at tracking and following us? What if he has his trackers, scouting teams to find us and then his..." I paused and glanced over at her, catching her gaze as I said, "Assassins?" Her eyes went wide as she leaned back in her chair, her hand coming up to brush some hair behind her ear.

"That would mean he knew the whole time. Not just about my mother and me but about others. It would mean he's been allowing low level Regens to resettle with us for decades and not telling anyone with the purpose of producing more."

"That's what I was thinking. He's been breeding his own Regens. Raising them with Purist values then sending them out to hunt us down. And kill us."

Silence settled between us as we both considered the idea and I knew it held possibility. There were so many options when it came to understanding the motives of someone who was so obviously stuck in a God complex loop. Any number of things could be true, this thought, another, two or three more or even all of them at the same time. The only way we would know would be to get some of these scouts to break and tell us something useful. Unless we could manage to capture and detain Father Rivers but somehow the prospect seemed easier said than done.

CHAPTER TWENTY-FOUR

WOLFISH WAYS

KAI'S JOURNAL - *Autumn Cycle, 2606 – 220 years after the event:*
We're still not any closer to knowing what to do with these wolves but in the meantime, watching the puppies get bigger is threatening to overload us with cuteness. On other fronts, my relationship with Hayley is thriving and we seem to be moving forward. I'm learning how to open up again, trust someone and be happy. It feels wonderful and I'm basking in it. Somewhere in the back of my head I'm waiting for the other shoe to drop, for her to hurt me or just decide I'm not worth the time and effort. I'm doing my best to ignore that side of myself since I know it's nothing but doubting myself and my worth. I deserve this, the happiness I'm finding with this girl and I intend to grab it with both hands and run with it.

I leaned against the door of the stall the wolf family was housed in thinking, my arms crossed over my chest as I listened to the whines, whimpers and tiny yips from the now month old puppies. They had opened their eyes and were stumbling around in an uncoordinated waddle which had been making me laugh. There was no laughter today however, I had far too much on my mind. I knew I needed to make some decisions, start planning but so much was at stake. I blew out a breath, grumbling at the end of the exhale and reached up to rub my eyes.

"Hey, I was wondering where you wandered off to."

I looked up to see Hayley approaching and despite everything weighing on me I smiled. She had been the only thing in my life the last few weeks helping me maintain any semblance of sanity. I pushed off the stall door and met her halfway down the aisle shaking my head. She slowed her progress, concern painted across her face as she reached out and took my hand.

"Is everything okay?"

"I don't know how to even answer that these days. There's so much going on, so many choices I have to make, people depending on me and its starting to get to me."

She nodded as she tugged me close and wrapped her arms around my waist, her head resting on my shoulder. I returned the embrace and we stood there holding each other for a few minutes in silence before she spoke again.

"It'll be okay. I know everything is piling up on you but you'll work it out."

"I sure hope so." I blew out a heavy breath and steeled my nerves for what I planned to say next. "Hayley?"

"Hmm?" She turned her attention to me and the smile I offered her must have given something away because her brow furrowed. "What's wrong?" It wasn't like me to allow my expression to slip, falter and show what I was thinking or feeling. It meant I was in a bad place emotionally and I needed to get myself back together. Somehow I knew Hayley and her answer to my upcoming question would play a big part in the process.

"Do you want to leave?"

"Leave? You mean leave here?"

"Yeah, the compound."

"And go where?" She seemed so confused I almost didn't have the heart to continue, but I pressed on.

"Home. Back to your father, your friends. The life you'd always known before my group captured you and brought you here."

"What? Are you serious right now?" Her face was painted with pure shock as she took a half step away from me. The loss of contact with her was a harsh jab to my system and while something deep inside me wanted to leave it there I knew I needed to press on. I had to know for sure, with total clarity what she wanted and if her plans included me.

"I wish I wasn't but yes, I am."

"Kai, this is my home now. My friends are here." She paused and stepped back over, brushing some hair out of my face. "My family is here. Why would I want to leave you and go back to that insanity?"

"I guess you wouldn't I just had to know for sure."

"Would you honestly just let me up and leave after everything I've learned about you and this place?"

"For the safety of my people I should say no but... If it would make you happy then yes, I would just let you leave."

"And that is exactly why I want to stay. I'm here because I want to be. And because I love you, Kai." She leaned in and pressed a gentle kiss to my lips before she added, "And don't you ever forget it."

I didn't attempt to hide the huge smile which took over my face at her words, she hadn't said them many times but I already loved hearing them. "I really hope you know I love you too."

"I do."

"Good, but just to be on the safe side, I think I'll remind you every now and then." I winked, she giggled and gave my hip a squeeze then pulled me closer. I suddenly remembered something I'd been wanting to ask her for a while but had been putting off in favor of other things. "Hayley?"

"Hmm?"

"How old are you anyway?" She flushed pink at the question as she turned her eyes toward the wall to her right.

"Uh, are you sure you want to know that?" I hooked a finger under her chin and forced her to look at me again, one of my brows raised to indicate she'd asked a stupid question. "Okay, okay. I'm nineteen."

"Oh wow." The flush on her cheeks intensified, shifting from a pale pink to a deep crimson in seconds.

"How old did you think I was?"

"I don't know actually. Something near thirty. Then again, I haven't guessed an age accurately in several decades."

"Well I don't know if I should be offended or take it as a compliment. Am I mature for my age or do I look old?" She quirked a brow at me and I guffawed at her.

"Thirty is old to you? Wow I must be some kind of ancient." I tried to look as offended as possible but knew I was grinning at her in spite of myself.

"Well..." She closed one eye and raised a hand up between us, waffling it back and forth a few times.

"Brat!" I grabbed at her, pulled her in against me and kissed her, silencing the giggles she had broken into. The halting of the noise didn't alter the smile on her face though as she leaned in and rested her forehead against mine.

"So," she said in a soft tone after several quiet moments had passed, "what do we start the day with?"

I sighed as I leaned away, dropping my arms from around her then reaching up to run one through my hair. "I suppose we pick something on the list and attack it head on."

"Attacking, sounds about right for the things you have to deal with."

I chuckled with a nod then glanced over my shoulder as I said, "Sadly the easiest choice I have to make is what to do with them." I pointed toward the occupants of the stall I'd been perched outside of when she'd come in and she offered me a compassionate smile of understanding.

"Yeah, that's an awkward situation. Honestly, do you think she'd let you get anywhere near the pups?"

"I don't know. I've been thinking about trying. Worst that happens is she bites the hell out of me and I have to take a day or so and heal." I chuckled and Hayley rolled her eyes, the movement followed by a grin before she sighed and dropped her arms from around me as well.

"Well, why not try now. No time like the present right?" Her tone said she was less than thrilled with the idea of me entering an enclosed space with a wild animal. I understood her hesitation but I knew I needed to try, regardless of the outcome. As long as the wolf didn't kill me I should be able to heal any wounds she inflicted. At least, I hoped I could.

I gave a short nod toward the stall and we moved to the door, checking inside one last time before I made any further moves at entering. The mother wolf was sitting near the back corner, the pups tumbling around in little balls of fluff between her and the door. I took a deep breath to steady my nerves, hoping I wasn't about to be chewed on and slid the lock from its cradle. Her eyes shifted off of her pups and toward the door as I eased it open a few inches. I was about to step in when she rose to all four feet, lowered her head and growled at the opening in her previously solid walled enclosure.

I paused as the fur on her back ruffled up, not sure if I should keep going. When her ears went back and she bared her teeth I almost backed up. It was then I remembered my demonstration with Prophecy for Hayley. If he and Genesis had the kind of intelligence which allowed them to understand us then maybe this wolf did as well. I cleared my throat, stayed right outside the door and made sure when I spoke my voice was smooth and calm.

"It's okay girl. I don't want to hurt you or your puppies. I just want to check on you and make sure you're all doing okay." The growling stopped and the fur on her back smoothed out, settling to its original place. The progress built a minimal amount of confidence in my idea and I continued. "That's good. Can I come in and check you all out?" Her ears came up as her head raised to its normal position but it wasn't until she leaned back and dropped her haunches into a sit that I felt comfortable to step inside.

Hayley kept quiet as I eased into the stall and slid the door closed behind me, my movements slow and deliberate so I wouldn't frighten any of the small furry family. The pups seemed curious about me from the second I stepped in and within three breaths I was surrounded by them. One had the hem of my pants in its mouth while another attempted to chew on my left boot. A third had discovered it could stretch to reach its nose up to the straps dangling from my belt and was tugging hard on them. The fourth was sprawled across my right foot, apparently using my boot to pet himself.

I let out a soft chuckle and shook my head at the puppies, every one of them already bigger than I would have expected for their age. I thought back, trying to remember some of the breeds we'd had when I was growing up and placed them at about the size of a five or six month old Labrador puppy. I glanced up, caught their mom watching them play and smiled at her. She seemed to smile back at me, her tongue lolling out like she was nothing more than a massive, happy dog. It was a sight I wouldn't soon forget.

I reached down and gently detached the little female chewing on my belt strap so I could walk without hurting her then set her a couple feet away. After disengaging the other three I made my way over closer to their mother. She sat staring at me, showing no further signs of aggression or wariness. I wondered if I really had managed to get through to her. I decided it was worth trying to talk to her again, tell her up front what I wanted to do and see if she understood it at all.

"I need to check your wound and make sure it healed okay. Do you mind if I look at it?"

She cocked her head to one side then slowly rose to her feet and turned so I could see her left side where the large gash had been. I eased forward, slow and steady so I didn't spook her and reached out to touch the area. It was solid and body temperature under my fingers, no signs of heat from infection or even scarring. The fur had almost completely grown back and it seemed as though she wouldn't have any evidence it had ever been there at all in a few more days.

"Well good, you're all healed up. I'm glad, you were in pretty bad shape when I found you." She huffed at me as if agreeing with the statement and then turned to look at Hayley where she stood outside the stall. "Can she come in?" She glanced at me, back to Hayley and then let loose a loud bark before letting her tongue fall out again and returning to a sit. "I think that was a yes."

She chuckled out a, "Yeah, I think you're right."

"Come on in."

Despite her laughter and agreement with my statement Hayley seemed hesitant to open the door and step into the stall. She finally took a deep breath, nodded to reassure herself and stepped inside. The minute she did she was pounced on by the four fur balls. She collapsed in a fit of giggles as they wiggled around and licked her face. I reached out to the female again, wondering if she would let me pet her. I was both shocked and relieved when she not only allowed my hand to contact her muzzle but then nudged into it further. I ran my hand up her nose and onto her head, scratching between her ears as I smiled.

"Well then. Who would have guessed? I should have known you would be this smart. Canines were intelligent critters even before the mutations. Sometimes smarter than us. At least that's what I always thought." The wolf seemed to be laughing at the comment and it made me chuckle. "I wonder... Would you like to stay here? With your pups? Plenty of food and safe places for them to play. No one hunting them down and hurting them."

I watched her gaze shift over to her puppies where they were still playfully mauling Hayley. She looked as if she were pondering the situation. One of the pups, the little cinnamon colored male who had been sprawled across my boot earlier, waddled over and crawled into my lap. I reached down to scratch under his chin, making him sigh as he closed his eyes, yawned then promptly fell asleep. It seemed the acceptance was enough for their mother to make up her mind. She rose to her feet, padded closer, laid down and put her head in my lap beside her puppy.

A minute later the female wolf was sound asleep, her head across my legs, one pup sleeping beside her muzzle and the other three curled up around Hayley doing the same. I looked them all over and shook my head, unable to believe what had transpired over the last few minutes.

"Did that seriously just happen?" I glanced over at Hayley and smiled at her question, it seemed she was picking up a habit of reading my mind.

"I was thinking the same thing. I can't believe it was so easy to get her to relax. I do think it'll be better for all five of them if they stay here. They really will be safer."

"Oh I know it... Who or whatever cut her open did a number on her. Best of they stay here behind the walls where they can be protected. Pretty sure we can let them out of here now though."

"Definitely. We'll stay a bit longer but when we do need to go we'll leave the stall open. This can be where they retreat to if the weather gets bad. I'll make sure everyone knows to leave them be if they see them." She nodded her agreement, the last thing we needed was someone in the compound seeing a massive wolf wandering around and have a bad, knee-jerk reaction. I wouldn't risk them being hurt after I'd promised they would be safe.

"Kai? What the hell do you think you're doing in there?" I shifted enough to look over my shoulder and grinned at the shock on Steph's face.

"I'm watching a wolf nap."

"Why? What happens when mama wakes up and bites your head off?" She was whispering, apparently worried about waking the sleeping wolves.

I chuckled and Hayley shook her head. Sometimes Steph could be hilariously paranoid and this happened to be one of those times. Obviously she hadn't noticed the mother in question had turned me into a breathing pillow. I pointed toward the mothers' head as I reached down and scratched the patch of fine, soft fur right above her nose. She shifted, yawned then looked up at me which made Steph tense visibly.

The gasp my runner let loose when a huge tongue left a slobbery trail up the side of my face was almost enough to make me laugh past the yuck factor. Almost, but not quite. I made a face as Hayley laughed then wiped the side of my face with my sleeve as the wolf hopped up and stood two feet away, tail wagging. She looked rather proud of herself for the impromptu bath she'd given me and it was the expression on her canine features which finally made me burst into laughter. The pup in my lap woke up, stretched and grumbled at me, causing me to laugh harder.

When I finally recovered I locked eyes with the female wolf and nodded toward the door. I stood and headed for it, her and the pups right behind me and Hayley trailing them. I turned and caught her gaze before I opened the door and smiled at her. "Okay, stay with Hayley or me for a couple days. I'd hate for you or the puppies to wander before everyone knows and end up getting hurt. Okay?" She actually thought about it for a minute then gave me a small nod, stunning me even further.

"Holy cow." I looked at Steph and the shock painted on her face was priceless, not that I could blame her for it.

"I know. Its nuts right? But she really does seem to understand."

I pulled the door open all the way and left it as I walked through, the female at my left side, Hayley on my right and the pups scampering around our feet. Somehow they managed to keep from tripping us as we all marched out of the stable and toward the center of the compound. Every couple minutes Hayley or I would be brought to laughter by the puppies. As we walked further from the stables I let my mind wander. I was deep in thought when a bump on my shoulder drew my attention toward my girlfriend.

"What has you thinking so hard?"

"Well, I've been trying to decide if I should name them since they'll be staying." I swept my arm to indicate the five wolves around us.

"Makes sense. It would make identifying them easier no doubt."

"That was my thought exactly."

"How about you ask their mama how she feels about that?"

"Good idea. Hey girl, I was thinking about giving you and your pups names. How does that sound?" The female looked at the pups then back to me. It seemed she agreed with the idea when she gave me her wolfish smile so I thought hard about what to call her. "Okay, how about... Shadow?" The low growl she let loose told me what she thought about the name so I held my hands out in apology and chuckled. "Fine, not Shadow. Ummm, Smoke?" Another growl had me tossing my hands up over my head, I was apparently bad at this.

"How about Ember?" I shot a look at Hayley when the female

barked happily, her approval of the name.

"Damn you." Hayley shrugged then giggled as the little cinnamon colored pup rose unsteadily on his hind legs and whined at me. I reached down to pet him, scratching under his chin which made his tail thump against my other leg. "And you little guy. How about... Hmmm." My brain kicked into overdrive as I tried to pick a good name for him. He seemed to be the most attached to me other than his mother so I had to assume he'd end up being a constant companion. "I like Flare." Mother and puppy both barked and tails wagged in acceptance of the name.

"Awww, there you go. You picked a good one."

"Great. The rest are up to you. The girls all seem attached to you anyway." She looked around her at the three female puppies winding and weaving through her legs chasing each other. Playful fluffs of fur, one black like mom, one a silver gray and the last a stark, shocking white like prophecy. All four puppies were already showing the beginnings of their mothers' green fur streaks. Their eyes had also begun to shift to the glowing radiation green of the Regen. They were beautiful animals and watching them, so many things ran through my mind.

"What's going on in that head of yours now?" I turned to look at Steph, having forgotten she was even there and couldn't help but grin. "You forgot I was here didn't you?"

"What? No of course not!"

"Mmhmm."

"Okay, maybe I did. I had a lot going on though so I can't be faulted." I offered her a small smile in apology which she returned as she shook her head. "Now that we cleared that up. I was just going over everything this could mean. Them staying here with us. This is huge."

"I'll say. I don't think anyone has ever allied with any of the mutated animals other than the horses we keep." She watched the puppies playing, Hayley chasing them, cuddling them as she caught each one.

"I've never heard of it happening before. We've always just been terrified of them. This could really change things in ways we never imagined." I had the feeling we might be on the road toward better things.

We had information which would change the way we dealt with the Purists and a new place to look for possible allies. If all the mutated species had the kind of mental comprehension and acuity the horses and wolves had, we were in an amazing new kind of world.

CHAPTER TWENTY-FIVE

WAKE UP CALLS AND ACTS OF DESTINY

KAI'S JOURNAL - *Spring Cycle, 2607 – 221 years after the event:*
Hard to believe all these months have passed us by and we're into another spring. I wish we had more information on the happenings in the world of Regens in Purist camps but none of the scouts or guards we've brought in are talking. Well, they are actually talking but nothing they've been saying makes any difference and not a word of it is useful. On the upside, the wolves have settled in and proven I made the right choice in letting them stay in the compound. They've been great to have around and I've gotten pretty attached to Ember and Flare. The female pups shadow Hayley any time we're out and moving about the compound, she seems to enjoy having them around. It's all very adorable. Now I need to stop spending so much of my night with this thing, end this entry, crawl into bed with my amazing girlfriend and get some sleep.

"Oof! Ember, get off you walking rug." I shoved the massive wolf off me before rubbing the sleep from my eyes. Talk about a rude awakening. I stretched, a grin spreading across my face as Hayley rolled over and buried her head against my shoulder with a grumble.

"Imf nh refy te b uf."

I stifled a chuckle, cleared my throat and brushed my lips across her temple as I asked, "What was that? Can you say it once more? Maybe in a language I recognize this time."

She removed her face from my shoulder, shot me a glare and repeated her comment without the muffles, "I'm not ready to be up. Hear it that time?"

"Yep, got it. And I know you'd rather still be sleeping but someone decided it was time to wake up."

I glared at the wolf who simply gave me the wolfish grin she was so well known for and thumped her tail on the floor. She seemed pretty proud of herself for the impromptu wake-up call if the expression she was wearing was any indication. I sighed and sat up, making Hayley whine beside me, making me turn back toward her and run my fingers through her hair. Propped on my elbow I leaned in and ran my nose up the edge of her ear, catching the grin tugging up the corner of her lips.

"Mmm, keep doing that and I'm definitely not getting up." I let out a soft laugh against her cheek for the comment then kissed my way back to her ear.

"Well then I should stop it. Come on, time to get up and moving... Sweetness."

"Oh you!" She swiped her arm at me as I leaned away from her with a laugh and slid from the bed. I'd taken to using the once hated nickname again in recent days. While it still wasn't her favorite sentiment she laughed every time, a sound which left her again now. The sudden release of the sound alone with my own caused Ember to bark, startling my girlfriend and halting her pursuit of me off the bed. She sat up and shot the wolf her second glare in as many minutes then huffed and climbed out after me.

"I'm gonna stuff that wolf one of these days."

I chuckled as the canine in question ducked her head low and let out a soft growl at the comment. In response, fingertips met head as my girlfriend walked by, giving the big wolf a hard shove. In an exaggerated move which spoke volumes about the intelligence our animals possessed, Ember unbalanced herself and fell to the floor on her side. She laid there and played dead as I went in search of and gathered all my clothes from around the small room. The second my feet were in my boots however, the ruse was up and she bolted off the floor and onto all four feet.

She was out the door first and found herself immediately ambushed by four half-sized, furry whirlwinds. Hayley tried to hide her grin at the scene while I could only laugh and shake my head. It was all very cute and touching, until one of the balls of rampaging fur broke free from the group and charged us. I gasped as I was tackled by the mass of reddish fuzz, knocked to the ground and covered in slobber.

"Ugh, just how I like starting my days, covered in wolf spit."

With a playful bark Flare bounded away to rejoin the rest of his family and I pulled myself off the ground. I heard a snort from my right and turned to find Hayley valiantly holding back what was sure to be a round of loud, attention grabbing laughter. I waved at her to get on with it and she let loose, collapsing to the dirt a minute later holding her sides. When she calmed and could breathe again I helped her to her feet and gave her a wicked smirk.

"Oh no, what? Kai, whatever you're thinking... Don't." I closed the gap between us and wrapped her in a massive, spit lathered hug which made her wiggle around in an attempt to break free. "Eww! Get off me, that's so gross. Ick!"

"Eww? Pfft, and here I thought you loved me."

I dropped my arms and gave her a dramatic pout I was sure she wasn't buying. Sure enough she narrowed her eyes at me and slapped me in the forehead with her palm. I laughed, she joined and ruffled my hair as I wrapped my arm around her shoulders and started for the archery range. Hayley had promised Faith, the teen girl from Oklahoma she would teach her how to shoot. Meanwhile I would be dealing with a new set of prisoners.

It had taken some time to haul in a new round after the first two. It appeared the Purists had figured out we were capturing their scouting parties and had been sending well trained, and well-armed guards with them. We'd taken a break for a few weeks and it had been enough to make them believe we'd given up it seemed. They began sending their scouts out without escorts once again and we had a new group in holding cells awaiting questioning.

The house Julia, Patricia, Hayley and the kids had been in before assimilating into our group now housed Gabriel, Raphael and the group of three we'd brought in after them. Others would be moved there once we'd gathered all the information we could from them. As predicted by myself and Hayley, each member of these new groups showed signs of being Regens. The heightened senses, enhanced speed and agility, quick healing and when we could get close enough to find it, the green ring around the iris. We'd even managed to find two Level Twos among their ranks which had shocked us all.

We approached the training area and I spied Faith already

present, working on stringing her own bow. I had to admire her spirit, precious few of my already trained scouting teams were willing to show up early for sessions to prep their own weapons without being ordered to do so. I grinned as I watched her fight with the bow, finally winning out, slipping the waxed string into place then letting out a triumphant whoop. Hayley bumped me with her shoulder and I turned to look at her, finding her sharing my expression.

"She loves learning all the little ins and outs of everything. She wants all the details." I nodded at the comment as we both turned to watch the girl again.

"How's she doing? I mean, honestly, is she showing any real skill?"

"Oh definitely. She's good with that thing, Kai." I stopped as we reached the fence, leaned my hip against the weather-worn railing and crossed my arms over my chest.

"Glad to hear it. Maybe in a couple years she can join a scout class for training."

"Really?" The shock in Hayley's voice made me glance in her direction and raise a brow at her.

"Yeah really. Why not?"

"She's just, really young." I understood what she meant but I also knew she wasn't very familiar with my training methods.

"She is, but it would be years before she was actually a scout. The teens generally begin training with the basics at fourteen or fifteen. Making and mending clothes, tending gardens, gathering and foraging. Things like that. The ones who show any special attention to things our guards or scouts would do on a regular basis have the opportunity to join those training sessions."

"The opportunity?"

"Yeah, the teachers let me know who seems interested or specifically inclined and I approach them with an offer to join one group or the other."

"So you don't force them to join? Just, pick them at random and order them into training?" I stared at her, stunned with my mouth hanging open an inch or so. The monster she'd been taught I was had become more and more horrific the more information surfaced. No wonder they were so scared; I was terrifying in their eyes.

"God no. No one does anything they don't want to do around here. I trust each and every one of my people to do the job they have because they chose it, they wanted it. There are some hiccups here and there of course."

"Like what happened when we were brought here." I nodded as I let my gaze wander the training arena then settle back on Hayley.

"Yeah, like that." Though I'd been debating how much of a hiccup the incident had really been recently.

"You have a look now, what's it for?"

"I've been thinking about that day a lot lately."

"Oh really?"

"Mmhmm. The thing is, the team that brought you in had been in my scouting ranks for a while. Several years actually and I would have sworn up and down Greer knew my rules."

"Okay, so what does that mean?" She cocked her head to the side, arms crossing over her chest mimicking mine.

"It means she conveniently forgot my rules long enough to haul you in here. The last few weeks I've just been wondering if maybe you were meant to be here. If I was meant to meet you, have you in my life. Sure seems like it these days, doesn't it?" She grinned at me, dropped her arms and stepped over to where I was standing.

"It does all feel a little like destiny, doesn't it?"

I nodded in reply to her question and she leaned in, pulling my arms away from my body and folding herself into them. I wrapped my arms around her so I could hold her against me, giving her a tight squeeze at the same moment I dropped a kiss on her head. It was nice to know she could see the higher plan of it all. I may not believe in everything the Purists did, most of my people didn't, but we did believe in something higher. Whatever the higher power might be had apparently wanted us to meet and I had to believe we were supposed to be together.

"Well, if destiny is what this is, I'll definitely take it. Bring on a little more of it actually." She chuckled against my shoulder at the comment and I smiled as I squeezed her again.

"Mmhmm, agreed. So, so much. Can I confess something?"

"Of course." She eased back so she could look up at me and I turned my gaze down to meet hers.

"Even after I'd decided I wasn't going to follow through on killing you, I wasn't sure I actually had it in me to like you."

"Oh really?"

"Yeah, really. But then you managed to weasel your way under my skin. Crawled in there and made me fall completely in love with you."

"I'm sneaky and full of surprises that way." I smirked as she giggled then I leaned down and pressed my lips to hers. I lingered for a few beats, savoring the feel of her kiss before I pulled back and looked at her. "For the record, you had the same effect on me."

"Oh did I?"

"Yeah, I'm in love with you too... My sweetness." She narrowed her eyes, leaned back and reached up to flick me on the nose. I laughed as I dropped my arms, taking her hands in mine and glanced over into the arena at the sound of an arrow zipping toward a target. When the arrow missed I heard an exasperated growl come from the girl at the other end. "I think maybe we should pause this until later. Faith needs some definite tutoring in aim before she hurts someone."

"Oh yeah. See you later?" I nodded, pressed a quick kiss to her forehead then released her so she could get to work.

CHAPTER TWENTY-SIX

CELL CROWDING

I LEFT Hayley at the archery range and turned toward the jail, stopping to look out over the wall of the compound. There was a storm rolling in and the clouds gathering overhead had turned a faint shade of pinkish purple in the early morning light. The sheet of rain I could pick out against the lightening sky would be overhead soon but it wouldn't stop our plans for the day. The archers would move inside, the people out gathering supplies would go on about their task as if nothing out of the ordinary were happening. Meanwhile I would be in the small, dark, cramped room of our jail, questioning Purist scouts who were reluctant to say the least.

I sighed as I shook my head, turning my back on the majestic scene in front of me and pulling open the door of the jail. Once inside my eyes adjusted quickly and I looked into the cell the new prisoners had been put in. I'd been told there were five of them total which was an unusual number to find. The scouting teams the Purists normally sent out were four strong for reasons no one understood. I couldn't help wondering if we'd managed to bring in a guard of some kind.

The idea was enough to make my heart race excitedly since we didn't often get our hands on soldiers of any kind. They were adept at slipping through our best guard ranks and vanishing into the woods. I turned my attention to the people now occupying the larger cell in the room. I looked them over, trying to decide which one I wanted to begin with when one decided to spit on my boots.

"Okay then, guess we'll start with you." I paused, leaned down and used the sleeve of my shirt to wipe the spit from my boot. It cleaned the dirt from the area and shined it up beautifully. "Thanks for cleaning my boot. What's your name?"

"Not telling you."

"Mhmm. All right. Well, you aren't getting out of this cell and into better accommodations until I at least have a name to put to your face."

While the comment wasn't completely true it held a little weight. Until we knew if they were from the same place as the others we'd picked up we wouldn't risk housing them together. Once we had names we would approach Gabriel, so far the most helpful of the last batch and find out if he knew them. If it turned out they were from the same compound, then we could house them together without risking too much information exchanged. Then again, maybe if I threw some of them from different compounds together and left a guard close enough to listen in on them we could actually get some information.

"Guess I'm staying here then."

"Are you sure? Because all it takes is a name, a few quick letters out of your mouth and we can get this ball rolling." I offered him an easy, casual smile in hopes of letting him know it didn't matter to me one way or the other. I couldn't care less if they stayed right where they were for the next month or six.

"Screw off." The words sounded as if they held every bit of venom he could spit at me but I didn't often let something as trivial as hatred phase me.

"Have it your way." I shrugged and turned my attention to the second man in the group, his deeply tanned skin and dark eyes blending into the background of the cell holding him hostage. "How about you? Feeling up to talking to me today?"

"Ummm…" He seemed nervous, twitchy and the way his eyes shifted to the first man I'd spoken to then back to me said something in itself. "No?"

The way he phrased his answer as a question before he glanced over at the first man again made me believe I'd been right, the other was their leader. It also told me this man was probably the lowest on the totem pole. As I huffed, brushed my hair back out of my face and looked at the rest of the group I realized there were only four people in the cell. I turned to the guard Luke had left on duty to watch them and raised a questioning brow. "Where's the other one?"

"Other one?"

"Yes, the other one. I was told there were five."

"Oh right, I keep forgetting that one. So quiet over there."

He pointed toward the cell next to the one housing the four men and when I looked into it I was stunned to find a woman looking back at me. It wasn't often these groups had women in them, the Purists finding women to be the weaker gender and refusing to use them more often than not. I narrowed my eyes at her, trying to get a better look and eventually she came into view through the shadows. I cleared my throat as I approached the second cell, focusing on its single occupant.

"Hi there."

"Don't talk to her, she has nothing to say to you either."

I couldn't see the woman's facial expression but the energy roiling off of her as she turned to look at the man I had presumed to be leader was palpable. You could cut the disdain with a knife, it was so thick it was obvious she hated him, and his commanding attitude. I had to open my mouth, something inside me wouldn't let me keep quiet on this one.

"How would you know she has nothing to say? Since you aren't her I'd say it isn't your call."

He glared at me and growled out, "It *is* my call scum. If I say she doesn't talk then she doesn't. Got it?"

I was about to open my mouth and give him a piece of my mind for the comment when a voice from inside the cell I was standing in front of beat me to it. "Oh shut up, Caleb." The man went wide eyed at her use of the name, his face turning deep red in anger. The reaction could only mean she'd used his real name, handing it to me after he'd refused to say it. I decided to keep quiet and see what else they might say while ticked off at each other.

"You know better than to use our names in this situation!"

"And you should know by now that I don't like being told what to do by halfwits who get us captured and locked up."

"Why... You... I could..." He was stammering and spluttering, obviously becoming angrier with her every second.

"You could what?" She stood as she spoke and turned toward

his cell, arms crossed over her chest. I could swear I saw the shadow of a challenging grin on her face.

He turned and charged the bars between the two cells, slamming his body weight into the barrier with a sound of rage sounding a lot like a roar. "You're lucky we're locked up woman or I'd show you the meaning of pain so intense you'd be begging me for death." Wow, this guy had some serious issues. I wondered how many Purist party leaders had this kind of psychopathic response to their authority being challenged.

"Oh boy, now I'm scared. Please. Caleb, you couldn't hurt me if you tried." He let out another of the roars and shook the bars between their cells causing me to raise a brow and shake my head at him.

"Is he always this... Intense?" She sighed, dropped her arms and nodded as she ran a hand through her hair. For a moment I thought I saw a handful of colored streaks in the golden locks but figured the dark was making me see things.

"Sadly he is. They always are. I've started thinking it's a prerequisite for leading a group."

"What? Intensity?"

"Minor insanity." I laughed outright at her comment since I'd been thinking much the same.

"Oh that's funny. And seems to be terrifyingly true."

"Yeah, terrifying. That comes close to covering it." She looked over as she spoke and I was stunned to find the faint glow of the irises of a Level Three staring back at me.

CHAPTER TWENTY-SEVEN

SHOCKWAVES IN REALITY

THIS WAS definitely a shock to the system and I almost reeled back, catching myself before I did so. I wasn't about to let her know she'd thrown me but I was in a frenzy mentally as I tried to piece together how she could be with the Purists. Her presence didn't make any type of sense and I needed a moment to process her mere existence. I didn't have the luxury of said moment though so I pressed on, pushing the voices in my head aside.

"What's your name? Or are you going to suddenly become as unwilling to talk as your counterparts here?" Thankfully I managed to keep my voice from wavering, showing none of the strange things I was feeling.

"It's Avril." I couldn't believe she'd given me her name so quickly and I wondered if maybe she'd made one up to get me to leave her alone. It wouldn't be the first time a Purist captive had done so but I almost always caught them in the lie after a quick conversation. I nodded as I pulled a chair over and seated myself close enough to see her but out of reach if she tried anything.

"Okay, Avril. Well I'm Kai."

"I know who you are, General. You're Conquest, winner of wars." I chuckled at the use of my nickname and had to admit it was growing on me a fraction more every time I heard it. After over two hundred years it was almost as comfortable to me as my actual name. Almost, but still not quite. I nodded and stared at my boots for a minute, allowing her some time to gather her thoughts before I bombarded her with another question, or twenty.

"Are you just gonna sit there or do you actually intend to talk?"

The words were snapped in my general direction and when I looked up she was glaring at me, arms crossed over her chest again. She was defiant, proud and not about to turn into a sniveling ball of captive goo because she was locked up. In another situation I could see myself being friends with this woman. Who knew, maybe there was still a chance of it happening.

"Oh, little fire in you, eh? That's fine, I like some spirit. I have several more questions but I've found most of your kind more than unwilling to actually talk to me."

It was not only the truth it was the understatement of the century. Most of the information I had managed to gather came from slip ups the scouts we had detained made. Usually while arguing with each other, often while questioning orders from a superior officer. I couldn't imagine letting my people get away with half the things these men said to their officers. Then again, I wasn't these men or their officers so my opinion was skewed and more than likely unwanted.

"Yeah well, not like they don't have a reason to be unwilling."

"Really? Because I can't imagine anything I've ever done to any of you before now that would warrant such an attitude."

"Being detained and stuffed in a cell tends to make people jumpy and uncooperative. More the men than women but as you probably noticed by now, there aren't many women in our ranks."

"I had noticed that and I was going to ask you why that is. Do Purist men just prefer to leave the women at home?"

"Ha! If only you knew how true that was." She paused as if considering whether or not she should continue. To her credit she didn't look to Caleb for permission, simply made the choice on her own, took a deep breath and forged ahead. "Actually they do, they believe that's our place. At home, cleaning, gathering, making things, cooking and raising children to further the population and the species. We have to rebuild mankind after all."

"Oh of course. So how did you end up out here with these knuckleheads?" My comment and most likely the word I had chosen to use made one of the men grumble under his breath. I rolled my eyes at him but refused any other outward sign of having heard anything from him at all.

"That's a very long story I'm not sure I'm completely comfortable telling you." Well I guess I couldn't expect her to hand me everything, she had to maintain some kind of barrier against me.

"How about an enemy friendly short version then?" She seemed to ponder the idea for a minute and then sighed and nodded.

"Fine. Basically, I'm just better at everything than these jerks." Caleb shook the bars between the cells yet again and started protesting her comment, loudly but we both ignored him. She pushed on, talking over the shouting man. "No matter how hard the officers at my base tried to fight it, they couldn't deny that I wiped the floor with them every time anything went down. They really had no choice."

"Huh, well, that sounds pretty interesting."

"Yeah. Besides, I informed them that if they didn't assign me to a team I would just tail them and end up right in the middle of it all anyway."

"Ha!" The more she talked the more I liked her. I was beginning to hope I could find a way to get her onto our side like I had Julia, Patricia and Hayley. If she could see we weren't her enemy, weren't what her leaders told her we were she would be an amazing asset to us. Not to mention it would be nice to have another officer with a little spunk and fire in her. She'd definitely keep me on my toes. "Well given the fact you're a higher level than they are, it all makes sense. You being able to outdo them I mean."

She cocked her head at me as a look of confusion worked its way across her face and she asked, "Higher level? What does that mean?" I cocked a brow at her since I wasn't sure if she was being so clueless intentionally. "We're all trained at the same level." The comment made me think she might not know what I was talking about, maybe it wasn't an act.

"No, I mean your mutation."

"What mutation?" The truth hit me in a sudden flash of clarity. Not only did the Purist leadership have Regens fighting for them, the Regens they were using didn't even know what they were. I was stunned into silence, only able to shake my head at the insanity of the entire thing.

My voice returned after a minute and I asked, "They really never told you?"

"Told us what?" Her eyes narrowed into a glare and she nailed me with the look which sent a shiver down my spine. No Level Three I'd ever met on our side would dare to look at any of the four of us Generals in such a way. Seeing those glowing green irises pinning me down with an angry intensity made my heart stutter in my chest.

"Damn. I knew your people were a bit on the secretive side but I had no idea they were keeping what you were from you."

"Stop being evasive and just tell me what the hell you're talking about!" Her shout was accompanied by a few harsh breaths and a rise in the flush I could make out on her cheeks. It was enough to silence Caleb in his protests and make him drop his hands from the bars. The look on his face said plainly he'd never heard her speak in such a way before. She was pissed at me and I knew I needed to tell her the truth even if she didn't believe it.

"Avril, you're a Regen."

"No. Not a chance. That's not possible, someone would have told me."

"It's true. You all are. I'd be willing to bet that those four are Level Ones, just like most of the other scouting teams we've collectively hauled in the last few weeks. You though, you're a Level Three. I'm stunned they managed to hide it from you for so long. Didn't anyone notice that you exhibit all the signs they tell you to look for?"

She shook her head furiously at the news and I figured she was unwilling to believe what she'd heard. It was a lot to swallow but she deserved to know the truth. Not to mention I was now stunned by the fact they had managed to put together groups of Purist raised Regens who seemed to actively ignore the signs in each other. Something had to be leading to the phenomenon and I was chomping at the bit to figure it all out. Every time I laced up one piece of loose information into a neat little bundle it seemed as if three more began to unravel.

Now I had to come up with a way of getting her to believe it which would be a feat in itself. I sat there lost in thought until she cleared her throat, pulling me out of my own head and back to the task at hand. I pushed out of the chair, needing to stretch my back and move around for a few minutes before all the excited energy boiled over. After pacing the short length of the room at least a dozen times I paused in front of the cell holding the four men again. After eyeing them as a group, scanning their expressions three or four times each I pulled my chair over and sat again.

"Okay guys, here's the deal. Names. That's all I want, your names. Not information or details or anything remotely fun or useful like that. Give me those four little pieces of information and I'll work on getting you out of this nasty cell."

"Why the hell should we believe you?" The boot cleaner had decided to open his mouth again. For a guy who had been refusing to talk, he sure did talk a lot.

"Why the hell shouldn't you? Have I lied to you yet?"

"You locked us up!"

"True, but I don't imagine any one of my people said you wouldn't be locked up. As a matter of fact, I'm fairly certain since they usually follow my orders to the letter when possible they told you up front you were being detained and held as prisoners."

"I... They... So?" I grinned when he stumbled over himself and I knew I'd caught him with the information. I'd be willing to bet he'd assumed I hadn't actually given the order to capture them and my scouts had done as they pleased.

"Ah, that's what I thought. So see, I have yet to lie, why start now? I sure don't gain anything from it." The darkly tanned man I'd spoken with earlier stifled a chuckle which grabbed my attention. I shifted to my right a few inches and smiled at him. "Seems your friend here is unwilling to see the truth."

The glare which took over the dark man's features at my words made me reel and I was thankful it was only mentally. He lowered his head a fraction and with brows deeply furrowed growled out, "He's not my friend." Even more proof these groups were sent out to work together whether they liked each other or not. I had to believe it made them weaker, more likely to make mistakes or end up arguing rather than working as a unit. It wasn't a game changer but the information could help us be better prepared to deal with them down the line.

"I apologize." His features softened, eyes returning to their normal set as he nodded his acceptance of my apology.

"It's fine. Most people assume we're all friends because we patrol together for weeks, sometimes even months at a time. Reality is we can't stand each other. I'm Saul by the way." Caleb, who I now knew was not Saul's friend glared at him, the hard set of his jaw showing how irate he was with the other man.

"I'm getting that feeling from most of these groups. I'll remind myself to not assume so it won't happen again. So, did you know you and your fellow scouts here were Regens, Saul?"

He shook his head wildly, eyes wide as he said, "No, definitely not. We've been taught all our lives that your kind are evil. The last thing we would think would be that we were like you. Most of us would rather die than live that way." I shoved my anger at the comment deep down inside, shutting it into a box. It wasn't his fault he was raised to hate those exactly like him and I wouldn't take my irritation about it out on him.

"How did they explain it all then? The ring around the iris, the enhanced abilities? In you and the boys here it might be pretty easy to write off as naturally occurring skill sets but her?" I pointed toward Avril, the faint green of her eyes visible in the dim space. The glow wasn't as bright as mine but it was there all the same. "How did they explain that away?"

"We're chosen." Boot cleaner Caleb spoke again before Saul had the chance and I focused on him.

"Chosen?"

"By God, to fight you." The words were strong, full of pride as he moved away from the bars between the cells and stopped in front of me.

"Ooookaaayyy." The drawn out word was accompanied by an eye roll which showed what I thought about the explanation.

"Go ahead and doubt it. Your disbelief doesn't change our destiny. We were chosen to rid the world of your kind and so we were gifted with some of your skills and abilities so we could be victorious."

I flat out could not help it, I burst out laughing. By the time I'd stopped and caught my breath I had rolled off the chair and onto the floor and the man was glaring at me. A muscle in the side of his jaw twitched in aggravation as he took a handful of slow, deep breaths. I assumed he was attempting to calm himself and for a moment I hoped it didn't work. When these guys were pissed they tended to run their mouths, I could use the break.

"I don't see why anything he said is funny." I turned to look at Avril as I returned to the chair and shook my head.

"Avril, these things we have, the differences, they aren't gifts or some kind of destiny at play. They're mutations and they only happen because we inherited them."

"Exactly, like we did." I sighed as I closed my eyes and rubbed my head while I counted to twenty then returned my gaze to her.

"No. We inherited these traits from our parents. We were born like this. It's really the only way it works. We mutate, Purists don't.

In order to show traits of the mutation you have to actually *have* the mutation which means at least one of your parents would have had to be a Regen."

Caleb, apparently unable to keep his thoughts to himself on the matter spoke up. "No. Not possible. Our people would never agree to even live with your kind much less have offspring with them. The children would be... They'd be..."

I raised a brow at the hot tempered man as he tried to find his words and finally asked, "They'd be what? Like us?"

"Abominations. Sins against the Father and the very Earth we live on. Monsters. So yes, pretty much like you." Despite having been insulted in the worst way possible I shot the man a cocky smirk as I shook my head.

"I admit; I've never been called a monster before. Don't think it suits me." I pretended to ponder the idea for a few seconds before I shrugged and turned back to Avril. "This has been a real treat but I think I need a break. I'll do what I can to find space outside this room for you and Saul. You'll be moved as soon as I can figure out other accommodations for you."

She stared at me in shock as I rose from the chair, an exact replica of the look painted on Saul's face. I pulled the chair over to its original place across the room, nodded to the guard and reached for the door before I heard, "Thank you, Kai." I looked over my shoulder at Avril, nodded with a small smile then moved to leave.

"What the hell about me?" I turned to look at Caleb when he spoke.

"What about you?"

"You said all you wanted was names. You have mine so can't I get out of here?" I dropped my hand from the handle and crossed back to the cell.

"I remember saying I'd get you out of here if *you* gave me your name. Since Avril is the one who gave it to me and you're still being a shit, I'll have to consider it." I watched anger slide across his face as he slammed his palms against the bars in front of me.

"Lying bitch!"

"I didn't lie to you. I just told you I'd consider it. Honestly, showing a little less hostility probably wouldn't hurt your case any." I shifted my gaze to Avril, gave her a quick nod which she returned and then did an about face and crossed back to the door. I got hold of the handle again and ignored Caleb heaving insults at my back as I pushed my way outside into the fresh air.

I started toward the locked down house to have a chat with Gabriel. If this group was from his compound, then Saul and Avril would be moved the next day. If not, well, we would cross that particular bridge when and if we came to it.

CHAPTER TWENTY-EIGHT

FAMILY CONNECTIONS

I GRINNED as I stepped into the house remembering the time I'd spent within these walls. The countless hours I'd spent sitting in one room or another chatting with Julia, playing with Nathan or trading silly stories with Hayley. Of them all the flashes including her were the ones I treasured most and they made me thankful for the near picture perfect recall I had. Every opportunity I had to hear her laugh was a blessing after the way we began our relationship. I shook my head, removing the thoughts since I didn't have time to stand around and reminisce.

After climbing the stairs, I paused outside the door I'd stood in front of so many times. I knew every dent, ding and scratch in the wood after what had to be hours staring at the thing, usually building up the courage to knock on it. Now the nerves attached to it were gone. The panic of rapping my knuckles against the portal no longer churned and roiled in my belly. It was once again simply a door. Strange how the occupant of a room could change its entire dynamic. I chuckled as I shook my head, raised my hand and knocked on the wood.

The door swung open a second later and the occupant offered me a sleepy smile. "Hello, General."

"Hello, Gabriel."

"Come on in." He stepped away from the door, crossed back to the bed and sat on the end of it as a huge yawn shook his entire body. I couldn't help but chuckle as he stretched his arms over his head to release the tension the yawn had left behind. "What can I do for you today?"

I shut the door then turned back toward him as I said, "We have a new set in the cells."

"Ah, need to know if they're from our compound?" I nodded and he eased back on the bed, leaning against the wall, his head falling back to rest against the cracked plaster. "Okay, shoot."

"Only names I got out of them were Saul, Caleb and Avril." His eyes shot open as he sat up and his gaze leveled on me.

"Did you say Avril?"

"I did." My arms came up, crossing over my chest as I tilted my head a bit.

"About your height, blonde, attitude for days?"

"That would be her." I grinned at his description but the expression fell away when he stood from the bed, turned and put his fist against the wall.

"Damn her!" His reaction piqued my curiosity but I didn't press, he needed to process and cool down before I tried to get anything more out of him. I'd almost reached the point where I no longer feared Gabriel but I'd now been reminded he was a large man and could be explosive. He took half a dozen deep breaths, his shoulders rising and falling with each. When he had calmed he turned and faced me again, saying, "Forgive me, General, yes I know them. Better than I'd like."

Now I was intrigued and couldn't help but ask, "Oh?"

"Saul is a decent kid but he is just that, a kid. He's not even seventeen yet. Not until Winter I believe." I was shocked at the information, the only tasks anyone under eighteen was given in my compound were gathering and basic housework. Nothing which could land them dead or imprisoned.

"What would possess anyone to send a sixteen-year-old boy out to do this job? Dear gods no wonder he was so scared."

"He'll pull through, he's a tough kid just a bit jumpy. Now Caleb, that man..." He paused and I wasn't sure if he intended to continue until he chuckled and finished with, "Is an ass."

"I'll agree with that assessment!" I laughed right along with him as I remembered my conversation with the man.

The laughter died away and his mood darkened from one

breath to the next, his expression going hard. "Then there's Avril." I nodded but said nothing, again letting him decide when to tell me whatever he cared to share about the woman. "She shouldn't be here." My plan to stay silent fell over dead at the deep, angry growl in his voice.

"Why? Because she's a woman and she doesn't belong in the wilds with the men?" My jaw set hard after I spoke, my temper flaring at the reminder of how the Purists saw women within their ranks. The feeling lasted a mere flash though as he shook his head, the anger fell away from his expression and a deep look of sadness took its place.

"No, she's as capable as any of those buffoons. Probably exceeds them actually."

"Then what is it?"

He looked up at me, fear and anguish evident in his haloed gaze which was now shimmering with barely restrained tears. "Because General... She's my little sister."

The news was like a solid punch in the gut and it rendered me speechless for several minutes. While I stood there dumbfounded Gabriel sat heavily on the edge of the bed and dropped his head into his hands. The staggered pattern of his breathing told me he had started crying but was trying his best to hide it. Not one to make attempts at turning an awkward situation worse I pretended I didn't notice, letting him release the tears he needed to shed in silence. When he finally looked up he wiped the last of the wetness from his cheeks and stood, moving to stand toe to toe with me.

"General, she can't stay in there."

"I'll do what I can Gabriel. I have to ask though, did you know? About her mutation?"

He sighed, shaking his head as he turned away from me, bracing one hand against the wall, his forehead leaned beside it. The two points took the majority of his weight as I watched him take two deep breaths. When he spoke, he was still facing the wall which meant I heard his words even though he spoke only a fraction above a whisper. "Yes. She's what you'd call a Level Three." The fact he didn't deny her mutation the way she and the other men had told me a lot. He released a heavy sigh, pushed away from the wall and turned to face me again. His expression had righted itself back into his usual features by the time he spoke again.

"Most of our ranks believe the hype they are fed, that we're chosen and that God gave us these powers. I don't happen to be one of those who follow with blind devotion. I do my job because I was trained to do it and I'm good at it but that's about all the drive I have. I had always questioned every word of it and since meeting you and your people I am more convinced than ever." I held my breath, not daring to hope he was about to admit what I begged for them to understand. "We are Regens."

CHAPTER TWENTY-NINE

NEW ACCOMMODATIONS

I EXITED the house an hour later with the knowledge Gabriel had given me so willingly despite the pain hearing of his sisters' capture had caused. I was determined to do everything I could to reunite them before the month was out but unfortunately, most of the success depended on her. I locked the door behind me, turned and took a deep breath as my eyes slid closed. I opened them again a ten count later, stepped off the porch and turned toward the archery range. I had to squint against the harsh light of the slowly dipping sun where it sat low on the horizon.

I couldn't believe I'd spent most of the day dealing with prisoners and interrogations. The thought caused me to yawn as I walked, exhausted and ready to fall into bed. Slipping into unconsciousness sounded wonderful, mere sleep would not suffice tonight. I was intent on making it back to where I'd left Hayley and see if she was still at her archery lesson with Faith. The ground was damp underfoot so I knew it had rained at some point while I'd been inside one building or the other.

They would have moved inside seeking shelter in hopes of allowing for better aim. Whether they had stayed there or even continued I wasn't sure of. I paused as I stepped in front of one of many small dwellings on the side of the compound I was in and stared at the place. I shut down as much as I could, letting my mind wander so I could take a break. My head had begun to pound hours earlier but I'd been ignoring it.

Most of the former houses which had survived the explosions during the event were already occupied. We did have a few which were too small for families with children however and the one I was looking at happened to be one of them. It had two bedrooms, one of which was much too small to really use for sleeping in. Before the event we had called such a space an office, now they were unusable space. The more I thought about it though the more I realized I could use such a space for all my supplies.

I smiled as I stepped up to the front door and opened it, slipping inside and surveying the open area we'd once called a living room. It was good sized and would easily allow two people, not to mention several massive wolves to lounge around. A fireplace sat against one wall and there were windows everywhere letting in the fading sunlight. I made my way to the back of the house and pushed open the door to the smaller of the two rooms. It was as tiny as I remembered it but I could store all my bow-making supplies and such in it with room to spare.

I left the smaller room and moved to the end of the hallway, pushing open the door of the larger room. I stepped in and scanned the walls I hadn't thought about in years. There was another fireplace in here, up against the outer wall. It would be perfect on those cold nights when even a second persons' body heat couldn't seem to warm you up. With my mind set I nodded, left the room and exited the house more intent on finding my girlfriend than I had been before.

"Hayley!"

I'd caught sight of her as I approached the outdoor archery area and couldn't wait until I made it across the yard to where she was standing. She was lingering outside the fenced area chatting with Faith and her mother and turned when she heard me shout her name. The smile which lit up her face almost made my stride falter. I would remember the expression for years to come I was sure since it outshone the sun behind her. She waved as I jogged closer, stopping in front of her.

"Hey. Haven't seen you all day. Everything go okay today?" I beamed at her despite the concern which crossed her face. I wanted to tell her my idea but knew she was inquiring about my visit to the jail.

My other news would have to wait a while but I couldn't tell her about the new information until we were alone so I only shrugged as I said, "Not bad. Tell you all about it later."

"Fair enough. So what were you all smiles about when you ran up?"

"I have an idea to run by you. Are you guys done here or do I need to hush and wait for a bit." I glanced from Hayley to Faith and back again as I hoped they were finished and we could leave.

"Nope we're done. Faith, you did great. We'll make an archer of you yet!"

"Heck yeah!" Hayley, myself and Andrea, Faith's mother all laughed at the girls' enthusiasm and I shook my head as I punched her playfully on the arm.

"Maybe we'll even make a scout of you, huh?" She beamed and the pride which crossed her mothers' face complimented it perfectly.

Hayley raised a brow at me before interjecting with, "Maybe so. First, this and next, horsemanship." We all nodded, said our goodbyes and I took Hayley's hand as we headed away from the range. "So, what's this idea you have?"

"You'll see, come with me." I led her out to where I'd been earlier and up the steps of the small house. Once we were inside I dropped her hand and gave her a nod as I said, "Go on, take a look around." After a few minutes she was back in the living room, standing in front of me with an appreciative smile.

"It's cute. Small but nice. Why isn't anyone living here?"

"It's just too small for any of the families with children and most of the couples who don't have them prefer the barracks with their friends." She nodded as she scanned the room again before returning her gaze to me. "I was thinking it might be the perfect size for a couple people with a small herd of wolves though."

I locked eyes with her as I watched understanding wash over her features until she beamed at me. She reached over and grabbed my hands as she asked, "Are you telling me you want us to move in here instead of living in that terrible, single room soldiers' quarters?"

"That's exactly what I'm telling you. What do you think?"

"I think we should do it tomorrow that's what I think!" We laughed together as I pulled her into a tight hug.

"Then we'll do just that. I've been meaning to get out of that nasty single room for years anyway. Never had a reason to push the issue though, until now." She nuzzled my neck as I finished the words and I chuckled at the tickle of her breath on my skin. "For now, I'm exhausted and I still have a full day of crap to catch you and Luke up on so, come on."

She lingered a few breaths longer then stepped back and I took her hand, leading her from the house and locking it up. Starting the next day, it would be ours but I did have a lot to report to my second before we could settle in for the night. The sooner it was done and I was asleep, the better.

We left the house behind with the knowledge it would be ours soon and went in search of Luke. We found him near the front of the compound giving orders to a group of guards. It was shift change and he was handing out stations and patrols. He tried to vary them so none of the guards ended up bored on their posts and lost concentration. It also had the added bonus of constantly shifting patrol patterns since no two guards walked the same patrol route the same way or the same pace.

I waited for him to finish handing out the orders then walked up, slapping him on the shoulder with a smile on my face. He turned to face me, beaming when he saw the pride I could be sure was written all over my face. "Hey. Good timing, just got the shift change finished."

"So we saw. I have some interesting updates I can't wait to share with you."

"Oh?" He glanced at Hayley like she would tell him what I was talking about before I had the chance to do it.

"Hey don't look at me, I haven't got a clue." He turned back to me and raised an eyebrow to which I shrugged with a small grin.

"What? You know how much I hate repeating myself. Let's go find Steph and Bradley so I only have to do this once." I gave him a quick wink which made he and my girlfriend laugh before we left the area in search of the other Captains.

CHAPTER THIRTY

NOT ALL SURPRISES ARE GOOD

KAI'S JOURNAL - *Summer Cycle, 2607 – 221 years after the event:*
The months keep marching right along and it bothers me that we haven't been able to pull any more information from these Purist captives. I'm beginning to consider the validity of letting Hayley talk to some of them. While I have the feeling she might be able to get more from some of the scouts I'm not sure it's safe to let them know she's out and about in the compound. Or that she's with us now rather than against us. The entire situation is exhausting and I do my best to not spend too much time dwelling on it. That's why I'm dropping the subject and getting some sleep now.

I laid in bed one morning, staring at the patterns in the ceiling above me as soft, even breaths caressed my shoulder. It was hard for me to believe over a year had passed since Hayley and the other women had been brought into the compound as captives. Almost nine months had lapsed since the night she had kissed me and the following moving of her into my quarters. We'd been in the small house I'd claimed for us for four months. I'd been shocked at how easily we'd settled in, as if neither of us had ever lived anywhere else, or with anyone else.

The fluidity with which we worked together, coexisted often shocked me and frequently scared me a bit. It was nice but something I'd never thought I would have again after I lost Laney. There had been more than a few years when I didn't ever want this feeling again. Now it was back in my life and I couldn't imagine why I wanted to ignore what I'd felt for Hayley. She had completed my life in a way I thought was impossible.

As much as thinking about Laney still hurt I knew she would be glad I'd found someone who made me so happy. If the situation had been reversed, I would have wanted her to move on. Guilt and heartache I'd suffered through for more than two decades after her death had been lifted and replaced by joy, companionship and love. The thought pulled a gentle sigh from me and made a small smile spread across my face. I closed my eyes again, falling back into the warm comfort of the woman sleeping peacefully in my arms.

I'd gotten a quick glimpse out the window during my daydreaming and found myself facing an overcast spring day. The drab gray light coming through the windows was enough to make me want to go right back to sleep. I turned, my eyes still closed and put my back to my girlfriend who responded by wrapping her arms around me and snuggling in close against my back. I was on the verge of following through with my plans for more sleep when a muffled yawn came from against my back. It was followed a short three seconds later by a gentle kiss on the back of my neck.

A whispered 'morning' blew a light swath of warmth down my neck and across my bare shoulder. It sent a shiver right down my spine and caused a sharp intake of breath at the same time. I shifted, rolled back over and wrapped my arms around Hayley once again. She adjusted, putting most of her body on top of mine so she was smiling down at me.

"Morning. Sleep okay?" My voice was rough with sleep but the raspy tenor only made her bite her lower lip as she nodded. Another yawn slipped free in the middle of the gesture and I chuckled at her for it. She made a face at me then turned enough to look out the window.

"Ewww, it's gross out there."

"Mmhmm. Storm rolling in. We'll probably get rained on most of the day."

"Lovely." I grinned at the word, huffed in displeasure at the information before she looked back down at me. I let my grin slip into a wicked smirk and she narrowed her eyes at me. Less than a breath later her full on smile turned into a sly grin. "And what kind of terrible things are you thinking, huh?"

"Why don't you come closer and find out."

I winked at her to which she quirked one pale brow before shifting her weight. The minor change in position allowed her to press her body down flush against mine. A deep purr emanated from my chest as I claimed her lips in a heated kiss. My hands slid down onto her lower back, pressing her even closer against me. The closeness combined with our usual lack of clothing allowed me to feel the sudden rise in her body temperature as she responded to me.

She shifted again, tilting her head to deepen the kiss right as someone pounded on the front door. With a grumble she broke away from my lips. "I swear to god someone had better be dead or carrying their own fucking arm..." I growled out as I forced myself to leave the warmth of our bed, and Hayley's body. She managed to giggle at my angry comment around the disappointment I could see in her eyes.

I yanked on my pants and the nearest shirt in an angry huff then stormed out of the room and down the hall toward the door. I flung it open and leveled an intense glare on Steph, making her take a half step back. She cleared her throat, crossed her arms over her chest and stared at my boots. She knew I was pissed and I was fairly certain she knew why if the flush on her cheeks were any indication.

"What?"

"Sorry to bother you, Kai, but we have visitors." My temper flared, of all the stupid things for her to interrupt my morning for.

"You pulled me out of bed for visitors? What the hell, Steph?"

"These aren't just any visitors."

"Whatever, tell them they can wait." I grabbed the door, having every intention of slamming it right in her face. Best friend or not, officer or not she had not started off on the right foot with me today.

I had gripped the edge of the door and begun the swing when she stopped the movement dead by saying, "Thea is here." I stood there and stared at her dumbfounded and unable to process what she'd told me.

"Say that again, I swear I heard you wrong. I thought you said Thea was here."

"I did, she is." I narrowed my eyes at her as I tried to determine if she was playing some kind of trick on me. I could count the number of times Thea had come to my compound in over two hundred years on one hand.

"Thea never leaves her compound."

"Well something she heard made her leave it now. All they would say was they heard some disturbing news and needed to speak to you immediately." One of the words she had used caught my attention and I fixated on it since news of Thea's presence was making my head hurt.

"They?"

"Trista and Lila are with her."

"Oh for the love of..." I growled, the sound putting a snarl on my face which made my head runner cover her mouth to stifle a laugh in spite of my anger. "Fine. Give me a few minutes to find decent clothes and let Hayley know what's going on then I'll be down."

She nodded, did an about face and headed back toward the meeting area we used. I sighed, kicked the door closed and made my way back to the bedroom. I found Hayley still sprawled out on the bed and still very much lacking clothes, not to mention blankets. My eyes raked over her toned frame pulling a pathetic whine from me and leaving a smirk on her face. She knew exactly the effect she had on me, I never tried hiding it.

I huffed and forced myself to dig through the pile of clothes in the corner for something not caked in dirt. Halfway through with a shirt in one hand and desperately seeking pants movement from the bed caught my attention. I risked a glance toward the area and immediately knew it had been a very good and all at once very bad idea. Hayley had shifted around and was now sitting on the edge of the bed, arms out behind her to prop her up. Showing her complete lack of shame in teasing me she hadn't bothered covering herself up with even the mostly sheer linen on the end of the bed.

"You coming back to bed, Babe?"

I whimpered, grumbled a few choice words under my breath then said, "No. Apparently the almighty Thea decided to leave her throne room and grace our humble compound with her presence. So I have to go see what the hell she wants." I set my jaw, fighting the growing urge to drop everything, crawl right back into the bed and make the other Generals wait on me for an hour, or three.

"She's actually here?"

The shock in Hayley's voice made me turn toward her again as I grabbed a pair of clean pants. She had grabbed the blanket and pulled it up around her. I wasn't sure if I should breathe a sigh of relief or mourn the loss of the view I'd had a minute earlier. I shook the mental image off and nodded at her then kept a close watch as she slid from the bed and mimicked my actions. Mostly clean garments in hand we both dressed in silence before I turned to her.

"Where are you going?"

"Umm, with you."

I chuckled at her comment and stepped over closer, wrapping my arms around her waist as I asked, "You think so, eh?"

"Oh I know so." She arched one perfect eyebrow at me and I couldn't help but grin.

"And why would you want to come with me?"

"Because I grew up hearing about this woman. She's supposed to be absolutely terrifying. I wanna see for myself." I rolled my eyes at her for the answer but knew I wouldn't be able to convince her to stay behind. Once the woman had an idea in her head it was stuck and changing her mind was like forcing a Mule to do something it didn't want to. Damn near impossible.

"There's no point arguing with you I suppose."

"Damn right." She pecked me on the nose, gave me a wink and then moved to pull away but I tugged her back.

"Well, I'm gonna try anyway. It's not exactly safe for you to come to this thing Hayley. It isn't just Thea; the other two Generals are here too."

"Ooohh, even more reason for me to go!"

I shook my head; she was actually excited about meeting three of the most feared Regens in the world face to face. She had to be insane. Then again, I thought, she had met me face to face which had turned out exceptionally well and I was one of those feared Regens. I blew out a puff of air and studied her, trying to come up with something I could say to make her stay behind.

"Hayley I..."

"Don't bother trying to talk me out of it." Damn, I swear she could read my mind.

"And why not?" I was pouting and I knew it.

"Because I'll only win. In the end, you'll let me go with you. I can even convince you without a fight."

"And why the hell would I agree without even trying to argue the idea out of you?"

"Because," she began as she leaned in closer, a wicked twinkle in her eye. When her lips met mine my heart stuttered, my stomach clenched and my knees went weak. I was powerless to pull away as my mind was wiped clear of everything I'd been about to use to change her mind. When she pulled away she lingered close enough that her lips brushed mine when she said, "You know what follows that later. At least, what *could* follow if I'm not pouting because you left me here."

I managed to whimper out a strangled, "Okay."

With a grin she dropped her arms from my shoulders and took a step back before she turned and left the room. Despite knowing I'd been bested I couldn't help but watch her walk away. The view was splendid. Once she was out of sight my brain kicked in again and I grumbled at myself. "Damn stupid hormones. Get in the way of my thinking and crap." I shoved my feet into my boots and went after her. One thing was certain, this would be a meeting to remember I could only hope it wouldn't end in chaos or disaster.

CHAPTER THIRTY-ONE

UNWANTED DEALS

WE'D TAKEN some time to finish repairing an old single story building near the northeast corner of the compound to meet in. The makeshift lean-to we'd been utilizing had decided to show its age and collapse. Thankfully no one had been present beneath the canopy when it fell or we could have been short a handful of scouts and guards. This new location was fully enclosed and in better shape than some of the other buildings near it. It hadn't taken much to get it in habitable condition and we'd been using it for gatherings for weeks now.

Despite my instincts telling me to be very careful at this meeting Hayley and I stepped into the room holding hands. The looks I got from Trista and Lila were fleeting but they spoke volumes about their presence. They were standing in my compound because they'd been dragged along by Thea which meant she was about to launch into a tirade. I took a deep breath as the taller woman turned to face me from her place across the semi-enclosed space. Her eyes narrowed at me then dropped to where I had Hayley's hand gripped in mind.

"So it's true then?"

"I can answer that better if I know what you're talking about, Thea." Light brown brows furrowed at my comment and I knew I was already on thin ice. Perfect.

"I think you know but fine, I'll humor you. Imagine my shock, my surprise, my genuine disbelief when Trista informed me you had taken a shine to a Purist scout. Then try to grasp how I felt when Lila proceeded to confirm the information."

"Why feel anything about it? It has nothing to do with you."

Hayley's hand tightened around my own and I knew she was telling me to stop poking the bear. Normally I would have agreed with her but she'd never dealt with Thea before. If I caved now she would believe she had the right to tell me what to do in my own compound. I wasn't about to let that happen so I stood my ground. I was prepared to go toe-to-toe with Death herself.

"It has everything to do with me, Kai! With all of us as a matter of fact. Don't you think this could bring all kinds of crazy down on us?"

"Why would it?" I threw a cautious glance at Lila when she questioned Thea, glad for her help but wondering what she was thinking. It was normally in ones' best interest to stay out of it if Thea's temper wasn't aimed at you. To do otherwise proved you were insane and wanted it to be.

"I honestly thought the two of you knew what she was and were keeping it from me. Now I see Kai has kept us all in the dark." My eyes narrowed as my train of thought ran ahead a few steps. I had a feeling I knew where she was headed with this and what she had discovered. Thea had a nasty if not useful habit of knowing things she shouldn't. Sometimes it worked for you but at times like this one it worked rather decidedly against.

"What are you talking about? She might not have out and told us she had feelings for Hayley when we were here before but we aren't stupid. We could see it. She wasn't actively hiding it just, fighting it." I offered Trista a small smile, glad she seemed to be back on my side in the matter. I wondered how long it would last once they knew the truth, or at least part of it.

"If only that were the extent of it. The relationship they've developed is bad enough. What I don't understand is how you can trust a White Guard sent to kill you, Kai. How do you manage that?"

There it was, the thing I'd feared the most. She had uncovered what Hayley was and why she was here to begin with. I had no idea how she'd managed it, none of us knew how she got her information. My gaze flickered to the corner where Trista and Lila were standing and I saw their eyes widen as they took in what Thea had said. I returned my focus to the eldest General and blew out a solid, steady stream of air through my nose.

I would keep my temper in check and discuss this calmly. It wouldn't do any of us any good if we got into a shouting match. I counted to ten, preparing myself to speak when I was beaten to the punch before I even reached two.

"No way, it can't be true. Kai?" Trista's distraction was perfectly timed and helped diffuse some of my temper, for the moment.

I took another deep breath, still needing at least a dozen more since my count had been interrupted then nodded at her as I said, "It's true. Hayley was a member of the White Guard and she was sent here to assassinate me." My hand came up to cut off the instant reaction I saw coming from Trista and Lila both. "*Obviously* that plan deviated and isn't the goal any longer."

"So says you. How do we know for sure?" I turned a glare on Thea, unable to believe she couldn't see the facts right in front of her.

"What's that supposed to mean? Thea, she's been living here free for months. If she wanted to kill me, she's had ample opportunity. On a nightly basis I might add." Rage flooded Thea's features and she took three quick steps toward me. In a rush of speed I hadn't realized she truly possessed Hayley pushed in front of me before Thea had finished moving. I leaned in against her back and whispered, "What are you doing?" to which she shook her head and trained her attention on Thea.

"Get the hell out of my way." Thea's voice was an intense and very angry growl as she stepped up into Hayley's face. To her credit she didn't so much as flinch despite Thea having a few inches on her. She simply stood there, her jaw set and her stance solid.

"No. Your issue isn't really with Kai."

"How dare you tell me who or what my issues may or may not be with or against? Move!" A flush of color had painted Thea's face and I was beginning to be concerned for Hayley's safety. The taller woman had a temper and she wielded it like a bladed weapon.

"I said no. I'm the problem here right? My presence, who and what I am? Fine, deal with me but leave her alone." I wanted to speak up, say something, anything but my ability to speak seemed to have abandoned me. In the face of Hayley standing in my defense against a woman she'd been raised to fear I found myself choked up and on the verge of tears. Pride shot through me and I couldn't come up with the words to pull her back out of harm's way.

"Oh you're going to wish you hadn't said that." Hayley took a deep breath at the evil smile turning up Thea's lips as she spoke. To her credit, even though I could feel her heart hammering hard against her ribs and the small but steady tremor rippling through her, she still refused to move. Thea shifted, looking over her shoulder and raised one chocolate brow at me. "You want me to let this go and leave you and your people alone, Kai?" I nodded and she shot me the most spine tingling, gut wrenching grin I'd ever seen. "Fine, I'll go." I almost breathed a sigh of relief until she followed it up with, "And I'll take her with me." Her gaze leveled on Hayley and fear kicked my brain full force into action.

"Not a chance." I pulled the smaller blonde behind me and got right up in Thea's face, my temper peaking again. "What good would that do?"

"Worlds of good. She can come to my compound for a few weeks so I can get to know her. If it turns out she really isn't a threat to you, she can come back."

"And why would I agree to that?" It was a ludicrous thought pattern and I wasn't about to agree to it. Hayley wasn't leaving the compound with Thea even if I had to incapacitate the other General myself.

"Because if you don't I will become a thorn in your side. You know how annoyingly distracting and intense I can be when I set my mind to something." She was right but I wasn't about to give in so easily.

"Thea, you've barely left your compound in two hundred years. You won't hang around here long."

"Maybe, maybe not. Then again, it's spring so resources are plentiful. How often do you gather supplies this time of year? Daily? Weekly? I'll bet you don't stockpile much since you can get out there and get more anytime." My temper flared even as my blood ran cold and I hoped she wasn't headed where I thought she was with the remark. "Makes me wonder, how long would it take you to run out of food if I barricaded your hunters and gatherers in?" My eyes narrowed and I saw red, not liking her threat in the least but I questioned how much of it was a pure bluff.

"No, there's no way you could manage that. It would take a good portion of your compound." The smile she gave me was shot through with evil intentions and I caught myself beginning to worry.

"Come with me, I need to show you something."

She waved me out of the building after her and with nothing else to do if I wanted to know what she was up to, I followed. She led the way to one of the towers my guards had erected years earlier and climbed to the perch at the top. I scaled the ladder behind her and upon reaching the platform followed the sweep of her arm as it arced across the horizon. What I saw ripped a gasp from me and blurred my vision, she had come prepared. I looked out at the thousand soldier strong main force of her army and knew she'd won, she could in fact blockade us from gathering supplies.

"I can order them to spread out and keep your people behind the walls or..." She swept her gaze down to the ground where Hayley stood between Trista and Lila, the two looking at her like she was some deformed creature which had stumbled out of the forest.

I tried to think of a way out of the situation but without the ability to forage we wouldn't last long, she knew my habits too well. During spring when times were good we only kept enough in the stores behind the walls to last two weeks, three at most. With her men keeping us in they could pillage our usual hunting and gathering spots all while keeping us from doing the same. I hung my head, knowing I was beat unless I could come up with a way to get around her very well trained fighters. I made my way back down the ladder, meeting Hayley at the bottom and shaking my head at her as she embraced me.

I pressed my cheek to hers as I hugged her back and whispered, "She's got enough soldiers with her to keep the compound surrounded, half her army is out there. She'll starve us out in a matter of weeks."

"Then I'll go." Those three barely audible words threatened to tear my heart out as tears stung the corners of my eyes. I shook my head as I pulled her closer, not wanting to let her go for fear of never seeing her again.

"No. I can't lose you. There has to be another way." I fought the flood back, refusing to let Thea see how heartbroken I was.

"There isn't, honey. I'll be fine, I can take care of myself. It's just a few weeks." I needed to argue, find another way to get out of this, she couldn't leave.

"Awww. Now isn't this just adorable. Come on, times wasting. Choices about the future of your whole compound to make and all that."

I bit the inside of my cheek as I fought the urge to turn around and punch Thea in the face. She would heal quickly from any damage the blow caused after all. However, the long term effects such an outburst would have on our future interactions kept me from acting on the impulse. I took a breath, shoved my temper back into place and pulled away from Hayley. She nodded her answer to my unspoken question and I sighed, defeated.

"Fine. But she better make it back here in one piece or you'll wish you'd never come here." I brushed some stray hair from Hayley's forehead, leaned in a pressed a quick kiss to her lips before I whispered, "I love you."

Her answering, "I love you too," broke through the last of my resolve and I had to turn and walk away.

CHAPTER THIRTY-TWO

DEPRESSION FUELED PLANNING

KAI'S JOURNAL - *Summer Cycle, 2607 – 221 years after the event:*

It's been days since I was forced into letting Hayley leave the compound and despite my attempts to cool my temper I'm still pissed. I could beat the hell out of Thea for this little fiasco and she'd better hope my girlfriend makes it back here in one piece or there will be hell to pay. Now I'm going to stop writing, put this thing away and try to get some sleep, not that I've been able to do much of that the last couple nights...

Three days after Thea's departure from my compound with Hayley in tow I was still sulking around like a moody teenager. I hated myself for being so easily forced into a corner, for being so predictable and for not fighting harder to keep her with me. I leaned back against the exterior wall of my old quarters with a heavy sigh and looked up into the deep purple sky. I'd had trouble sleeping without the familiar warmth of her body beside me. While the idea she'd become such a needed part of my daily life was heartwarming, it also hurt like hell. The sound of someone sitting down beside me made me turn my head and I managed to offer Steph a small smile though I didn't feel it.

"Hey. How ya holding up?"

I snorted, shook my head and responded, "I'm not."

"Fair enough. I gather you aren't sleeping."

"Nope."

"Are you at least eating?" I turned my head and glared at my best friend, hating when she played mother hen with me. I knew she was looking out for me and had my best interest at heart but it was still obnoxious. "Okay, I'll take that as a no. Try to relax, Kai, she'll be back."

"How can you know that? Thea is a real piece of work. I don't trust her as far as I can throw her. She's always been so damn secretive with us all."

Her eyes narrowed down, brow furrowed and she offered me a snort for the comment as she replied, "And you've been so open and honest with the three of them?" The question earned her a return glare as I pushed to my feet and brushed myself off.

"You know what, Steph? Screw off." I turned to leave and she surged to her feet, grabbing my arm to stop me.

"Kai, wait. I know you don't want to hear that but it's true. The four of you don't share anything. You're the most uncooperative and closed off allies I've ever met. I don't even know how you make it work."

I started to protest, wanting to argue the point, tell her she was wrong and we managed to work things out fine. I wanted to tell her I wasn't secretive, fight the comment by telling her I was totally open with the others. As much as I wanted to do it, I couldn't because she was right. I still wanted to hate her for it though. I attempted another glare but knew it fell short when she pulled me into a hug.

I grasped at my faltering irritation, wanting to cling to it as long as I could. Angry was familiar, it was easy, it had some drive behind it. At least if I was angry I wasn't depressed. I sighed, giving up my feeble hold on my temper and hugging her back. Sure I was pissed off, who wouldn't be in my place? Below the surface rage roiled a deep, dark chasm of pain, loss and heartache so profound I was worried I wouldn't be able to function if I let it take hold.

The last of the anger slipped away into the darkness and I released a heavy sigh. "I'm sorry, I know I'm a mess and I'm slipping but I can't stop worrying. I don't know where they are or when she's coming back. Or even if she's okay."

"I know, but it'll be okay. I think Thea understands, despite all her bluffing and bravado that if anything happens to Hayley you'll be after her for it."

I nodded against her shoulder and then released my hold so I could take a step back, putting her at arm's length. I stood there and stared at her, letting the silence hang between us as I attempted to piece my ragged emotional state back together. As much as I wanted to break down and lock myself in the house until she returned I couldn't let Hayley's absence stop everything in the compound. I had people relying on me and I needed to pull myself together and start acting like their leader.

"I guess I just needed some time to wallow. There's too much to do right now though and I need to get it together. A weakness was exposed when Thea made her threats. It's time we make sure something like that never happens again."

"Good. Nice to have you back. General." She flashed a smile at me and I grinned back unable to hold out against her perky enthusiasm any longer.

"Well we'll see if my being back as you put it does us any good in the next several months. Get Luke, Bradley and Willow then meet me at the house. It's time we made some plans."

She nodded and then left to follow my orders without another word. Thea had exposed our weakest point during months of plenty, a rusty link in the chain I hadn't even registered. Once we implemented my ideas and any new ones the others might have it would eradicate the problem. If things worked as I hoped, I'd have to thank Thea for strengthening my compound when I saw her again. I smiled to myself as I turned and headed off toward the house, letting out a sharp whistle as I walked, bringing a thickly furred loping shadow out of the inky darkness.

"Hey girl."

I reached out as I spoke the words and let my fingers run through the thick, soft fur of the wolf who had trotted up beside me. Ember had filled out nicely since the night I'd found her months earlier and she was a truly amazing creature. As stunning an animal as she was she paled in comparison to the largest of her four offspring. Flare charged up after a handful of yards and came to a skidding halt in front of me, a wolfish grin on his face. His cinnamon colored fur had a soft gleam to it in the light of the full moon overhead, the streaks of eye-catching emerald flecking the pelt glimmering. His eyes glowed the same unearthly green as his mothers, and mine.

"You're a pain Flare. Come on, let's go home. Where are the girls?"

At the inquiry as to where his three sisters were Flare looked over his shoulder toward the front of the compound. I knew the question had been a stupid one, the three young female wolves had latched onto Hayley from the first day. She was their person and when they hadn't been allowed to accompany her when she left with Thea they had taken up watch at the front gate. The three of them, Hestia, Sol and Luna hadn't moved from their post since the gates had closed behind Hayley three days earlier. I shook my head as I continued toward the house, Flare and Ember falling into step with me.

"I'll take them some food later and make sure they're doing okay."

The comment was as much for Ember as for myself. I could tell the anxious mother wolf was worrying about her daughters, grown up enough to take care of themselves or not. She hefted out a sigh, bumped her shoulder against me as we walked and then trotted ahead to play with Flare. Sometimes it still caught me off guard how human their actions and thought processes could be. I made my way across the porch of our house, stopping at the door and biting back the wave of emotions assaulting me.

"You can't avoid the place until she comes back. Just get in there and deal with it, Kai." I was talking to myself now, beautiful.

Flare padded up beside me and nudged me in the hip with his nose, letting out a soft whine as he did. I knew he could tell I wasn't thrilled about the prospect of walking into the place alone. I took a deep breath, squeezed my eyes closed and opened the door. I eased my eyes open as I stepped over the threshold and my breathing shuddered before I could get the flood under control. Everything spilled over as the familiar scents of the place surrounded me.

I forced it all back down, now was not the time to fall apart. It would have to wait until after I met with my section leaders, my Captains. As if on cue there was a knock on the door and I turned to answer it finding Luke, Steph, Bradley and Willow on the other side. I waved the foursome into the house and closed the door behind them before leading them into the living area. They settled into comfortable spots as I worked on getting a fire lit so we would have light, and a little warmth.

"Okay." I began once I had the fire going, brushing my hands off on my pants as I stood and turned to face them. "I'm pretty sure you're all wondering why I pulled you in here to chat in the middle of the night. Right?" Four heads nodded as I looked at them all, each one appearing a bit frazzled and in need of a few more hours of sleep.

"Definitely. I'm dead on my feet, Kai."

"I know Luke, and I am sorry for dragging you out of bed. I'm sure you've all noticed that I've been a bit out of sorts the last few days since Thea left with Hayley." Four more nods but none of them commented, which I was thankful for. "I won't lie to you, most of that is just me missing Hayley and not handling her absence well. The rest, that's a different creature completely. Thea exposed a huge fault in our system, our habits and it scared me. As little as she actually leaves her compound she was still able to learn so much about our usual methods, how long would it take a group of trained Purist scouts to do the same?"

"I wondered the same thing." I glanced at Willow and gave her a small nod then leaned against the wall, arms folded across my chest.

"Why didn't you say something to me about it?"

"Honestly? I was giving you some time to process everything that happened. I was planning on giving you tonight and then approaching you tomorrow sometime."

"Glad to hear it. As the head of my gathering and supply teams I'll need you involved in this process more than anyone else."

"And what process is that?" I smiled at her, hoping she would be willing and able to implement some of the things I had in mind.

"We need to seriously rethink our entire system. Not just during this time of year but all of them. We spend most of the year with less than a month of supplies in storage and it was just made very clear that we could be cut off from restocking with as few as eight hundred men." Four nods once again and knowing they were following my thinking bolstered my confidence in the idea. "I intend to find a way to store more. I'd like us to have *at least* three months of supplies in this compound at any given time."

"Three months? Kai, that's a feat. None of the compounds can manage that I don't think. Even Thea." Bradley was right of course but I couldn't let that deter me.

"I know, but there has to be a way. I want us to put our heads together and figure it out. We can do this, the five of us working together."

CHAPTER THIRTY-THREE

OLD HAUNTS AND STRANGE MEMORIES

AN HOUR in the only headway we'd made was working out when we could meet over the next several weeks without taking too much away from the compound. My Captains were each needed in their daily roles and removing them for long periods of time wouldn't be wise. I had to work around their training schedules, meals and even sleep. It finally became obvious we could only meet late at night or very early in the morning. Each gave their opinion and we discovered not a single one of us wanted to be up before dawn.

The timing for our gatherings decided, we set to work figuring out what actually needed to be done to improve our situation. If we could triple our usual stores during every season we would be safer from the type of event Thea had tried to pull on us. I also had a few ideas skipping around my brain for ideas on how to be sure we could get in and out of the compound even when barricaded. I was certain we could find a way to dig a tunnel system to move to and from the woods which would be virtually impossible to detect from the wall.

With the times set for us to meet we were all too tired to begin any type of planning for the how of making it all work. All the details would have to wait until the following day, after we had each managed to get some decent sleep. I was fairly certain the others would be back in bed and sleeping soundly the minute they returned to their quarters. For me however the deep, peaceful slumber I so desperately needed was being elusive. I had expected it to be but it still left me agitated as I tossed and turned, unable to find any kind of position which felt right without the familiar body of my girlfriend beside me.

I laid in the room surrounded by silence and the scent of Hayley fighting off the depression threatening to take over again. I could keep it in check if there were people around but the minute I was alone it reared its ugly head. Before I could stop it a tear slipped down my cheek but I refused to acknowledge it by brushing it away. I'd already cried more since meeting her than I had in the previous ten years combined. Keeping everything locked away wasn't necessarily the best way to handle life but it was how I had operated for the last hundred years or so.

I growled at myself when several more tears slipped free then turned on my side and tugged over the handmade pillow Hayley used. I hugged it tight, burying my face in it and tried to think of anything other than where she might be, if she was safe. After reminding myself I was in the house alone and the nearest building housing other people was well over five hundred feet from the only window in the room I gave in. I dropped the defenses I'd been clinging to so valiantly and released all the pain I'd been holding back. I sobbed into the pillow, cleansing myself of all the worry, the pain and the insecurity I'd been feeling until I finally slipped into the beautiful emptiness of sleep.

The next day came quicker than I would have liked thanks to having wasted most of the night sulking and planning, then crying. I rolled over, putting my back to the window and the offending sunlight streaming through it. I covered my head with Hayley's hand-stuffed pillow but the action did little to allow me to get back to sleep since it only succeeded in washing me in her scent. I huffed, pulled the pillow away and sat up with a yawn. I shot a useless glare at the window before I slipped out of bed and rifled around the room for clothes that didn't smell like either horse or wolf.

The apparently absurd feat finally accomplished I left the house and made my way across the compound toward the stables. I stepped into the large structure and smiled when the smell of grass and horse wafted over to me. I'd always loved the smell of the stables, since the day I'd been given Prophecy and had to visit the building regularly. A real smile pulled at my lips for the first time in days and when it made guilt begin to surface I tamped it back down. I knew Hayley wouldn't want me feeling guilty about being happy while she was away.

The elation I'd been feeling was swept away when a familiar head appeared from a stall down the aisle. The forlorn whinny Genesis let out made my heart ache in my chest. The bond the two forged had been instant, strong and she missed the woman as much as I did I was sure. I walked down the wide aisle, my heart in my throat and my stomach lurching uncomfortably. I reached out and rubbed the silky nose snuffling at me and sighed. I knew she was hurting and not sure where her person had gone, it had been something I'd tried to fight Thea on when she refused to let Hayley take her horse.

"I know girl. I'd feel so much better if you and Luna were out there with her. At least then I'd know for sure she was safe."

I regretted my decision to keep the wolves a secret from the other Generals now, after the fact. If I'd told them about the five canines everything could be different. If I'd only let them see the bond we'd formed with them and how we interacted Hayley might have protection out there. Instead she was relying on Thea and her soldiers to provide her with the safety and security she was used to inside the compound. I wasn't so sure I trusted Thea enough to be okay with it all, as a matter of fact, I knew I didn't.

Maybe Steph had a point and I should work toward being more open, more honest with the other three women. The worst I could imagine coming out of it would be to end up being thought of as weak or too willing to give in to the demands of those under my protection. At best we might find a better way to interact, be stronger and better able to protect ourselves and our people. I scratched Genesis under her chin and made up my mind. Once we had our new plans made and underway and Hayley was back home safe I'd attempt to open up lines of communication with Thea, Trista and Lila.

It wouldn't be easy; I'd never been the sharing type. It had taken Laney years to get me to open up and it had been her insistence which had forced me to drop my walls around Steph. They had been the only two I trusted completely; until Hayley came into my life. I sighed with a shake of my head. It seemed no matter what I attempted to think about my mind always drifted back to her. I missed her more than anyone would ever guess and I took a few minutes to marvel at how deeply she had wormed her way into my activities.

I shook myself out of the thoughts threatening to drag me under, slid the lock on the stall to let Genesis out then walked back toward the entrance and let Prophecy join her. They stood in the doorway framed by golden rays of sunlight and watched me with an intensity which might have unnerved me if I hadn't been dealing with it for so many decades. I managed to smile at the two horses and give them a wave. Obviously it was enough to convince them I would be okay since they turned and trotted out of the stable to get up to whatever horses do in their spare time. I lingered in the aisle staring out the doors until a hand on my shoulder pulled me from my thoughts.

I nearly jumped out of my boots before looking over and seeing Faith standing beside me with a sheepish smile on her face. She ducked her head slightly as she said, "Sorry, Kai, I didn't mean to sneak up on you."

"You really didn't. I was just lost in my head again. Seems to be happening more often lately." She nodded as she removed her hand from my shoulder then ran it through her hair. I thought for a moment before asking her, "What are you doing out here?"

"Oh, ummm."

"Its fine that you're here Faith, I just didn't know you'd been coming out to the stables."

"Okay well, Hayley brought me out here a few days ago to meet the horses. Dirge kinda attached himself to me."

I gave her a big smile as a chuckle slipped free from her and I laughed. "Oh boy. He's a fireball, that one. Keep an eye on him if he's picked you as his rider." She looked shocked at first and I wondered if she thought I'd be angry at her bonding with one of the horses. The sound of his name being spoken drew the horse to stick his head over the top of his stall door. I leaned over and kissed him on the side of his nose which caused him to snort and toss his head. I glanced back toward Faith finding her looking less shocked, the expression slowly replaced by a bright smile which lit up her young face.

"So you don't mind if I learn to ride?"

"Of course not. Most of the scouts and gatherers are terrified of the horses because they're so big. We even have trouble getting a decent number of the guards and soldiers on them so the more people we have who ride, the better."

"Oh good. Hayley said you wouldn't mind but I was still worried." I chuckled at her again as I shook my head.

"You know what? Hayley knows me pretty well so if she tells you I'll be fine with something; I probably will be." She nodded then turned toward the door when someone called her name and we watched as her mother appeared in the open doorway.

"Oh there you are. I figured this is where you'd be, you're already attached to that horse. Sorry if she bothered you, General."

"Not at all and I've mentioned before, please call me Kai."

Andrea nodded, Faith waved at me and I returned the gesture as she joined her mother and they left together. I decided I needed a walk around the compound before my evening meeting with my Captains so I left the stable. The next few hours were spent exploring parts of the compound I hadn't personally been into for years. Small, private nooks I had once used to escape when we'd first settled the area so I could think and plan without interruption. Now those same spots seemed small, dark and isolated rather than the inspiring crannies I remembered them as.

I turned away from the last of the dark hideouts with a shake of my head and a light chuckle then turned myself toward the house. I still didn't feel quite right going to the place I'd come to think of as home without the one person who had made it feel like one in the first place. The thought was still in the front of my mind as I stepped onto the porch. I couldn't wait until Hayley was back and I didn't have to walk through the front door alone any longer. For the moment I didn't have a choice so I pushed it open and made my way into the living room where I'd be meeting my Captains in a short time.

I crossed the room and worked on getting a fire started, sometimes it could take a few tries. I wanted the room to be a bearable temperature when the others showed up. I could admit to myself when no one else was around that I had been keeping the place somewhat drafty. Shivering had been helping me ignore the loneliness I'd been working on waiting out. I had completely forgotten what it was like to be in a relationship, have someone I didn't want to be without. Now it had all come back to me and it was threatening to tear me apart if I didn't get her back soon.

I smiled to myself as I remembered the days before the event, a time when we would have called this thing Hayley and I were doing dating. Back then she would have been called my girlfriend, I still liked the sound of it even if few people used it anymore and had taken to calling her such. She seemed to like it as much as I did or at least hadn't bothered asking me to stop using it. There were so few of us left we tended to settle down with whoever irritated us the least early in life.

Things were so different now, relationships weren't like they used to be before hell rained down on us. Back then we had time choices, plenty of other people to pick from for our mates, the ones we would spend the rest of our lives with. These days there were so few people left, not to mention the rift between the two separate types of humanity so finding a totally compatible mate could be difficult. Things were uncertain and lifespans were variable among our side to say the least so we made the best of the time we had.

The fallout of this type of situation, the kinds of everyday perils we came across and the lack of decent numbers in the population meant we took whatever we could get and fast. We went from friends to married with children, well some with children, in what felt like days sometimes. It was the best way to do things since the odd of meeting someone you could really connect with were slim for most people. I almost felt bad for having been given the opportunity twice; almost. I shook my head at the thought as the fire caught, blazing and crackling as I stood and crossed the room to my usual seat to wait.

CHAPTER THIRTY-FOUR

NOT SO URBAN PLANNING

ONCE WE were all gathered in the living area of the small house I took a minute to compose myself, using the time to study each of the people present. I trusted each of them with my life and with the lives of every resident living within the walls of the compound. I smiled to myself at the thought, knowing we might not always get along but if it came down to the wire, they'd have my back, no matter what. I let them chat and joke for a bit longer once I'd taken in my fill of looking them each over. After a bit I cleared my throat to get their attention then pushed to my feet and began.

"Okay guys, we know we need to put our heads together and come up with a few ways to keep more food inside the walls. That said, Luke?" He focused on me and I braced my hands on my hips as I asked, "How long do you think it would take a group of your guys to put up a solid plank fence around some of the wooded land at the back of the compound?"

"Not sure, would depend on how big you wanted the space and how many of my guys you want me to use. Why?"

"We'd need something pretty big, I'm thinking that bringing a big herd of deer or two inside the compound and keeping them in a large fenced area near the back might be a good idea."

"Sounds like a plan. I think we could have a couple decently sized pens put together in a couple months if I use about half my guys." I nodded, about to tell him to go for it when he added, "But can I suggest putting up four or five instead of only two?"

"Possibly. For what reason?"

"If you're planning on bringing deer in, why not use those wolves of yours to herd in some of the wild boar in the area. They breed like rabbits and they're pretty good eating if you ask me."

"Perfect. Go for it."

"And while we're on that thought, speaking of rabbits." I grinned at him and he chuckled with a small shrug. "Hey, they breed fast and are great for stews."

"I agree. Okay, so your men, as many as you can pull and still keep the walls guarded, are on making those pens. The quicker they're ready the sooner we get animals in them. Now, that gives us the crops we grow in the spring and summer, deer, boars and rabbits inside the compound. Any other ideas?"

I caught the grin on Willow's face just before she said, "What if we find a way to bring some fish inside the walls. There's close to a dozen huge buildings at the back of the compound still in decent condition. We haven't even given them a second look as far as I know since they aren't living spaces."

"Good point. They're all across the river in that little valley near the outer wall. We should head out there tomorrow and check them out Willow. Steph, you and Bradley should come with us. Luke, get your guys started on those pens first thing." They each nodded at me and I grinned at the ideas we were managing to come up with. "Okay, any other ideas anyone?"

"Well, we all know I'll vote for bringing some turkey inside the walls, suckers are tasty." I laughed at Steph with a shake of my head and turned to Luke.

"All right, so add on a turkey pen to that list. Try to get at least one pen per animal done in the first run. I'd like to start bringing them in and getting them settled before the weather changes."

He nodded as he responded, "Yes ma'am. We'll start with the boar pen. They'll need the most space and it'll take your wolves some time to get them into it while we work on the others."

"Perfect. Okay, I think if we can find somewhere to keep some fish year round we might actually be set." I'd had an idea bouncing around in my head for a better part of the day and I decided it was better out now than later. "I had a thought earlier today. I hate that over and above the fact Thea caught us without enough food inside the walls, she would have been able to keep us in indefinitely with so few soldiers. It scared me. There has to be a way to get some tunnels under the walls and out into the woods.

Concealing them outside will be easy enough, we'll have to brainstorm covering them up on this side. It'll probably take some scouting and talking it over to work it out so we can save it for later. For the time being, let's get some rest and then meet back here in the morning. Except Luke, he has planning and building to do."

We went our separate ways for the night with plans and ideas for the next day. As soon as Luke and his men had the first boar pen finished I would send the wolves out to bring a herd back. I kicked the door closed once everyone had filed out and made my way down the hall to the bedroom. It had been almost a week since Hayley had left with Thea. Being in the room without her at night was still hard but I was making the best of it. Steph was right, she would be back soon enough and then she never had to leave again.

I woke with a jolt the next morning as someone sat on my back and I reached back to swipe at them, getting a laugh in response. The weight lifted off of me so I could turn over and once I was on my back I glared up at Steph. She stood there, flashing her usual obnoxious grin at me and I had the urge to throw something at her. So I did. The feather-filled lump hit her in the face and started a pillow fight which lasted until a sharp knock sounded against the door frame.

We stopped in an instant, both turning to look at the door and breaking into laughter at the look on Bradley's face. He seemed stuck somewhere between stunned and horrified and it couldn't have been more comical. I yanked the second pillow out of Steph's hand, smacked her with both before I dropped them on the bed then gathered my clothes. Once I was dressed I led the two out onto the front porch where Willow was waiting for us. The grin she wore told me she had sent him inside on purpose and I had to applaud her devious streak.

"Everyone ready?"

Three nods greeted me in answer so I led the way to the stable. We weren't about to walk to the back of the compound. It would take us all day to reach the river on foot thanks to the overgrowth which had taken back the parts we rarely used. From what I remembered of the place back before the event, it had been some type of spiritual retreat. A place for people to come and rest, relax, get away from their everyday lives for a while. Some people stayed a day or two, some for weeks and others lived in the retreat year round, working the land and seeking truth.

It was this original use which left the compound offering housing, working farmland and the stables we still used. It had been free of plumbing, electricity and the like back before those things ceased to exist. I opened the door of the stable as my mind wrestled free of those days, the ones before all hell broke loose. I was needed in the present, the here and now so I needed to focus so we could make some progress. I knew there were something along the lines of eleven buildings at the far end of the compound we hadn't bothered digging through. Now I found myself hoping they would yield something of use to us, something to help keep us alive.

We saddled up the horses, Prophecy prancing around like he hadn't been out in days which I realized in the moment, he hadn't. I'd been so wrapped up in my pain, my heartache over Hayley's departure I'd forgotten all about taking him out. I would have to make it up to him over the next few days, remind him I still cared before he took it personally. Bradley saddled his stallion Javelin, Steph worked a bridle onto her mare Keeper and Willow got her gelding Hercules tacked up. We'd always picked on her for the name she'd given the little guy since he was, in fact, the smallest horse in the stable.

Once we had the horses tacked and had mounted up we left the building and turned the beasts toward the path we would have to take. I doubted it would still be clear after so many years without use but we would only find out if we tried. We made it through close to fifty acres, almost halfway before the path became overgrown and hard to pass. Undaunted, the horses pressed on, crashing through the brush as if it wasn't there. We came up the river, finding it still swollen with the spring melt runoff but not as bad as it could have been.

Thankfully it barely qualified as a river most of the year, only becoming big enough to worry about during the spring. We trudged down alongside it until we found a place where it widened out and the flow slowed to a crawl. After wading the horses in and across we worked our way slowly down the slope on the other side toward the first of the buildings. It was a tall thing, looking much like another stable or possibly a barn of some kind. We broke the rusted padlock off the door so we could push our way inside and what we found made me grin from ear to ear.

I knew the minute I laid eyes on the contents of the barn we would be able to take some work off Luke and his men. The small structures the larger building housed were ones I had seen before and knew well as chicken coops. We hadn't seen many chickens in the last hundred years since they didn't survive mutation well but I did know they could make great housing for rabbits. With a little care, cleaning and repair they could be ready for use in a matter of days. Near the back were several other types of cages I didn't recognize.

Willow stepped up beside me, a grin on her face and pointed to one of them as she said, "Squirrel cages. I never saw one in person but my grandpa had pictures of them from the farm he grew up on. Showed them to me dozens of times when I was little."

"Squirrels, huh? Sounds promising." I grinned as I decided to have Luke figure out how to get them fixed up as well. I wasn't about to argue with yet another possibility for food given our situation. "This is a great start, hopefully the rest will prove just as useful." The others nodded then followed me out of the building and on to the second one.

The next structure turned out to be an old storage barn, falling apart at the seams and unusable for anything other than spare lumber. We left it and headed for the third, having seen the low, long structure from the hill. It was somewhere around eighty feet from one end to the other, a good sized building and appeared to be built of stone or something like it. It was narrower side to side but it still spanned something close to thirty feet.

The roofline towered over us, standing nearly twenty-five feet up and I stared at it as I dismounted to try the doors. There were two of the massive, fifteen-foot-tall things with the latch set in the middle. I worked it free of the layer of rust attempting to hold it in place then yanked it loose. Once it fell away the doors swung open rather easily and I stood out of the way as one swept out and the other in. We stepped inside, letting our eyes adjust to the dim lighting before we moved through the entry area. Once we stepped into the main room of the building I was stunned with what I saw, what we had found.

High set windows let a flood of natural light into the space, making it bright and well lit. The center of the room held a dropped area which almost appeared as if it had been scooped out. It looked to me like the pools the recreation center had when I was a kid. My brain kicked into high gear as I registered what it might be and I scanned the room intently. There, to one side was a pipe coming from the wall, a crank set onto it and I almost jumped for joy as I prayed it would still work.

I made my way over to it and grabbed the handle on the crank, finding the screw mechanism it was held by rusted and refusing to budge. I fought with it for a minute before I waved Bradley over to help me. The look on his face told me he had no clue what he was looking at and as the others joined us they looked similarly confused. I chuckled at them, showed Bradley what needed to happen and then explained.

"It's a gravity pump. I'd be willing to bet this pipe is connected to the river up there. We open this valve and the water will run down and fill this pool here."

"Okay..." Steph gave me a weird look as she glanced at Willow then back to me and continued, "And how do we keep it full without overflowing and without having someone up here day in and day out watching it?" It was a good question but I had the feeling I knew the answer.

"There's probably..." I paused and looked around the edge of the pool, my eyes lighting up when I found what I was looking for. "There!" I hopped into the massive dropped area and walked to the opposite corner from the pipe, pointing to a small opening near the bottom. It was round, just over half the size of the fill pipe and had a mesh cover over it which showed a very minimal amount of rust. "That's the drain. I'd be willing to bet this one runs down under the back wall and dumps back into the river where it curves around the compound."

"So it continually circulates?"

I nodded at Willow and reached a hand up to have her pull me out as Bradley fought the valve free. As he raised the block, cold water spilled through the pipe, filling the pool in a steady stream. It would probably take all day to fill, it was massive. If I had to guess, I would assume at least as long as that old swimming pool from the rec center. It was sixty feet long, at least twenty wide and I estimated around eight feet deep since the edge was well over my head.

"Leave the valve open, we'll finish checking this building out then move on and let this fill up."

We moved on through the space, finding strange alcoves set into the walls at equal intervals and it took me ten of them to figure out what they were. The floor of the tenth was visible and the blackened area of stone under the layer of dirt gave away its purpose.

"Fire pits. They're fire pits to keep it warm in here so the pond won't freeze in the winter." Steph, Willow and Bradley agreed with the assessment and we left the building in high spirits. "We couldn't have asked for a better find. It means we'll have to send some of your workers up here in rotations year round to keep the fires going and make sure it doesn't drain too fast but I think we can handle that."

"I agree." She said with a nod as we mounted back up on the horses to check the other buildings. "Besides, I can think of several of my people who would jump at the chance to come stay out here and take care of these things. This and the rabbit barn."

"Good, then once they're ready to go we'll work on a rotation and who to put in it." She grinned as we turned the horses toward the next building, excited to see what else we would find.

The rest of the buildings made me wish we had thought to explore them earlier. Two more barns we could adjust and repair for small animals. One set up for birds which would make a perfect place for Steph's turkeys and another pond building. The last four were in terrible condition overall but had some bits and pieces we could use for repairs and new buildings. I would have Luke and his men raid them for extra lumber and such then flatten what was left.

Overall it had been a productive day and I was feeling better and better about our chances of keeping ourselves fed in the future. The things we'd aimed to get finished dealt with we headed back toward the part of the compound we already used. We chatted about the possibilities for the tunnels as we rode, trying to decide how to go about digging them and where to even put them.

"You know," Steph said after a few minutes of silence, "I think they'll be easy enough to get started if we pick unusual places to place them. I know there's a weird dirt patch on the back side of the training arena in the stable. It never gets used, is big enough to hold four or five people and is concealed unless you know it's there."

"She's right!" Willow piped up excitedly, her face lighting up as she fought to keep from bouncing in her saddle. "I've been back there several times getting things this brat tossed over the wall while I wasn't looking." She gave Hercules an affectionate pat to soften the blow of calling him names. I grinned when he huffed and tossed his head at her.

"Yeah I know the spot." I was picturing it in my mind as we spoke about it and I knew it would be the perfect place to put one of the tunnels. "I think that's a good place for the first. There's a similar type space in the new meeting area and in the archery barn. That's three already. I think we need at least seven or eight and we'll have to head out into the woods to find places for them to emerge that aren't easy to stumble across." Three nods met my words and then silence fell over the group as we tried to come up with more places to put the entrances.

By the time we made it back to the stable the sun was low in the sky, the day had faded away around us but we had a full set of plans to run with. We got the tack off the horses, brushed them out and then turned them all loose to graze for the night.

I watched the four of them run off into the open space to the side of the building and laughed as they sprinted around and played. Sometimes I wondered what they were thinking, wishing they could speak so we could know what was on their minds. I knew Prophecy would have some crazy things going on in that head of his so I could only imagine some of the others.

I glanced over to the open door of the stable to find Genesis standing there alone, watching the others frolic. Her head hung low, her ears tilted back and she looked about as defeated as I'd been feeling the last few days. I sighed as I turned and walked over to her, knowing there wasn't much I could do to make her feel better but needing to try anyway. I reached up and ran my hand up her to the middle of her forehead and she let out a heavy huff.

"I know girl. I miss her too but she'll be back. Eventually..." She seemed to understand I was feeling as down as she was about Hayley's absence. She moved to drape her head over my shoulder, nickering softly in my ear. It felt like she was hugging me and I realized she was doing exactly that, giving me a horse hug. The thought made me smile a bit as I reached up and wrapped my arms around her neck, giving her a squeeze.

"It'll be okay Genesis. I promise, even if I have to walk to Thea's compound in three weeks and bring her back myself, it'll be fine. All right?" She gave me a toss of her head which approximated a nod in horse language then took a step back, turned her head and perked her ears toward the other horses. "Hey, go play. She would want you too, we can't stay depressed the entire time she's gone. That would just be pathetic, eh?" She tossed her head again, taking my words as all the permission she needed. She tore off across the empty space between the stable and the other animals, brushing past Prophecy in a flurry of speed.

He whinnied, reared up on his hind legs then tore off after her, leaving a cloud of dust and a very confused Javelin behind him. I laughed as I watched he and Genesis nip and hip check each other. They had bonded more in the last few months even though I'd been sure they were as close as possible before. I also couldn't help but notice the slight curve of extra weight Genesis had put on. If we were lucky, we would be welcoming the first ever Level Four mutation foal born into our world within the year. The prospect was exciting and I could only hope I wasn't seeing things.

I shook my head with a heavy sigh then turned away from the playing creatures. As much as I would love to stay and watch them all evening, I had other things to attend to. I made my way to the front of the compound, seeking out Luke, anticipating telling him everything we had found. Unless Steph had found him first, she had a big mouth and loved stealing my chances at big news, it was her favorite pastime. I grinned as thoughts of my friends flickered through my mind. I was glad to have them and I wasn't sure what kind of mess I would be without them to keep me from spiraling out of control.

CHAPTER THIRTY-FIVE

MAKING PLANS

AFTER FINDING Luke and discovering Steph had yet to tell him my wonderful news, I filled him in on the things we had found over the course of the day. He was as excited as we had been at the prospect of less work with better results. We grabbed some food and made our way to the back wall, leaning against it and waiting for the rest of the Captains to join us. Once they were all present I decided we needed more solid planning for the tunnel system I had now decided absolutely had to be implemented.

"Okay guys, we need to get these tunnels started. It'll take months to dig them and if we get caught in the middle of the task when the first freeze hits we'll be out of luck. So, we have the starting points picked. Ten in total, now we need to scout the woods and find places to end them. Here..." I grabbed a short stick I'd been carrying around with me then leaned forward. I began drawing a rough approximation of the side of the compound we used regularly. Once I had the walls worked out I plotted out the general spots we would be putting the tunnel entrances.

We sat and looked at the dirt for a few minutes, each one of us studying the diagram with an intensity which spoke volumes. We had varying talents, trades and understandings we could apply to placing the pathways. In the end it was Willow who set one up first, grabbing the stick from my hand and tracing a line through the brown surface. "I think the line I drew leads into that small clearing where the river does the switchback." I nodded at her estimation, she was right, if it wasn't in the clearing it would be damn close.

"Perfect place. It's easy to get lost in that part of the woods if you don't know the area so it's unlikely anyone would be back there to stumble on the exit by accident. Great work Willow."

"Thank you. The others should be easy enough to hide once we can get out there and start looking around. We're just so close to the situation it's hard to come up with places we think are hidden."

I grinned and nodded because she was right. These woods were home to us, nothing seemed hidden or secret, none of the area felt unexplored or dangerous they were simply our woods. Once we could get out there on foot, or horseback and begin actively looking for places to end these tunnels we would see things differently. I leaned back against the wall once more, crossed my arms over my chest and flashed a smile at the small group seated around me.

"You've all been great the last few days. I want you to know how much I appreciate each and every one of you and the things you do for me, for everyone here. We'll set out tomorrow and start scouting for places to put the rest of those tunnel exits. I want them planned and the digging started within the next three days. We have to get on this right away if we plan to have them dug, cleared, reinforced and passable before winter descends on us again."

They all nodded their understanding then we went back to our dinner, falling into comfortable silence once again. I knew I could count on every one of them to get the job I needed them to do done. I didn't have to worry or stare them down. Everything would pan out and by the time winter hit once more, we would be safe from Thea's scare tactics. I couldn't wait to have it all completed, knowing I'd done anything to put my people at risk left an ache in my system I couldn't shake. I had to protect them, no matter what it cost me to do so.

Kai's Journal - Summer Cycle, 2607 – 221 years after the event:
Not much to report today, well, I guess that's a lie. We found some buildings we can use and we're beginning preparations to use the ones we can reform then tear down and repurpose the ones we can't salvage. The next step is to find places for these damn escape and gathering tunnels to come up out in the woods. That's a problem for a time when I'm not sitting in the dark alone about to pass out from lack of sleep. As hard as it's been

to settle myself and get any real rest with Hayley gone I have to push the issue and get by until she's home again.

The next day began bright and early even though I had no desire to get up and moving. I was exhausted from tossing and turning all night since I was still having trouble getting a decent night of sleep. I forced myself to roll out of bed, grumbling as I pushed to my feet and stretched my arms up over my head. My back popped as my knees protested the treatment. Everything was sore and I was about to make it even worse. With a huff I tugged on clothes and left the house, heading for the stable to meet a scouting team Bradley was supposed to be hand-picking for our task.

I dropped the hand I had up to shield my eyes as I stepped into the building, finding a group of eight milling about the entry. I grinned and placed a friendly slap on Bradley's shoulder as I walked by, grabbing his attention. I moved into the middle of the small group, taking stock of how many we had who weren't scared of the horses. I saw three we could put on horseback and send a bit further out which would keep Willow, Bradley and myself from having to do the furthest searches. I waited for them to realize I'd arrived and the eventual hush which fell over the group.

"Okay everyone. I'm sure Bradley already explained what we're up to out there today." Nods from each were my response so I continued. "Good, here's what I want to do. The three of you I know are trained for riding, go get your horses tacked up and meet us back up here in a few minutes. Your orders will be slightly different and we'll get into them once we're mounted up and ready to leave." The three I'd mentioned departed without a word to do as I'd instructed.

I turned my attention back to the rest of the group gathered and gave them a quick once over. I knew each of them well and trusted them to do what was asked of them and keep the secrets of what was being implemented if ever captured. "The rest of you. I'll assign grids to each of you. We need each and every one of you to find a safe, secure and fairly hidden area to put the exits for these tunnels. They need to be difficult to find, we don't want them easily stumbled upon by Purist scouts." I waved them in closer, handing each a hand drawn map of a section of wood outside the compound.

"Those of you not on horses will be checking the areas closest to the walls. While we want several of the exits as far out as we feel comfortable digging before winter, having a handful closer won't hurt. You each hold a map I've drawn of a various section of woods. Search it, find somewhere we can bring these tunnels up and take your map with the location marked to Luke. Remember that we can't cross the river easily so if you choose an area across it, make sure you come talk to me before taking your location to Luke so I can approve it. Understood?" They all nodded, glancing at each other then back to me and I gave one short nod in reply.

"Good, head out, you have the day, if you need longer we can send you back out tomorrow but I kept the areas to a decent size you should be able to search easily in a single day. Meet back here at sunset and we'll make sure no one needs that approval I talked about." They all turned and exited the building leaving me standing there with Bradley and Willow. I turned to look at my Captains with a smile on my face.

"You look happy, but tired." I nodded at Willow's remark, feeling every hour of sleep I'd lost the last few days.

"I'm drained. I can't seem to get any decent sleep without Hayley next to me." Bradley gave me a sad, knowing smile then glanced at his wife. I knew they understood my predicament. If anything ever happened to one of them the other would be completely lost. I could tell neither of them was sure what to say so I waved the whole thing off as I said, "No time to dwell on it though. We have things to get done." They nodded and I was sure they were glad for the reprieve from my weird emotional states.

We were saved from any further need for small talk when the three scouts I'd sent for their horses reappeared. Their mounts were saddled and ready to go which meant we were running behind and needed to catch up. "Just give us a few minutes to tack our horses and we'll head out. Wait for us outside, mount up and get your horses warmed up and ready for a day out in the woods." They each nodded then led their animals out into the field beside the barn to get them walking.

I moved to Prophecy's stall, nuzzling him as I stepped in to check him over. I'd been neglecting his exercise lately and he was looking a little bored, and maybe a bit chubby. He bumped my shoulder with his nose and I chuckled as I swatted at him. "Stop it you, we have serious things to take care of today." As usual he seemed to understand perfectly, his demeanor switching instantly as he dropped his head a few inches so I could slide his bridle on. Once I had him tacked up I made my way outside to find Bradley and Willow already waiting with the scouts.

"All right. We'll be working in pairs today since we're heading a bit further away from the compound than I'm comfortable with any of you venturing alone. Kyle you're with Willow, Greg with Bradley and Greer..." The woman gave me a small, sheepish grin and I knew she was wondering if this was further punishment for her slip up months ago. She was almost finished with her second round of training and while she didn't know it, I was well over her mistake. I knew she had learned her lesson and wouldn't be repeating it in the future. "You're with me." She nodded as she patted her horse on the neck, a move I recognized for what it was, a nervous twitch.

The two Captains and I mounted up and the six of us heeled our horses toward the gates. Once we were outside I pulled ahead of the small contingent, turned Prophecy to face them and held up a hand. "Okay, your Captains know where I want you searching. Stick with them, follow their commands. I don't want anyone out of their scouting partners eye line for any reason. We don't know when or where we'll encounter Purists as far out as we're headed and I'm not taking any chances. Everyone have their bows?"

Five nods met my question, each of them raising their weapon so I could see them. "Good. Plenty of arrows?" Five quivers, each filled to capacity without being jammed rose into my line of sight and I nodded my approval. "We're set then. Bradley, Willow?" They both met my gaze when I looked at them in turn and I finished with, "Take care of them, I expect to see you all at sundown."

"We'll all be here, General." I gave Bradley a warm smile, followed it with a sharp nod then turned Prophecy and waved them on their way.

"Come on, Greer, let's get this party started." She nodded but heeled her horse to follow without a word. I knew I needed to talk to her, make sure she understood I wasn't still upset with her. It was for that very reason I had chosen to pair up with her myself, it would give us a chance to chat. We rode in silence for several minutes before I cleared my throat and looked over at her. "Vega is looking well." I gestured toward her big chestnut mare and she grinned at the comment.

"She's doing wonderfully. I admit when you sent me back through training I didn't expect to end up on a horse. I'd never given it a thought the first time through." She leaned forward in her saddle and patted the mare on the side of her neck earning her a happy whicker in response.

"Well I'm glad you managed to bond with her. The more people we have on horseback the better off we are."

"I can understand that." She let out a soft, nervous chuckle as she leaned back into place on her saddle. She cleared her throat, her gaze fixed on the forest in front of us as she said, "Look, General, I..."

"Greer, wait. Before you say anything I feel like I should tell you something."

"What?" The word was spoken hesitantly as she shifted her gaze over onto me. I could feel the nervous energy rolling off the poor girl.

"Relax. I just wanted to tell you that I'm not mad at you. I never really was. I felt like I had failed because I obviously hadn't made my training as clear as I should have. You're back in because I needed time to adjust the program and send someone who had already been through it back in for a second round. You messed up, yes but that's to be expected. No one is perfect. I'm not the type to hold a grudge." She exhaled loudly, her shoulders slumping and she looked like I had removed the weight of the world from her back.

"Thanks for that. I've spent the last few months worried that I really mucked up and pissed you off. Though, I'm glad to have gone back through training. It means I got to meet Vega here." She grinned down at her horse, the mare responding to her words by tossing her head and giving us some horse chatter. We both chuckled at her before looking at each other once again.

"Sorry I didn't tell you sooner. I've been a little preoccupied lately."

"So I noticed." I caught a glimpse of her smirk out of the corner of my eye as she added, "If you have to be completely distracted, you picked a distraction that's easy on the eyes at least."

I laughed outright as I said, "And I'll make sure I tell her you said so!" She paled, her eyes going wide and I couldn't stop the snort which tumbled free at the expression. "Settle down, she'll think it's funny."

"If you say so." I nodded in affirmation and we settled into a steady pace toward our destination in the woods. The conversation remained light, even teasing at times and I finally got to know Greer as a person for the first time.

CHAPTER THIRTY-SIX

BAD NEWS

WITH THE search of the woods behind us and spots chosen for every one of the tunnels we would be digging to exit I was ready to drop. I shuffled into the house, not feeling lost and depressed to be in it alone for the first time. I was too damn ragged to feel anything other than the need for my pillow. I dragged myself down the hall and into the bedroom, kicking my boots off as I crossed the room. I fell onto the bed without bothering to take any of my clothes off, I smelled like horse and dirt and I doubted I could have cared any less. I mustered enough energy to drag Hayley's pillow over, pulling it half under me and burying my face in it as I slipped into the blissful darkness of sleep.

Kai's Journal - Summer Cycle, 2607 – 221 years after the event:
I'm thrilled to report that we made great progress through the afternoon. Spots have been picked and construction within the walls is underway. With any luck we'll be set up with new food supplies and routes in and out of the compound before winter hits again. I'm doing everything I can to find things to occupy my time and keep my mind off worrying. Next step is, well, I'm really not sure but I'll figure something out. For now, something resembling sleep so I can attempt to function tomorrow.

When I woke the next morning I was thankful all over again

for the rapid healing we possessed. It meant all the scrapes, bruises and muscle pulls I'd acquired the day before had healed while I was asleep. I rolled onto my back, stretched and then looked over at the window. The dingy gray light filtering into the room told me it was cloudy out and the soft rumble in the distance meant a storm was approaching. I rolled out of bed, swapped out my clothes for ones not covered in forest grime and yanked on my boots before leaving the house.

Sure enough, the minute I stepped off the porch a raindrop hit me in the forehead. I turned my face up to the sky and blinked as several more droplets landed on my face. We could use the rain but I was glad we'd had a clear day to search the woods before this storm rolled in. I returned my gaze to the landscape, let out a yawn then stretched again, still trying to finish waking up. I linked my fingers behind my head and tried to make a list of the things I needed to do over the course of the day. The first on my list was to head out and check on the progress Luke and his team had made the day before.

I got my bearings, turned in the right direction and dropped my hands to my sides as I started walking. I wasn't in any kind of hurry, not having much I could do on other tasks until the rain let up. I was a few feet past the stable when a sharp whistle cut through the air, grabbing my attention. I spun on my heel to find Steph running toward me so I paused and let her catch up.

"What?"

"Kai, its Hayley."

"She's back?"

"Umm, no... She's uh... There's been... She..." I raised a brow at the hesitant stammer she seemed to have developed. She was making me nervous which had chased away the last of any tiredness which had been lingering.

"Steph, spit it out, she what?"

"She's missing."

"She's what? How?" I could feel the rush of heat as my temper flared but I held it back, whatever had happened wasn't Steph's fault. With the anger stifled, fear swept in to take its place, leaving a cold shiver racing up my spine.

"We just got a runner from Thea, they were ambushed on the way back to her compound. Seven of her scouts and two soldiers were killed, twelve total wounded and they took Hayley."

I set my jaw, pushed past her and made my way toward the

front of the compound as the rain began to come down in sheets. I ignored the fact I was getting soaked, I wanted some answers. I barked out a harsh 'move it!' when I reached the gathered crowd of people near the gates. They parted when they heard my voice and I stepped right up to the panicked looking runner they'd been surrounding. I must have looked as irate and panicked as I felt because the second he turned his gaze on me he shrank away. He backed up three steps and ducked his head, looking at his feet.

"What happened?" I did my best to not growl the words out at the poor kid, it wasn't his fault either but I was having trouble maintaining my composure.

"We were ambushed, General. I don't know how many, it was hard to tell in the chaos but there were at least seven I saw. Purist soldiers."

"Seven? Only seven and they got the jump on you with all those soldiers around?"

"Ummm, not really. The General sent most of the soldiers on ahead after we left. She only kept four with us for the trip back."

"She what?"

I seethed, wanting nothing more than to go find Thea and rip her a new one for her error, or rather errors, multiple. She had promised me Hayley would be safe and now she was in the hands of the people she had turned her back on. A prickle worked over my skin as I tried and failed to suppress the thoughts creeping up on me. What if they had discovered what she'd told me? What if they knew about our relationship? Either one of those things could land her locked up, or dead.

I fought back the wave of nausea the thoughts threatened to bring with them and took a deep breath. I turned toward Steph and found Luke standing beside her. After scanning the crowd and finding a handful of the guards I trusted present I focused on my second again.

"Luke, I need you here supervising the new construction but I need a handful of guards."

"For?" He had one brow raised at me in question but the expression on his face told me he knew what I was up to, he just wanted me to say it.

"They have Hayley; they aren't keeping her. I'm going to get her back. But first, I'm paying Thea a visit." He winced and I knew deep down he was glad he would be skipping this mission.

"Okay. I'll round up a few for you. I won't let you leave with less than ten though." His concern was painted across his features and it managed to cool my temper a few degrees.

"I'm fine with that. Actually, if you could, make it more like twenty, I don't trust that we won't be ambushed as well." He nodded and went to gather what I knew would be his most trusted guards to travel with me. "Greer?" I had seen the young woman's face in the crowd and made a split second decision to take her with me. After the ground we'd gained the day before I felt comfortable returning her to the daily tasks she was used to performing.

"Yes, General?"

"Get together a group of nine scouts who are good with a bow and can ride. Meet me at the stable as soon as you can."

"Umm, yes, right away, General." She seemed confused for a minute but then gave me a small grin before she turned and ran off to do as I'd instructed. I watched her leave, did an about face and made my way back toward the house. I needed a few things if I was heading out to confront Thea and god knew how many Purists. Steph caught up with me halfway there and fell into step beside me.

"This is suicide, Kai."

"No it isn't. It won't be easy but what in life worth doing is?"

"Fine. But I'm going with you." I stopped and turned to face her as I shook my head.

"No, Steph, you can't. I need you here. You, Bradley, Luke and Willow know what I'm trying to accomplish here. I need every one of you working on the issue while I'm gone. I expect some major steps in the right direction when I get back."

"You really think I'm just going to step back and let you go out there without me?"

"Yes."

"And why would I do that?" She crossed her arms over her chest defiantly and I mirrored the action.

"Because despite the fact that you drive me insane and you're a royal pain in my ass most days, you're a good soldier. I gave you an order and you'll follow it."

"Damn you."

I smirked as she dropped her arms to her sides and huffed in defeat, I'd gotten the upper hand with the comment and we both knew it. I continued the walk to the house, left the door open so she could follow me in and gathered my things. I tossed my full quiver and bow over my shoulder and went for the front door. Once we were outside I closed it and started for the stable, Steph on my heels. Greer and the group she'd picked were there waiting for me when I walked up, the soldiers Luke had hand selected standing behind them. Without being told he had only brought those who were capable on horseback, he knew I'd want to move fast and being on foot wouldn't do.

"Good, all of you get your horses and saddle up. We'll grab some supplies and get on the road."

I was thankful when no one questioned my orders or asked any questions, simply dispersed to follow the command so we could leave. We all tacked our horses, mounted up then made our way to the store houses to gear up and gather supplies. Three extra horses were tacked down with food and other various things we might need. Once everyone was armed we made sure saddle bags were full as well, one thing we had learned was you could never have too much food with you in the woods. Packs stuffed and strapped into place we started for the front gate and what could be the worst mission any of those present had ever been assigned to go on.

I whistled as we approached the gate and all five wolves raced for our group, startling a couple of the horses. They settled down quickly when they realized it was Ember and the pups and a few even gave Flare nudges with their noses as he passed them. I turned in my saddle to look at Steph as she chuckled out, "At least you're taking them with you."

"Definitely. If I'd just been honest and upfront with the other Generals about them when they were here, Hayley might have had Luna with her and she'd probably be safe right now. I'm done keeping secrets."

"Glad to hear it. Be careful, okay?"

"I will." I righted myself in the saddle as the gates were pulled open and shouted, "Let's move!"

CHAPTER THIRTY-SEVEN

CONFRONTING DEATH

I WAS determined to catch up to Thea before she made it back to her compound and I'd been lucky enough to land a group who all had horses with Level Three and Four mutation as mounts. We could kick them into high gear, run them faster and longer than those with lower levels. They'd all still have trouble keeping up with Prophecy but I'd have to make it work. The second we no longer had the gates in sight I spurred my massive white stallion into a gallop and took off. The others followed suit, keeping up as best they could after taking into account the pace I'd set.

We ran hard the first day, stopping when it was obvious we would all drop if the horses didn't get water and we didn't eat something. I opted to save as much of the food rations we'd brought along as I could and hunt whenever possible. We caught dinner to save our packed stores, smoked it over the fire while the horses grazed and then managed to get some sleep. I went with a smaller guard detail overnight than usual since we had five massive wolves with us keeping a lookout as well. I felt safer than I ever had outside the gates with Ember standing watch less than fifteen feet from me.

I was up before dawn hunting with Ember at my side, ripped from a less than peaceful sleep by dreams fraught with visions of

Hayley hurt and in danger. Once it had become apparent I wouldn't be resting I'd packed my things and set out with the big female wolf in tow to catch some breakfast. With Ember panting beside me and an armload of small animals tossed over my shoulder I trekked back toward camp. I heard movement before I saw anyone and Greer's frantic voice reached my ears as I broke through the brush and into the clearing. The panic on her face when she turned to look at me came close to wrestling the laughter I was fighting back from me.

"I wish you could see the look on your face right now."

"Well I wouldn't have this look on my face if you wouldn't disappear in the middle of the night alone and worry the living hell out of all of us!" I could understand her worry and even a mild dose of irritation but she needed to watch her tone.

"Whoa! You need to take a step back and check your attitude, Greer."

"Kai, you vanished without telling any of us where you were going or when you'd be back. You do know we're here to protect you, right?"

"Yes, I'm aware. So are the wolves and I had Ember with me. I was fine and I managed to catch us some breakfast. Relax, I was careful. Now let's get these cleaned and cooked so we can eat and get moving."

She huffed out an exasperated sigh but nodded and took the bundle from me to get started on cleaning and cooking them. It was written all over her face how much she wanted to keep arguing the point with me but she'd chosen to back off and let it go. I knew they would worry but I needed the time and space out in the woods to get my head on right. We didn't know what lay ahead and I needed to be prepared for anything. I ruffled the fur on the top of the big black wolfs head and moved to gather up the last of my belongings.

Once we had all eaten we re-tacked the horses and got underway again, heading toward a point where we hoped to catch up with Thea. I'd calmed considerably in the last few hours but I still had a few choice words for the other woman when we caught up to her. Flashes and flares of temper or not I was seething and probably would be until we got Hayley back. I sat in my saddle, reins loose and Prophecy leading the way. I trusted him to get me where I needed to be with a minimum of hassle, he did his part by treading as lightly as possible so as not to unseat me.

We rode at a slower pace than the day before for the first three hours since we were mired down in the muddy underbrush of the woods. It had rained enough the day before to breach the cover of the canopy and only stopped right as we reached the place we made camp. The result was everything being disgusting and mucky. Once we left the forest and hit the plains it dried out somewhat so I pulled my focus back to where it needed to be. I gave Prophecy a light kick, leaned forward some and let him go. He took off like a shot and the others in the group followed suit as fast as they could get their horses moving.

I was pushing the horses, not to mention the people in my group to the edges of their stamina and endurance. I could have slowed down, given them an easier pace, stopped at regular intervals and actually gotten some decent eating and resting in. Doing so would mean falling even further behind Thea and I was hell bent on catching up to her as soon as I could push us there. I hated dragging other people into my emotion driven push but everyone insisted on protecting me so, they were along for the ride. None of them were complaining yet so I would keep driving forward at this ridiculous pace I'd set and hope we caught up before the arguments started.

As it turned out we only had two more days to travel before we caught up to Thea and her group. The injuries her people had sustained in the ambush caused her to set up camp until they healed. It had cost them time but allowed us to find them quicker. I pulled Prophecy to a halt right outside the small camp minutes before sunset. I was out of my saddle and striding toward the center of the group when Thea stepped out in front of me.

"Kai, wait."

I wasn't in the mood to wait or to talk by this point and rather than giving her a chance to explain or even trying to talk, I punched her. She took the hit, then a step back and held her hands up in front of her trying to calm my temper. I was fuming again, the sight of her sending red hot rage flowing through my veins. The hit had helped and the anger began to ebb away slowly, leaving the ache of loss in its wake. My vision cleared and I got a good look at Thea, realizing how ragged and exhausted she looked.

"I... I'm sorry, Thea." I shook my head with a sigh, I was pissed off at her but after more than two hundred years I should have a much better handle on my temper.

"No, don't apologize. I deserved that outburst. I know I came into your camp strutting and preening like a damn peacock but I was just worried Hayley was some kind of spy. That she really was after the four of us and using you to get to the rest of us."

"Yeah you did. And I was so set on not trusting you to let you walk out of my camp with her without sending the one thing that could have saved her." She cocked her head at me, a questioning look on her face. I let out an ear piercing whistle that brought all five of the wolves to my side and caused every one of Thea's group, the General included, to tense. "It's fine. No reason to be on alert, they won't hurt you. They've been living at my compound for months now."

My voice was low, drawn and showing every bit of the guilt I felt for not letting Thea know about the canines. If Hayley had been able to take one of the girls with her she might not have been taken. As if fully aware of my state of mind Flare nudged his way under my left hand. Ember did the same on the right, a low, pitiful whimper resonating from her as I scratched the top of her head. I glanced to my right and caught sight of Luna, head hanging and looking bedraggled, as if she'd lost her best friend. Well, I guess she had if I thought about it.

"They've been living with you? And no one has been hurt?" Thea's voice ripped my attention away from the white wolf and back to where she was standing.

"Yeah. I found Ember here injured out in the woods one day." I gave her head another scratch and she leaned against my hip heavily. "I brought her back to the compound so she could heal and it turned out she was pregnant. She ended up giving birth to these four in our stable." Thea's eyes went wide with shock and I nodded at her, knowing her mind was working as hard as mine had been when it happened.

"These are her puppies?"

"Mmhmm. They are. I realized not long after they were born she had the same ability to understand us as the horses do. I just talked to her and she started to trust me."

"How old are these pups?" She glanced at Flare and then over to the girls, watching them intently.

"Hmmm, let me think, they're somewhere between eight and nine months now." She nodded as she looked them over again, her gaze landing on the massive white form sniffing her way around the camp.

"What's that one doing?"

"Which? Oh that one there, the white one?"

"Yeah, what's it up to?"

"She. Her name is Luna. She's been Hayley's shadow for the last several months. She's been keeping watch since they day you left the compound with her best friend. I'd assume she can smell her all over the place and is wondering why she can't seem to find her. Luna, come here girl."

The big wolf trotted over to me as I dropped to one knee and took a gentle hold on her muzzle with both hands. "She isn't here, honey. Someone took her." She whined at me as she tucked her tail tight between her legs and tried to back away. "I know; believe me I do. But we'll find her. I promise okay?" She huffed at me but then seemed to accept my promise and sat down, her head settling in my grip.

"I can understand why you'd keep them a secret, Kai. If they are this attached to you two I can only imagine what a powerful weapon they could be. Not letting anyone find out about them is probably best. But you need to know you can trust Trista, Lila and me." I sighed as I planted a light kiss between Luna's eyes and dropped my hands from her face to stand.

"I know, Thea. I need to learn how though. It's no secret the four of us have never worked well together. We keep our distance, work alone and stay out of each other's way. It's been that way for two centuries."

"That's true, it has. But maybe it's time for a change." I turned to face her, offering her a small, faint hint of a smile at the idea. Maybe we were finally starting to think along the same lines and would be able to work together.

"I think it is time, past time actually. We've always had more going for us than the Purists have but we would never work together to stand against them."

"You're right. And I'm willing to admit my attitude played a big part in that. I'm older than the other three of you and so I took it upon myself to think I was doing everything right. I put the rest of you at a distance and just did things my way."

"Well, to be fair, so did we. I let myself think that because you were all older than me you wouldn't listen to my ideas so rather than trying I just stayed away and did my own thing."

"Wow, we're a mess aren't we?" I chuckled as I nodded at her, agreeing completely. We were a total disaster and we had no one to blame for it but ourselves and our inability to talk to each other. "Well, how about we fix that, starting today. I can't move my men until tomorrow, they healed up just fine but they used a lot of energy doing so. They need another day to regain some of it before we start pressing toward home again. Stay with us tonight, eat, rest your horses and we'll head out tomorrow. We'll resupply and get a good night of sleep at my compound then head up to stop in and see Lila."

"Okay, I can agree to that. Then what?"

"Then we have some version of this conversation with her. I have the feeling she and Trista will be easier to convince than I was. It took all of this to make it hit home how divided we've been."

"Sounds like a plan to me."

"Oh, and Kai?"

"Hmm?"

"For the record... In the few days I spent with her after we left your compound, I really got to know Hayley. She seems like a great girl." The praise for her made me smile though the expression was a faint glimmer of its former self.

"Yeah, she really is."

"Mmhmm. I don't believe she's a spy and I seriously doubt she still wants to hurt you. As a matter of fact, I'd be willing to bet she would lay a beating on anyone who would dare to hurt you."

I let out a soft chuckle as I laid a hand on her shoulder and said, "I'd be willing to take that bet."

"I do hope you realize that girl is head over heels in love with you." A flush crawled its way onto my cheeks following the widening of my smile her words elicited and I ducked my head to hide both. "And from that look I'd say you feel the same."

"I do."

"Then let's get our shit together and go get her back."

CHAPTER THIRTY-EIGHT

REOPENING WOUNDS

KAI'S JOURNAL - *Summer Cycle, 2607 – 221 years after the event:*
The weather has been brutal out here and even though it's the middle of the summer cycle the nights and early mornings are a bit cold. The fact that I'm spending these cold nights alone hasn't helped. Now that my nightmares have become a bit more of a reality than I like it's been even more difficult to relax, and to warm up. Fear has a vice grip on my entire being and I won't be at ease until we find Hayley and I know she's safe.

I woke to a light drizzle the next morning, crawled out from under my blanket and shivered when the chilled air hit my skin. I'd fallen asleep between Flare and Ember and hadn't realized how warm they'd been keeping me, until I was clear of them. Gooseflesh snaked up my arms as I dug through my saddlebags for something warm to throw on over my loose tunic shirt. My fingers closed around a sweater I'd thrown in the bag at the last minute and I pulled it on without looking at it. A breeze kicked up the minute I had it settled over my torso, wrapping me up in the odor permeating the sweater.

The familiar scent of Hayley whipped around me and my heart stuttered, my stomach clenching tight. I was glad I hadn't managed to eat yet but without a full stomach to focus on I found myself fighting the urge to cry. I bit the inside of my cheek, closed my eyes and pulled in a deep breath, filling my lungs with the crisp morning air. A hand settled on my shoulder so I turned, opening my eyes to find Greer standing in front of me. The expression on her face was pure, uninhibited sympathy and as much as I wanted to hate seeing it there, I couldn't.

"We'll find her."

"Here's hoping your optimism pays off. At this point I don't know what to think, they've had her for a couple days now. Who knows what they might have done to her." Even thinking about it made me shudder and I mentally kicked myself again for being so secretive and keeping Luna from going with her.

"Look, I know you're the General and you're a hell of a lot older than I am but you are also *way* too close to this situation to think about it clearly so I want you to listen to me. Okay?" I nodded as she caught my gaze with her own and held it. "Good. So yes, they have her no, that's not good and it sucks. But, think about it, Kai. She's been living in the compound with us for months. I seriously doubt they know she's been out of captivity for most of that time. I'm sure they do think she's managed to gain some kind inside information." She had a point though I wasn't sure what kind of difference it would really make.

"I doubt they'll care. They'll assume she's been corrupted."

"I don't know. I'm thinking they'll want to know what she found out, they won't know she's been compromised. I doubt she'll out and tell them she's in love with you, she struck me as a hell of a lot smarter than that. She'll find a way to keep herself safe."

"You're probably right."

"Of course I am." I laughed as I rolled my eyes at her then gave her a friendly punch to the shoulder.

"Thank you, Greer. I needed that."

"Anytime. Now let's get everyone up and moving so we can get out of here." I nodded my agreement then turned to rouse the rest of my group so we could make the most of the day.

I knew Thea was anxious to get back to her compound even if we would only be turning around and leaving again a day or so later. She needed to resupply and trade out the men who were still regaining their strength for well rested troops. Once we had those things taken care of we would start the trek toward Lila's territory. It was a place where I was sad to say I'd never bothered to stop. The others had been to my compound more than I could count with the exception of Thea who had set foot on my land only a handful of times.

I would have to make sure we all worked together to spend more time in each other's company. It would mean traveling more often but I wouldn't mind as much once I had my girlfriend back. I'd spend most of the year wandering between the compounds without complaint if I had Hayley by my side.

Kai's Journal - Summer Cycle, 2607 – 221 years after the event:
There are a multitude of things I miss about the world pre-event. A couple of those things are cars and planes. While I never had the opportunity to fly I did spend a decent amount of time in cars back then. They were efficient at getting you from place to place quickly. Quick is something I'd give almost anything for right now. Being on horseback with a handful of weary, healing men on foot means the trek to reach Thea's compound is taking days. She told us over dinner that we should be there tomorrow barring any catastrophic happenings. Once we resupply and find fresh troops we'll be on our way again. Then comes the trudge toward our next destination which should only take a few days if all of Thea's troops are trained for riding.

I was daydreaming, as I had been for the last few days as we traveled. I knew I didn't need to watch where we were heading, Thea had the lead and Prophecy was content to follow Ghost. My job was to stay awake and seated which I could do as my thoughts wandered to Hayley, again. My mind circled back out of its depressing loop when I heard the metallic squeal of gates being opened. I blinked a few times to force my eyes to focus and stared at the massive construct which was Thea's outer wall. Everything kicked back in and I led the group inside the compound so the guards could shut the gates.

The groan of the soldiers pushing them closed behind us made Prophecy sidestep. I took in my surroundings and was surprised at how different Thea's compound looked than my own. While mine had been a spiritual retreat once upon a time hers had been a science and technology research facility before the event. You could still see the old scanners on some of the doors which had once read fingerprints and retinas before allowing entry. I shook my head as I thought about everything we'd depended on all those years ago.

We eased the horses to a stop in front of a large building and dismounted, unloading everything from the saddlebags and getting their tack off so they could cool down. Prophecy proceeded to drop and roll in the courtyard, kicking up a massive cloud of dust and making the nearby children laugh. When he stopped a few minutes later he got back to his feet then turned to me with a toss of his head and a whinny. I was coated in a layer of dust which he apparently found amusing. I glared at him as I dusted myself off, coughing here and there.

"Steph is right; you *are* a jerk." He pranced around in obvious glee over being labeled as such. My horse was weird.

"Hey, he's no worse than my butthead here."

At the mention of himself in a less than stunning way, Thea's massive dapple-gray, Ghost, head-butted her, knocking her forward almost five feet. She turned and swatted him on the nose with a stern look to which he simply mirrored Prophecy by tossing his head and prancing around. The two nickered to each other then turned and trotted off into the compound together leaving us simple people shaking our heads. I worked as much of the dirt from my hair as I could then turned to Thea, about to say something about our crazy animals when a shout came from my right. I glanced in the direction of the angry voice and saw a dark haired man with a scowl on his very red face yelling at someone.

The person he was pissed at came into view a moment later with an equally angry look on her far too familiar face. I went wide eyed and turned to look at Thea who sighed, shook her head and moved to get between the two.

"Hey! Enough! Both of you need to back up." She stepped between the two bodies, arms out and a hand braced on each of their chests.

"Thea, you need to get her under control! She's a damn loose cannon and I'm tired of it!" The anger on the man's face hadn't diminished even a fraction and I could see the twitch in his jaw.

"Loose cannon? What the hell Horatio, I am not!" The woman attempted to reach the man but Thea's hand on her chest stopped her from getting close enough to touch him.

"Oh aren't you? I don't appreciate walking into *my* training arena and finding *my* soldiers already bloodied up and worn out because *you* thought I was taking too long. You have no right to interfere with my methods, Claire!" I stepped up closer to the rapidly unraveling situation, not at all happy to see her time with Thea had done nothing to curb Claire's temper.

I was about to open my mouth and give Claire a piece of my mind when Thea spoke up, her voice resonating through the area. "Hey! I said it's enough already. Look, you two haven't been able to agree on a damn thing since Claire got here. I swear I told you to work together and it seems to me you've been doing everything but what I expect of you."

The two shrank away from their leader and I had to admit a certain amount of fear of her myself. She had a very commanding presence when she decided to set that tone to her voice and let it fly. I cleared my throat and the pair looked at me, Thea's gaze following a moment later.

"What the hell are you doing here?" The bite in Claire's tone made me go wide eyed and take a sharp breath in. I hadn't expected her to still be so angry more than a year later. Her banishment from my compound had been brought on by her own terrible behavior but I had to figure she didn't see it that way. Apparently she blamed me for all of it and it definitely appeared she wasn't settling into her new home or the new role she'd been given in it. I wondered how Thea was managing to tolerate her attitude.

The woman huffed when I failed to respond to her, shot a look at Thea, glared at Horatio and then turned on her heel and stormed away. The situation momentarily diffused, Thea sighed in relief and turned her attention to the man. With a furrow of her brow she pointed a finger at him and just stared for a minute.

"You. I expect better from."

"General, she…"

"I don't care what she did." She cut him off as she poked him in the chest. "The fact is she's been here for a year; you've been here your entire life. You know what I expect from you, what kind of behavior I tolerate and what I will put my foot down on. She's still learning these things and as I would expect from anyone coming from another compound, she's pushing her boundaries, testing my limits. If you have an issue with her or the things she's doing, bring it to me. Do *not* engage the woman in shouting matches. Do I make myself clear?"

"Yes ma'am, General. Very."

"Good. Now go get your men together, we have to resupply and pull new soldiers. We have a new mission to set out for." He nodded, turned and headed off to follow her orders, leaving the two of us standing there watching him go. My people had fallen back several yards, not wanting to be caught in the crossfire if things went to hell but my keen hearing was still picking up bits of conversation. They were all buzzing about what had happened, most of them remembering Claire from her time in my compound.

Thea turned toward me, anger set in her features and irritation blazing in her bright green eyes. Somehow I knew I was about to be on the receiving end of her rage and I wasn't looking forward to it. She stepped right up into my face and took a sharp breath in, apparently attempting to calm her temper a fraction before trying to speak to me.

"You sent her here. It was you who brought this down on me, my compound and my Captains. This is the pinnacle of how badly we work together. When you have a problem, you dump it on me. Now I'm stuck with her anger, her violent temper and her insubordination. Thanks for that."

Without giving me a chance to respond she shoved past me, nearly knocking me on my ass and stormed out of the clearing we'd been occupying. I regained my balance, turned and stared after her in complete shock. I knew I'd taken a leap when I'd sent Claire to her but I hadn't realized I'd upset her so badly. I shook my head in an attempt to calm my ragged nerves and turned toward my people.

"Well, that was, terrifying. Come on guys, let's go find somewhere to settle in for the night. I get the feeling we won't be getting the grand tour after that display." Greer stepped up beside me and bumped my shoulder with hers.

"At this point, I think we're lucky to still be inside the walls. She was really pissed off."

"Tell me about it." I bumped her back, we both managed small smiles and then led the rag-tag group I'd brought with me deeper into the place to find somewhere to sleep.

Kai's Journal - Summer Cycle, 2607 – 221 years after the event:

I'm more than a little confused by Thea's outburst. I can understand that she's upset about me just dropping Claire on her the way I did but she might be over-reacting slightly. Part of me thinks I should find her tomorrow and try to talk to her about it. The rest of me thinks that's a terrible idea and I should leave her alone until she's ready to talk rather than pushing her and making it worse. Since I'm not sure which option is the right one, I'm going to sleep on it and see if things are any clearer in my head in the morning.

The next morning, I was ripped from a less than peaceful sleep by someone sitting on the edge of the bed I'd found to occupy. I turned to face the body, peeked an eye open and caught sight of Thea's profile in the pale light of the still rising sun. She was staring down at her boots and I wondered, once my brain kicked in and thoughts began processing, what she was doing sitting there. Leaving aside the fact any normal person wouldn't come to visit me after a blowup like she'd had, it was also strange to see her so early. The few times she had been to my compound she had proved herself a night owl.

I managed to sit up and prop myself on my elbows as I yawned. It was too early to be awake after the fitful night I'd had. The nightmares of all the horrific things which might be happening to Hayley were plaguing me endlessly and keeping me from getting any type of rest. I sighed and looked over at Thea, reaching out to tap her on the shoulder. She responded by looking at me and I raised a brow at her before realizing I was lit from behind by the window and she might not be able to see it.

I grumbled as I forced myself to sit up all the way and asked her in a raspy tone, "Hey, what's up?"

"I'm really sorry about yesterday. I was angry and I took it out on you."

"Well yeah, of course you did. I'm the one who sent her here. Her and her damn attitude problem."

"As true as that might be, that wasn't why I blew up at you." I shifted so I could get around her, crawled from the bed and pulled on my sweater. The mornings this time of year were still a bit chilly and if I was going to attempt being out from under the blankets I needed another way to keep warm. After shoving my feet into my boots, shivering from the chill they held after being exposed to the air all night, I turned to face Thea.

"Okay, why did you blow up at me then?"

"Umm, can we take a walk, I'm not sure I can have this conversation sitting still."

"Sure, come on." I led the way out of the room I'd found the night before and then let her take the lead since it was her compound and she knew better where to head.

We walked for several minutes in silence and I took the time to study my ally. She was still staring at her boots, looking a bit sad and completely defeated. I wasn't used to seeing her this way and it was unnerving. Thea had always been the tough one, too cocky and headstrong for her own good and picturing her any other way but commanding was heart-wrenching.

"Thea?" I barely got her name out before she stopped, turned her gaze up into the cloudy sky and shook her head. I could just make out the shining trails the tears had left on her cheeks and the mere fact she was crying threw me.

"You have to believe me; I wasn't angry at you."

"So you said. Once again though, if it wasn't me, what was it?"

"It was me. I've been angry at myself."

"What reason would you have to be angry at yourself?"

"Because I don't know what to do. And I really hate not knowing what to do, Kai."

"Do? About what?" Those were the only words I could manage in the moment. I was having trouble wrapping my mind around Thea actually crying and coming up with any deeper thought was proving difficult.

"Claire."

"Claire? What about her?" I worried I was about to have to negotiate a way for the woman to stay for a while until I found somewhere else for her to go. I couldn't imagine Trista or Lila would be keen on taking her in if Thea couldn't even handle her outbursts of temper and violence.

"She's rude, insubordinate, violent, rash, and..."

I watched her for a moment, expecting her to continue and when she didn't I prompted her with a gentle, "And?" She sighed, turned her gaze down from the progressively graying sky and looked at me, eyes shimmering with unshed tears.

"And I think I'm in love with her."

About the Author

Kaden Shay is a 30-something crazy-cat-lady in-the-making who currently resides in Arizona with her partner and miniature zoo, which does currently include 4 cats. When she isn't writing or playing mom to several fur-kids she's singing, playing guitar, or playing online video games.

Kaden grew up in a very musical household and was singing with her family early on in life. Having an English teacher for a dad gave her a love of the written word and encouraged her to begin her own path toward writing. She spent middle school and early high school penning poems, songs, and short stories before beginning her first book at age 16 (a project she still hasn't completed)!

Her furry family, currently consisting of two dogs, four cats, and several rodents, is always available to help her procrastinate in finishing projects.

More from Kaden Shay!

In a world where Vampires reign and humans have two purposes, food or entertainment, can a human woman hope to become more than someone's next meal?

Enter the world of the Vampire Elite, a High Council of ruling Vampires who govern the world from their own blood-driven perspective. Silver, the daughter of their leader, Ayana and her Lycan mate Ianos is the world's first and only hybrid. She's also the future leader of the Council. With a chip on her shoulder which competes with the expanse of her mother's sizeable territory and a disdain for human life, she is frequently the cause of problems within their ranks.

When she finds herself sharing space with a human woman who isn't afraid of her, who challenges her at every turn, how will she react? Will her mounting confusion about her connection to the human tear apart her last strand of self-control? Most importantly, can a hybrid who has always hated humans ever learn to love one? All these questions send ripples through Silver's life when Angel enters the picture, turns her world upside down and makes her feel things she never thought possible.